# "You look pale. Are you okay?"

"I'm fine," Carver said. "Just wondering what it is we're about to open. Please, go on."

Brigid read the whole chant that had been written onto the knife, drawing from her incredible memory to interpret the ancient symbols as best she could.

*Beware! I am the bringer of Death, the Destroyer of Souls, the alpha and the omega, the vanishing point. Mourn now the end of your life's journey, for all shall fall before my power, their family line expunged from all histories, their bodies returned to Tiamat. I am the blade Godkiller. Gaze upon my bloodwork and lament.*

"This is the symbol for Enlil," she explained as Kane and Grant returned to the discussion at the display cabinet, "but it's been altered."

"Altered how?" Kane asked.

Brigid pointed to the knife's hilt before looking up at Kane and Grant. There was clear concern in her emerald eyes. "It's the name of the knife's owner," she explained. "I think it means Son of Enlil."

**Other titles in this series:**

# James Axler

# Outlanders®

## INFINITY BREACH

A GOLD EAGLE BOOK FROM
# W★RLDWIDE®

TORONTO • NEW YORK • LONDON
AMSTERDAM • PARIS • SYDNEY • HAMBURG
STOCKHOLM • ATHENS • TOKYO • MILAN
MADRID • WARSAW • BUDAPEST • AUCKLAND

Recycling programs
for this product may
not exist in your area.

First edition May 2010

ISBN-13: 978-0-373-63866-6

INFINITY BREACH

Copyright © 2010 by Worldwide Library.

Special thanks to Rik Hoskin for his contribution to this work.

**Printed in U.S.A.**

Headlong themselves they threw
Down from the verge of Heaven, eternal wrath
Burnt after them to the bottomless pit.
—*Paradise Lost*
John Milton 1608–1674

## The Road to Outlands—
## From Secret Government Files to the Future

Almost two hundred years after the global holocaust, Kane, a former Magistrate of Cobaltville, often thought the world had been lucky to survive at all after a nuclear device detonated in the Russian embassy in Washington, D.C. The aftermath—forever known as skydark—reshaped continents and turned civilization into ashes.

Nearly depopulated, America became the Deathlands—poisoned by radiation, home to chaos and mutated life forms. Feudal rule reappeared in the form of baronies, while remote outposts clung to a brutish existence.

What eventually helped shape this wasteland were the redoubts, the secret preholocaust military installations with stores of weapons, and the home of gateways, the locational matter-transfer facilities. Some of the redoubts hid clues that had once fed wild theories of government cover-ups and alien visitations.

Rearmed from redoubt stockpiles, the barons consolidated their power and reclaimed technology for the villes. Their power, supported by some invisible authority, extended beyond their fortified walls to what was now called the Outlands. It was here that the rootstock of humanity survived, living with hellzones and chemical storms, hounded by Magistrates.

In the villes, rigid laws were enforced—to atone for the sins of the past and prepare the way for a better future. That was the barons' public credo and their right-to-rule.

Kane, along with friend and fellow Magistrate Grant, had upheld that claim until a fateful Outlands expedition. A displaced piece of technology…a question to a keeper of the archives…a vague clue about alien masters—and their world shifted radically. Suddenly, Brigid Baptiste, the archivist, faced summary execution, and Grant a quick termination. For

Kane there was forgiveness if he pledged his unquestioning allegiance to Baron Cobalt and his unknown masters and abandoned his friends.

But that allegiance would make him support a mysterious and alien power and deny loyalty and friends. Then what else was there?

Kane had been brought up solely to serve the ville. Brigid's only link with her family was her mother's red-gold hair, green eyes and supple form. Grant's clues to his lineage were his ebony skin and powerful physique. But Domi, she of the white hair, was an Outlander pressed into sexual servitude in Cobaltville. She at least knew her roots and was a reminder to the exiles that the outcasts belonged in the human family.

Parents, friends, community—the very rootedness of humanity was denied. With no continuity, there was no forward momentum to the future. And that was the crux—when Kane began to wonder if there *was* a future.

For Kane, it wouldn't do. So the only way was out—way, way out.

After their escape, they found shelter at the forgotten Cerberus redoubt headed by Lakesh, a scientist, Cobaltville's head archivist, and secret opponent of the barons.

With their past turned into a lie, their future threatened, only one thing was left to give meaning to the outcasts. The hunger for freedom, the will to resist the hostile influences. And perhaps, by opposing, end them.

# Chapter 1

*October 31, 1930*
*Somewhere in the South Pacific*

Hiding amid the foliage, a beautiful woman peered through a set of compact binoculars in the direction the U.S. naval base. Demy Octavo was a tall, shapely figure, sheathed in a formfitting outfit of soft brown leather that clung to her every enticing curve like poured mercury. Matching leather gloves on her hands accentuated her long, elegant fingers, and a pair of matching handguns were strapped to the swell of her hips. The compact pistols were modified versions of the Beretta Model 1915, and their silver handles were engraved with the columnlike symbol of the Fascist party along with the motto *Viva La Morte,* or Long Live Sacrifice. Octavo's tight-fitting ensemble left only her head uncovered, but for the moment her striking features remained hidden behind the binoculars.

Octavo's skin was tanned to a wonderful bronze shade from hours spent reclining on the beautiful golden beaches of the Mediterranean, and she had carefully painted her lips a luscious, rich color known as falu red. Her long, dark hair swung freely behind her, cascading over her delicate shoulders like a waterfall, loose strands catching now and then on the island breeze. Her hair was a shade of brown so dark as to be almost black, and her tresses held a slight kink that was pleasing to the eye.

Demy Octavo was on a mission, sent to the South Pacific by her government under the auspices of Benito Mussolini himself, tasked to acquire important American military secrets. And yet, hidden in the natural cover of the island's green-and-yellow ferns, the gorgeous Signorina Octavo did not watch the naval base. Instead, she had turned her binoculars to the skies above, where a single-seater airplane cut through the air, its engine buzzing like an angry hornet. The airplane was an experimental model, one not yet in general production. Sleek lines swooped back from the aircraft's pointed nose cone, where an intake unit sucked in a stream of air to hurry its passage through the cloudless blue skies above the rolling waves of the Pacific Ocean. A glass blister protruded midway along the sharpened length of the dartlike aircraft, like a bubble on a stream, and a figure could be seen sitting within, piloting the strange vehicle with grim determination.

Demy Octavo knew that plane and she knew the figure who guided it through the azure sky. The pilot's name was Abraham Flag, a gifted scholar and full-time adventurer who had done more for the American government in the past five years than any other man.

Tales of Abraham Flag's exploits were splashed across the front page of every newspaper in America with alarming regularity, but those stories could only scratch the surface of Flag's true contribution to the well-being and sanctity of the Land of the Free. However, Flag himself was no government employee. He worked for an even more noble cause, one he had described in his few rare interviews to the gentlemen of the press as "the continuance and evolution of mankind."

The beautiful Signorina Octavo had clashed with Flag on several occasions in the past when her goals had conflicted with his own. They had met on the moonlit streets of Paris, Octavo armed with only a stiletto blade hidden in her stocking top beneath a cerise evening gown, and Flag armed with nothing but his keen intellect as they vied for possession of a meteorite of breathtaking mineral worth. They had become close then, as they found themselves in the romantic City of Lights, but, when he had realized the wicked government that Octavo represented, Flag had resisted the woman's abundant charms. Instead, Professor Flag's determined spirit had remained focused solely on preventing the invaluable meteor from falling into the wrong hands.

Even now, as Demy Octavo tracked Flag's plane with her binoculars, she recalled those tender moments in Paris, before Flag had discovered the nature of her real mission. He had left with the meteor, and she had been forced to report her absolute failure to Mussolini. A man not renowned for his even temper, Mussolini had erupted with rage at the news.

Octavo watched the remarkable plane as it swooped around in a long, banking curve, almost as though its extraordinary pilot was taking one last, long look of the tiny Pacific island before deciding to land. Octavo knew that was not the case— Italian intelligence operatives had learned of the discovery in question three days ago when they had intercepted an urgent message that had been wired to Flag's New York apartment, requesting his assistance as swiftly as possible. Flag himself had been out of the country at the time, working in his fabled Laboratory of the Incredible, where he was not to be disturbed, and so two of his frequent colleagues had gone in his stead. It had been two full days before Flag himself had responded to the U.S. Navy's summons to confirm this appointment with mystery, a further day for him to reach the island from his laboratory in the Antarctic. Octavo smiled wickedly at the thought—Flag's other commitment had given her time to charter a mail plane via New Zealand, which had brought her close enough to the tiny island to drop in the waters and swim ashore, unseen by the patrolling military.

The island itself was barely more than a pinprick on the map, a little-known territory of the United States of America called Isle Terandoa. Less than a decade before, the whole structure had been below the water, but a shift in the tectonic plates had revealed the atoll, and the U.S. had been quick to organize a small naval presence there. Tucked away between New Zealand and the western coast of South America, Terandoa had been used as a test site for the Navy, a place where they could try out prototype seagoing vessels well away from public scrutiny. More recently, the tiny island, which was no more than four miles square, had played grudging host to a team of archaeologists whose tedious excavation work had been seen as a dangerous compromise to security by the local Navy commander, a proud man called Edmond Kinver. Against Kinver's requests, the brass in Washington had insisted that a small team from Harvard be given access to Terandoa, and so he had curtly accepted them, fencing off each area that they studied and hurrying them along in their painstaking work. That was, at least, until the head of the archaeological team, a man called Ross Moorcroft, had made an unexpected discovery. Moorcroft had brought his discovery to the attention of General Kinver, and soon after the call had gone out for Abraham Flag's expertise.

The steady drone of the airplane's engine grew louder to Octavo's ears as Flag brought the sleek one-man craft in to land on the single airstrip inside the naval compound. The powerful lenses of Demy Octavo's binoculars followed the aircraft's descent and landing, and she waited patiently to see what would happen next. Five seconds passed, then ten, until finally that strange glass bubble that rested atop the arrow-shaped craft sprang open, flipping to one side on a hinged arrangement until it hung at the starboard side of the aircraft. A moment later, the pilot's hand emerged and the powerful form of the mighty man of adventure vaulted from the cockpit, his booted feet gliding down the short run of steps that had been molded into the side of his unique aircraft.

As Flag's toe struck the black tarmac of the landing strip, General Kinver, who stood to attention, offered the fabled adventurer a brisk salute. Two dozen sailors wearing smart dress uniforms stood to attention behind their general in the blazing midday sun, and from the end of the baking runway two men in civilian dress watched the proceedings. The first of these men had bright red hair and his shoulders were so wide that he reminded one of a football player still wearing his shoulder pads. The wide man's name was Barnaby B. Barnaby, and he was an archaeologist of some renown. Beside Barnaby stood a much shorter man who wore an ill-fitting suit with a dark, sombre tie and a fedora hat. The man's name was Anthony Pontfract, though he was known to his friends as "Little Ant." Little Ant was a master linguist who was able to speak and read several dozen languages fluently and instinctively apply that knowledge to numerous others. Both men had a long history of accompanying Flag on his endeavors, and their companionship dated back to a period in the Great War when all three men had been incarcerated in a notorious prisoner of war camp.

Crouched amid the foliage almost one thousand yards away, Demy Octavo, the glamorous Italian secret agent, was unable to discern the words that were spoken. Thus, she simply watched in silence as Kinver exchanged pleasantries with Flag, patting him on the shoulder like an old friend as the smartly dressed squadron of his best men stood rigidly to attention at the side of the airstrip. Barnaby and Little Ant made their way along the airstrip to meet their friend, with Little Ant hurrying along to keep up with Barnaby's distance-humbling strides.

It had been just a few months since Octavo's most recent encounter with Abraham Flag, but the adventurer's appearance still surprised her, making her heart flutter for just a moment like that of a giddy schoolgirl. Flag was an immense man, over six feet in height, with wide shoulders, muscular arms and sturdy legs. As such, the first impression he gave was not one of size so much as of exceptional power. Demy Octavo had been witness to several of Flag's superhuman feats, and she knew that it was more than simply an impression of power that this singular man exuded. He wore his dark hair close to his skull, swept back from his high, intelligent forehead in the tidy style he had favored since his military days during the Great War. His eyes were a piercing purplish-blue, like two magnificent amethysts set beneath his unlined brow. He wore a casual shirt beneath a flight jacket of brown leather, similar in color to Octavo's own outfit. His shirt, like his pants, was a shade of deep blue, complementing and exaggerating the color of his fascinating, unearthly eyes.

Flag and his two associates strode alongside General

Kinver toward the main office building of the small naval base. Watching from afar, Demy Octavo was impressed in spite of herself to see Flag turn to the waiting sailors and salute them, taking a few moments to honor them for coming out to greet him in the roasting Pacific sunshine. Demy Octavo watched as Flag and his companions disappeared into the main building with the commander at their side.

Once the four men had disappeared from view, the beautiful, dark-haired Italian agent took the compact set of field glasses from her eyes, folding them in on themselves on a butterfly hinge mechanism before replacing them in the protective casing that she wore strapped to the small of her shapely back. Then, carefully scanning her surroundings for guards, Demy Octavo slowly pushed forward through the thick foliage, closing in on the mysterious objective that she and Abraham Flag shared.

ABRAHAM FLAG narrowed his eyes momentarily as he and General Kinver stepped out of the bright sunlight and into the relative darkness of the two-story administrative building, allowing his remarkable eyes to adjust and letting his other senses assess his new surroundings. Flag was a man unlike any other. His natural senses—smell, hearing, touch and taste, as well as his eyesight—were disciplined to an incredible level of prowess, and he relied upon those senses to sift through great swathes of information that the average man might easily ignore or miss altogether. Abraham Flag maintained the firm belief that every detail might hold a crucial warning, a pivotal fact that would yield its secrets if only one took the time to consider it fully. And unlike most men, Flag was able to consider those facts at lightning speed, such was his prodigious intellect.

"Where is the artifact?" Flag asked in a voice whose rich timbre both commanded authority and put its listeners at their ease.

Barnaby spoke up, his voice booming in the corridor as he led the way to a closed door. "The commander gave over an office just through here, Abe," he explained as he pushed open the door. "We've spent the last two days trying to work out what this thing is made of."

Flag stood stock-still in the doorway and looked across the room to the artifact. Resting on a work top, surrounded by Barnaby's notes and a series of spectrographic photographs, was the artifact. It appeared to be a knife, its blade thin but stretching almost the length of a man's forearm, like the *itak* machete used by the Filipinos for combat. The blade and hilt appeared to be of a piece, and as Flag stepped closer, he realized that they had been carved of stone. Its surface glistened under the lights of the room, like a polished volcanic stone, and Flag saw indentations all along its surface—writing. He glanced at the writing for a moment, instantly recognizing the ancient characters from a language that dated back several millennia. There appeared to be at least three dozen tiny characters etched into the blade's surface, and Flag presumed that a similar number would be apparent were he to turn the weapon over.

Barnaby B. Barnaby spoke up as Flag looked at the weapon. "It's at least three thousand years old, Professor. I'd estimate maybe five or six thousand years."

Flag spoke without looking up from the object on the desk. "What does it say, Ant?"

Little Ant had already pulled a small notepad from his ill-fitting jacket's breast pocket, thumbing through its dog-eared pages in anticipation of his ally's question. "It's ancient Mesopotamian, Chief," the famed linguist explained. "There's quite a lot of it, and there are characters here I don't even understand, but the essence of it is a war chant, like a song. It says 'Beware! I am the bringer of Death,' et cetera."

As Little Ant spoke, Abraham Flag reached into his own jacket and produced a pair of white cotton gloves of the thinnest of material, which he then placed over his hands. Wearing the gloves, Flag carefully lifted the stone knife and held it close to his gaze, running his eyes along the writing there. Working in silence, Flag flipped the knife over and scanned the characters along the other side of the blade before speaking once more.

"A war chant?" he repeated thoughtfully. "Did you find any indication to whom this chant was addressed, or who the owner of the knife might have been?"

"Nothing like that," Little Ant admitted, "but I did find one name on it."

"A name?" Flag encouraged, his purple-blue eyes flicking up to lock with the linguist's.

"'Godkiller,'" Ant read from his notes. "I think it's the name of the knife itself."

# Chapter 2

*Early twenty-third century*
*Antarctica*

White on white. That's what the Antarctic was. That's *all* the Antarctic was.

Grant stood beside the cooling hull of his Manta craft, looking at the monotonous landscape that surrounded him. It was white as far as the eye could see, a freshly laundered sheet, stretching to the north, south, east and west. On closer scrutiny, Grant could make out that here was snow, there was ice and, billowing across it all, tossed about in the currents of the fierce winds, icy flakes of snow and snowy flecks of ice.

Snow and ice, white on white. Until this moment, Grant, who by any estimation was a well-traveled man, had never appreciated quite how many different gradations of white there could be.

Grant was a huge man, his skin like polished ebony, with black hair, close-cropped atop his scalp and shaped around his lips in a gunslinger's mustache. Though he wore a puffy white jacket and pants, there was no disguising his powerful frame. There was a bulky lump on his right sleeve, the only evidence of the hidden sidearm Grant carried there.

As he turned back to the Manta, somehow relieved to see

its obtrusive bronze form amid this white canvas, Grant pulled at the fur-lined hood of his jacket, raising it over his head. He didn't feel cold, even out here in the arctic chill that was dipping to 40 below, but the wind was howling in his ears like a wolf howling at the moon. The shadow suit Grant wore beneath his jacket helped keep him warm. The shadow suit was a remarkable weave of advanced technology that provided a temperature-controlled environment for its wearer, along with protection against radiation and environmental toxins, as well as some protection from blunt trauma. Despite these incredible properties, the shadow suit was wafer thin, a one-piece bodysuit finished in black that could be easily slipped beneath other clothes. It was like wearing a suit of armor, but with none of the associated restriction of movement.

As the wind churned up the snow like a flight of doves, Grant stepped into the protective lee of the Manta craft and began to speak, seemingly to no one but himself.

"Kane?" he said. "I can't see shit down here. Are you planning on landing anytime soon?"

Kane's firm voice came to Grant's ear a moment later, sounding so clear that he might be standing next to the man in a sheltered room far away from the blizzard's howling winds. The communications were routed through Commtact units, top-of-the-line communication devices that had been found in Redoubt Yankee years before. The Commtacts featured sensor circuitry incorporating an analog-to-digital voice encoder that was subcutaneously embedded in the mastoid bone. Once the pintels made contact, transmissions were picked up by the auditory canals, and dermal sensors transmitted the electronic signals directly through the skull casing. Theoretically, even a completely deaf wearer would still be able to hear normally, in a fashion, using the Commtact.

As well as offering radio communications, the units could also be used as translation devices, providing a real-time interpretation of foreign language if sufficient vocabulary had been programmed into their data banks.

"Cool your jets," Kane grumbled over the Commtact. "I'm bringing her in now."

Before the final syllable of Kane's proclamation had concluded, Grant saw the dark shadow appear overhead, dipping through the swirling snow, and a moment later the graceful shape of the Manta craft settled on the white blanket of snow beside him.

The Mantas were alien craft, left on Earth for millennia before being discovered by Grant and Kane during one of their exploratory missions. The beauty of their design was breathtaking, an effortless combination of every principle of aerodynamics wrapped up in a gleaming bronze finish. They had the shape and general configuration of seagoing manta rays, flattened wedges with graceful wings curving out from their bodies. The elongated hump in the center of the craft was the only evidence of a cockpit. The Mantas featured a wingspan of twenty yards, and a body length of almost fifteen feet. Finished in a bronze metallic hue, the surfaces of each craft were decorated with curious geometric designs; elaborate cuneiform markings, swirling glyphs and cup-and-spiral symbols that covered the entire body of the aircraft. The Mantas were propelled by two different types of engines—a ramjet and solid-fuel pulse detonation air spikes—allowing them flight in the skies and outside of the atmosphere.

Grant watched as the cockpit to the second Manta opened and two figures stepped out. Like him, both of them were dressed in white, wearing fur-lined jackets and white pants.

The first figure was a woman in her mid-twenties. She had vibrant red hair that trailed down her back like a burst of evening sunlight. Even as she stepped from the graceful wing of the Manta, the woman was bunching her hair back behind her head, pulling it away from her face as the Arctic wind blew it about her face. After a moment, she tied her hair back and looked up at Grant with her warm, friendly smile, her emerald eyes glinting with a furious intellect. Brigid Baptiste had been a crucial part of their triumvirate ever since Grant had joined the operation known as Cerberus. While her high forehead pointed to an intellectual aspect, her full lips suggested a more playful, passionate side; in truth, Brigid Baptiste was both of these and more besides.

Behind the attractive figure of Brigid Baptiste, the third member of the field team exited the Manta's cockpit, even as the snow started to settle on its sloping bronze wings. This was Kane, Grant's longtime partner, whose friendship was unquestioned, whose loyalty was unswerving. Grant had known Kane ever since their days in Cobaltville where they had been initially partnered as Magistrates, the strong-arm force that kept the citizenry in check. Whereas Grant was powerfully built and bulky, Kane was tall and lean with most of his bulk in his upper body. It had been said that Kane's physique was like a wolf's, and often his temperament was similarly inclined. He was pack leader, loner and scout. Like Grant, a bulky lump showed beneath the wrist of Kane's jacket where he held his sidearm for quick access.

"Seen anything interesting?" Kane asked as he greeted Grant.

"Snow," Grant grumbled, his deep voice sounding like a rumbling volcano.

Kane looked around before turning back to Grant with a self-deprecating grin. "Kind of samey, isn't it?"

Grant nodded, his own mouth breaking into a grin.

"*Monotonous,*" Brigid corrected them both without looking up from the portable radar device she was consulting in her gloved hand, "is the word you are looking for. 'Samey'? Honestly, who taught you two to speak?"

Kane glanced over Brigid's head and caught Grant's eye as the redheaded woman began walking away from the two Mantas. "You know, you'd never believe she used to be a librarian," he said flippantly.

"That so?" Grant replied. "You'd think she'd let us forget once in a while."

"Ha." Kane laughed. "She never lets anyone forget anything, isn't that right, Baptiste?"

Glancing up from the tracking device, Brigid fixed Kane with a disparaging glare before turning back to the readout screen she held in the palm of one hand. Although meant in jest, Kane's observation touched on a crucial aspect of Brigid's personality. The woman had what was colloquially known as a photographic memory, or, more accurately, an eidetic one. Brigid could study any image for just a few moments and commit it to memory in vivid detail, with the ability to draw from that memory again and again with total recall.

In her previous career as an archivist in Cobaltville, Brigid's incredible powers of observation had put her in a critical position during the discovery of a worldwide conspiracy intended to subjugate humankind. Her subsequent work with Kane and Grant at the Cerberus redoubt had been primarily concerned with uncovering and overthrowing that conspiracy in all its many evolving forms. Even now, the presence of the Cerberus trio in the harsh environment of the Antarctic was tangentially related to that far-reaching scheme.

Their boots sank into the thick snow as the three figures trekked away from their Manta craft. Kane glanced back, watching for a moment as the swirling whiteness settled on the still Mantas. The two craft were already dappled with a thin coating of snow, and would doubtless be hard to spot in another hour or so. It struck Kane then that anything could be hidden out here—anything at all—and they might never see it.

Kane dismissed the thought. "Everyone remember where we parked, okay?" he instructed, his tone light. "Baptiste, I'm counting on you here."

Brigid cast Kane another withering look as she continued to lead the way across the Antarctic wastes. "You think you're funny," she said. "Emphasis on 'think.'"

"Lighten up," Kane said as he brushed snow from his sleeves. "I'm just trying to keep things cheerful."

"Oh, you're very trying," Brigid snapped. "I've had to listen to this blather for the full three-hour trip over here."

"Really?" Grant asked, unable to hide the note of pity from his tone.

"The first hour was okay," Brigid assured him. "The second I started wishing we'd found a parallax point so we could jump here instantaneously instead of using the Mantas." Parallax points formed a hidden network of nodes stretching across the globe and out into other planets that allowed the Cerberus warriors to jump via the quantum ether through use of an alien device called an interphaser. The system allowed for almost instantaneous travel across vast distances, but it relied on specific locations; no parallax point, no interphaser jump.

"What about the third hour?" Kane grumbled.

"Wish I was dead, wish I was dead, wish I was dead," Brigid muttered, the words streaming into one.

Grant looked at Kane and shrugged. "I think she's joking, buddy."

"Because she *thinks* she's funny," Kane said.

"Oh, touché." Grant chuckled, applauding.

They had walked just eighty yards across the snowbound wastes when Brigid Baptiste stopped in her tracks and pointed ahead. "It's right there," she said.

"Where?" Kane asked, shielding his eyes with a gloved hand.

"I don't see anything, either," Grant added, scowling.

Peering in the direction that Brigid was indicating, they saw a continuing expanse of whiteness. Out here, the sky was white, a thick blanket of clouds reflecting the ice and snow below them. Snow flurries continued to fall across their vision, a dappling of white across the whiteness of the background. Kane relaxed his eyes, surveying the wash of white that stretched before him. As he did so, he noticed the shadow. It seemed almost incongruous as it stretched across the snow, pouring out across the white blanket in a gray, indistinct pattern that was easy to miss. The sun was ahead of them, Kane noted, pushing the shadow of the structure toward them so that its apex almost touched their booted feet. They had landed the Mantas barely one hundred yards from it, and yet it had remained utterly invisible, disguised in the harsh, white landscape.

Kane raised his arm, drawing its shape in the air with an outstretched finger. "There," he said. "You see it?"

Grant squinted, trying to cut down the dazzling effect of the sun on the white snow as he sought the thing that Kane could see. Beside him, Brigid checked the readout of her palm-sized tracker device before peering again into the swirling whiteness.

A sudden lull in the wind brought with it a break in the dance of the falling snowflakes, and for a few seconds the majestic structure stood revealed.

It was white, like the ground and sky around it, so white that it seemed to exist only in the shadows it cast. Its leading edge stood just twenty-five yards from the three Cerberus warriors, and it stretched far back into the snow-packed ground. It was difficult to estimate its actual size, for it was clear that the structure had been mostly buried by the snow. Yet the evidence of it was there, a rough circle of struts and spines that dominated the land for almost a quarter mile, becoming more crowded near to what was presumably the center.

There were other parts, too, they now realized as they gazed all around them. Struts stuck up here and there, like shoots from a hopeful plant. Kane looked behind him at the path they had just trod. Their footprints were already losing their shape as the swirling snow filled them in, and in another few minutes they would be gone completely as nature painted over them, obliterating any trace that they had ever existed. And over there, just a few feet from where they had walked but a minute before, another strut poked from the ground, rising up in a point that towered to twelve feet above them, twice the height of himself or Grant. As remarkable as it seemed, they had walked right past it, taking it for a natural feature of the snow-laden environment, a stalagmite striving up to the skies. Kane's eyes flicked upward, and he smiled as he saw that there was nothing above the strut, nothing to drip down and create the beautiful stalagmite that twinkled in the frosty sunlight.

Brigid released the breath she hadn't realized that she had been holding. "It's colossal," she gasped.

"See," Kane said, "I'd have gone for *big* and maybe *samey.*"

"It's so beautiful," Brigid continued, ignoring Kane's remark.

Still shielding his eyes, Grant stepped closer to Brigid, peeking at the display screen of the tracking device she held. "You think this is it, then?"

"Oh, this is it, all right," Brigid assured him, never turning her attention from the magnificent spires that jutted from the white landscape. "The secret laboratory of Abraham Flag."

# Chapter 3

The wind picked up again, and snow swirled around them as they stood there, admiring what little they could see of the fantastical structure. After a few seconds, Kane turned to Brigid, who still stood with her mouth agape as she admired the magnificent spires of the buried building.

"I think we'd better find a way inside, Baptiste," he told her, "before my, er, frozen assets fall off."

"What?" She turned to him, mystified. "Sorry, Kane, I was just…"

"It is beautiful," Kane agreed. "But let's not wait to see what it looks like inside. That's why we came here, isn't it?"

Brigid nodded. "It is going to be very exciting seeing what's inside there," she said as she jogged forward, leading the way. "I can feel it."

Kane followed the red-haired woman, while Grant brought up the rear, as she compared the electronic readout she held to the structure around her. Brigid's instrument held a portable sonar device, as well as a computer memory containing the plans that they had found for Flag's so-called Laboratory of the Incredible. The plans had been discovered among other sensitive information that had been held as encrypted files on a computer drive that Kane, Brigid and Grant had found on a mission in North Dakota a few months previously. The computer had contained a wealth of military information dating back over two hundred years to the final days of the twentieth century, before the nukecaust of 2001 had changed everything. Decrypting the files was proving to be a laborious process, teasing out the information one tiny thread at a time. The first useful file to be decrypted from the North Dakota hard drive had contained information relating to a secret weapons project near the Russian-Georgian border. The weapon, code named the Death Cry, promised to be of devastating use against a race of alien invaders called the Annunaki, who had been manipulating the human race since their earliest days. However, a confluence of events upon finding the Death Cry had resulted in the device going off in a level of the quantum plane generally reserved for matter transfer, though thankfully not a plane that the Cerberus team accessed.

The scientists working at Cerberus had continued in their endeavors to decrypt further files from the database in the hopes of finding something else that might be of use against the Annunaki. Their latest discovery had been the incomplete schematics to a fabled research laboratory from the 1920s. The Laboratory of the Incredible had been the rumored workplace of Abraham Flag, an adventurer and explorer of some renown, whose exploits had abruptly halted on All Saints' Day, 1931. A master of many scientific fields, Flag had been conducting research that was years—decades even—beyond that of his contemporaries. However, he had chosen to keep many of his remarkable discoveries to himself and, upon his disappearance, a persistent rumor had it that the man's fortresslike laboratory contained numerous treasures, from nuclear reactors to a functioning cell phone that required no broadcasting network for its operability. The truth of these rumors had, to Brigid's knowledge, never been proved, but clearly Flag's hidden Antarctic retreat had been a matter of some concern to the U.S. military.

Guided by the information from the North Dakota database, the Cerberus field team had traveled to the Antarctic and pinpointed the Laboratory of the Incredible as best they could. Only here, on the ground, was the enormity of the structure becoming apparent.

Kane, Grant and Brigid spent almost an hour searching the immediate area, looking for a point of entry into the strange construction, but other than the spires and bumps, there seemed to be nothing but deep snow.

"I think it got buried," Brigid announced after they had spent a full twenty minutes just trekking around the perimeter of upthrust spires.

Kane looked at her, his brow furrowed.

In reply, Brigid shrugged. "It's been here a long time," she said. "The natural weather patterns cover everything with snow over time." As she said it, she unconsciously shook her head, and settling snow fell from her ponytail of bright red hair.

"Guess we're making our own entrance," Kane decided, producing a compact tool kit from inside his Arctic jacket. The tool kit was roughly the length of Kane's forearm, and it featured a weatherproof pouch of soft leather that snapped together so that it could be placed snugly into the inside pocket of his jacket. The kit contained several compact tools, including a lock pick, a glass cutter and a digital lock jammer.

As the wind and snow blew about them, Kane pulled out a handheld buzz saw and snapped together an acetylene torch from the leather pouch. Then he set about finding a place to start working, with Grant and Brigid dogging his footsteps.

As Kane selected a mound from which one of the curious icelike spires protruded, Grant turned to Brigid and asked why anyone would design a building that needed to be constantly dug out of the snow.

Brigid shrugged. "Maybe the owner preferred it that way," she suggested. "Abraham Flag was, by all accounts, a fascinating and unique individual. He liked his privacy."

"So Lakesh was saying back at the base," Grant responded, recalling the briefing that the Cerberus team leader, Mohandas Lakesh Singh, had given them prior to dispatching the Manta craft. "But what's the big deal about all this anyhow?"

"If that military record was correct," Brigid explained, referring to the coded file they had found on the North Dakota computer, "there's a strong possibility that Flag gained control of an ancient Annunaki artifact. It's that artifact that caused him to go into hiding."

"What sort of artifact?" Grant asked, brushing snow from his sleeve.

"A weapon," Brigid said.

"What kind of weapon?" Grant asked. "A nuke?"

"Well, what kind of weapon does a god carry?" Brigid replied enigmatically.

"A lightning bolt," Kane growled, not bothering to look up from his work at the mound, "if what we found Marduk using in Greece is anything to go by."

"We'll see," Brigid said diplomatically.

Kane's eyes met with hers and Grant's for just a moment, and the hint of a smile crossed his lips. "I'm saying lightning bolt," Kane said. "Anyone care to take a bet?"

"Kane…" Brigid began, her expression frosty.

"Giant hammer," Grant cried, snapping his fingers. "I say it's a great big hammer with a handle as tall as Brigid. A hammer that can…knock down mountains."

Kane laughed. "Sure, that's likely," he said, an edge of sarcasm to his tone.

"You never heard of Thor?" Grant snapped back.

"Whatever." Kane laughed. "I'll take the bet."

"Baptiste?" he prompted.

Brigid shook her head, her ponytail of vibrant red hair whipping about her with the rising wind. "I can't really…"

Brigid offered a resigned sigh. "Okay. I say it's a…dagger."

"A dagger?" Kane repeated dubiously, while Grant worked beside him, hefting the hunk of reinforced glass away. The hunk of glass was large, almost as tall as Grant himself and it clearly weighed a great deal. Yet Grant seemed to lift it with almost no effort, such was the man's strength.

"A knife," Brigid continued thoughtfully, "made of stone that features…"

"Features?" Kane encouraged.

"Writing," Brigid finished. "A stone knife with writing down both sides that promises the death of godly enemies. Satisfied?"

Kane raised his eyebrows, impressed. "Pretty specific, Baptiste," he said. And then, after a moment's thought, he asked, "How much inside knowledge you got?"

"Me?" Brigid replied, offended.

"Come on, spill," Kane insisted.

"If you'd bothered to read Lakesh's notes, you'd have seen…" Brigid began.

"Notes?" Grant spit. "Did you see how thick that report was? The file was like the Prophesies of Whathisnamus."

"Nostradamus," Brigid corrected automatically.

As they spoke, Kane swept snow aside and pulled back a hunk of glistening metal from the ground. The edges were a little jagged, but it had the rudimentary appearance of a door into the snow. "Okay, kids," he announced, "we're in."

Seconds later, Kane clipped a powerful xenon flashlight to his jacket's lapel and clambered through the door, his two partners following him.

Making their way through the makeshift doorway, the three Cerberus exiles found themselves standing on a ledge about seven inches across. Leading the way, Kane walked along the ledge, kicking several small objects aside that appeared to be nothing more than paperweights.

Together, they made their way along the ledge until they could jump down to what appeared to be a series of steps running along the towering walls of a vast chamber. They found themselves in a high-ceilinged area that reminded Brigid of a chapel. Remarkably, Kane's flashlight beam was redundant; the area appeared to be lit through some hidden process that granted the ceiling a soft, pleasant glow. The glow was more than enough to light the room, and it almost seemed to be natural light, rather than artificial.

The chamber stretched on for almost eighty feet, with a width of half that again. The high ceiling gave it the air of a cathedral, and Brigid found herself looking up in wonder at the enormity of the place. The ledge that they had initially dropped onto had led to a series of shelves that doubled as steps. The shelves stretched all the way up all four walls, with a few items placed sparsely along their lengths. Everything was the color of ice, white and blue and crystal clear.

As they peered all around them, the three explorers saw

twin rows of glass cabinets spaced widely apart in two perfectly straight lines that led to the exit doorway. Each of the
cabinets held a mismatched item of some description, and
Brigid found herself drawn to the one nearest to where they
had climbed down the shelves. Inside, she saw an old-
fashioned barrel organ, finished in lustrous mahogany with a
large wheel at each of the four corners of its base. She leaned
closer, peering at the strange item until her forehead brushed
against the cool glass of its containment box.

"So," Kane asked, "what is all this?"

Brigid turned away from the cabinet. "Storeroom?" she
proposed with some uncertainty.

"You said this place had become buried," Grant said,
"which means we're at the top of the building. Meaning it's
an attic full of junk. Nothing unusual about that."

Kane glanced around him, checking several of the cabinets.
The nearest held an empty wooden chair, and in the one beside
it a single bullet rested on a plinth. "Trophy room maybe," he
suggested. "Where old man Flag kept his treasures."

"I wonder what they all mean," Brigid said, her quiet voice
echoing through the vastness of the chamber as they made
their way toward a doorway at the far end of the room.

Kane gestured to the large wooden throne that stood inside
the nearby cabinet, indicating the strange ideographs that
decorated its surface. "Looks like Egyptian writing," he said.

Brigid glanced at it for a second. "Aztec," she corrected him.

Trailing behind them, Grant cast his eyes across all the curiosities in the vast room. "So, what was this Flag guy?" he
rumbled, his voice echoing in the room. "Some kind of col-
lector of junk?"

"He was an adventurer, like us," Brigid explained, leading

them past the cabinet with the bullet inside, checking her portable scanner with a furrowed brow.

They stepped out of the room of curiosities and found themselves on a balcony containing an old-fashioned radio receiver. The balcony overlooked a huge area that stretched farther than they could readily make out. The area contained two desks and several comfortable seats, but the vast majority of it was dedicated to what appeared to be a scientific laboratory. The lab was stocked to an almost obsessive degree, featuring equipment whose nature Kane couldn't even begin to guess. Above and to the sides, the walls and ceiling appeared to be made of pure ice, twinkling in place as the light played over its smooth surface.

"This is nothing like the schematics," Brigid said as she consulted the palm-size tracker screen.

"Schematics can be wrong," Kane reminded her with a shrug, his eyes still fixed on the level below them.

"Not these," Brigid told him, tapping at the portable screen with her fingernail. "This is a portable sonar unit. It should be able to give us an accurate representation of where we are."

"And…?" Kane encouraged warily.

"According to this," Brigid said, showing Grant and Kane the display, "we're standing in a wall. I mean, right inside a *wall*."

Kane felt decidedly uncomfortable when he heard that, a jab of fear running through his spine. Irritated, he calmed himself, demanding that he behave rationally. "It's just an empty, forgotten redoubt, same as dozens of others we've visited," Kane stated firmly, making his way along the balcony toward a stairwell. The stairwell was built in a subtle curve that doubled back on itself, forming a double helix.

"What does it mean?" Grant asked. "Is your dohickey on the fritz?"

"It's tracking us just fine," Brigid assured them. "No, this is something far more subtle. I think that this place, this Laboratory of the Incredible, has stealth technology that can confuse tracking systems, so that it cannot be spied upon."

Pushing back his hood, Grant ran a hand over his cropped hair and whistled. "When did you say this place was built?"

"I'd say 1920-something," Brigid replied. "Nobody's quite sure. Flag would disappear for months at a time, and there's every possibility that he built this place in sections as he required it. Likely, I'd say."

"Any idea how?" Grant asked.

"He used some kind of sonic drill, I think," Brigid said. "A pretty powerful one."

Kane looked around at the glasslike walls. "Stealth technology," he said. "For a building. In 1920. You have got to be kidding."

"Professor Flag was a scientist of exceptional ability," Brigid reminded him as she followed down the stairwell with Grant at her side. "Years—perhaps decades—ahead of any of his peers."

"So the guy was a genius," Grant said.

Brigid considered Grant's statement for a few seconds before she responded. "That term might actually be construed as an insult," she said. "The man was extraordinarily intelligent. 'Genius' doesn't even begin to scratch the surface."

Stepping from the curved stairwell, Kane walked a few paces across the laboratory and looked all around. "Any idea what this Flag guy looked like?" he asked as Brigid and Grant came over to join him.

"I've examined the photographs in the Cerberus database," Brigid began.

"Let me guess," Kane interrupted. "Six foot six, square jaw, short dark hair—military style?"

Brigid nodded. "Why do you ask?"

"Because he's standing right behind you," Kane said.

# Chapter 4

Brigid and Grant spun, turning to face the stranger who stood where Kane was indicating. Grant's Sin Eater handgun snapped into his hand, propelled from its hiding place at his wrist holster.

The Sin Eater was the official sidearm of the Magistrate Division, and both Grant and Kane had kept them from their days as Mags in Cobaltville. An automatic handblaster, the Sin Eater was less than fourteen inches in length at full extension and fired 9 mm rounds. The whole unit folded in on itself to be stored in a bulky holster just above the user's wrist. The holsters reacted to a specific flinching of the wrist tendons, which powered the pistol automatically into the gunman's hand. The trigger had no guard, as any kind of safety features for the weapon had been ruled redundant. Thus, if the user's index finger was crooked at the time it reached his hand, the pistol would begin firing without delay.

Beside Grant, Brigid Baptiste's hand whipped down to the hip holster where she stored her trusted TP-9 tactical pistol, a bulky, automatic handblaster in dull black finish. The butt was almost central to the unit, making it appear almost like a square block finished by the wielder's hand.

Although Brigid's training was recent, all three Cerberus warriors were schooled in numerous forms of combat, from hand-to-hand martial arts to the use of knives, pistols, rifles and antitank weaponry. Furthermore, all three had the honed, lightning-fast reflexes that familiarity, muscle memory and combat awareness brought. In short, Brigid, Grant and Kane could more than adequately acquit themselves in any given combat scenario.

Right now, however, combat was not required. Grant and Brigid relaxed as they saw the man now standing before them. It was Abraham Flag, all right, although to describe him as "standing" was not entirely accurate. He was held upright inside what appeared to be a glass cylinder. The clear glass of the cylinder was somewhat obscured by a bluish, misty gas that floated within, through which they could see that the man inside was naked. His eyes were closed and, despite standing upright, he seemed almost relaxed, as though in a deep, dreamless sleep. Large metal pipes fed the cylinder, and Brigid noticed a control podium off to the right. No noise exuded from the strange construct, but the misty gas drifted in languid, faltering curlicues within the tube.

Kane's laughter came to their ears, as Brigid and Grant relaxed. "Boy, you two can really move when you want to," he said when they glared at him, still chuckling as he spoke.

Grant holstered his Sin Eater with a casual flick of his wrist, while Brigid made her way across to the control podium that was attached to the strange cylinder by a series of wires and copper pipes. There were controls integrated into the flat surface of the desk itself, like paintings on the reverse of a glass pane, and a foolscap notebook rested atop the unit. Brigid brushed dust from the glass work top and looked at the information displayed there. A series of dials was set beneath the glass of the unit, their needles held steady at about the three-quarters mark on their respective gauges. Beside them, a seven-digit analog counter slowly turned, and Brigid watched for a few seconds as the wheel to the farthest right ticked past 3 and rolled on toward 4. Then she picked up the notebook and flicked through its pages, finding that it was full of calculations written in blue ink with an elaborate hand.

"What do we have?" Grant asked as he and Kane strode over to join Brigid at the podium.

"He's a freezie," she said. "Cryogenically frozen and held in stasis here since—" she ran her finger along the index page of the notebook before flicking through several pages and finding the information "—November 1, 1930."

Kane whistled in amazement and paced over to the glass cylinder to take a closer look at the man inside. He was a muscular individual, well-built and broad shouldered, with a firm jaw and high brow. "He doesn't look much more than— what?—thirty-five, maybe forty."

"This is cryogenic research," Brigid said, indicating the book, "far in advance of anything Professor Flag's contemporaries would have been working on."

"The guy's a supergenius, remember," Grant stated.

"Supergenius or not, this is really quite remarkable," Brigid told them both. She closed the notebook and placed it back on the glass work top. "You can be the smartest Neanderthal in the cave, but it still won't do you much good to design a computer until someone develops the microchip. Flag's notes here indicate that he bypassed so many hurdles with regards to the limitations of the technology around him. I mean, look at him. He's a 250-year-old man, and he has been perfectly cryogenically preserved."

Kane looked at the impressive man standing before him in the glass cabinet. "Kind of vain, though, isn't it?"

"What?" Brigid asked.

"Why freeze yourself?" Kane asked. "Dead is dead—why prolong it any more than you need to?"

"I don't think he died, Kane," Brigid considered. "I think maybe something terrible happened back in 1930, and this was his way of keeping out of its path."

Kane knocked the cylinder with the edge of his fist. "Yeah, great job. Happy 250th, Sleepy."

Kane stepped away from the cylinder and headed back into the vast laboratory area, peering this way and that. "Anyway, let's go see if we can find this knife thing," he said. "Hopefully there's a map somewhere. I don't want to be wandering around this place forever."

Brigid and Grant followed, spreading out so that the three of them could scope out the vast Laboratory of the Incredible as quickly and efficiently as possible. Working swiftly and methodically, they checked work surfaces and desks, opened cabinets and looked beneath wipe-clean work tops, pushing aside notebooks and Bunsen burners, beakers and glass tubes. There were bottles and jars full of strange concoctions, and many of them appeared to hold crystals or small deposits of salt. Kane presumed these had once been liquid, too, but had evaporated over the vast passage of time since anyone had last walked through this strange and startling laboratory.

"You think he'll ever wake up?" Grant asked, calling across the room to Brigid as he peered behind a rudimentary spectrograph.

"I only glanced at his notes," she admitted, scanning the

shelves of a freestanding cabinet, "but it looked like he couldn't finalize the wake-up protocols in time."

Leafing through some loose papers at a desk, Kane stopped what he was doing and looked over at Brigid warily. "In time for what?" he asked.

"I don't know," Brigid said. "Do you want me to read the notebook, or do you want me to look for the knife?"

"Well, let's start by…" Kane began and then his words tailed off. Suddenly, like an anxious rabbit, he stood to his full height and looked off to the far end of the room. "You hear that?" he asked, his voice a whisper.

"What?" Grant asked, keeping his own voice low.

Silently, Kane indicated ahead of them to where a brightly lit doorway waited. With a swift hand gesture, he stalked toward the doorway, encouraging his partners to follow.

"This had better not be another joke," Brigid muttered as she pulled the TP-9 from its holster once more.

Kane hurried forward, his body low as he made his way to the doorway. Peering inside, he observed that it opened into a short corridor that led to another doorway just a dozen paces ahead. The noises were coming from beyond the second doorway.

Grant edged up beside Kane, giving his partner a concerned look. "What have we got?" he whispered. Grant had known Kane for years, and he knew that his partner had remarkable instincts, what Kane would call his "point-man sense." In reality, the point-man sense was a combination of spatial awareness and the refined use of Kane's other senses to become almost spiritually at one with his surroundings. In their days as Cobaltville Magistrates, Kane's point-man sense had saved Grant's life on more than one potentially lethal occasion.

Kane made a face before he stepped into the brightly lit corridor. His face said it all: whatever it was, it was probably trouble.

Grant held his hands loose at his sides as he followed Kane along the walkway, walking on the balls of his feet so as to make as little noise as possible. From the far end, where the vast laboratory stood, Brigid waited, TP-9 in hand, scanning the corridor and the doorway that led to the room beyond.

Reaching the doorway, Kane held up his hand, instructing the others to wait but to hold their positions. There were definitely noises coming from the next room, people's voices and the sounds of movement. Warily, Kane eased forward on silent tread and peered through the open doorway.

The room beyond was roughly hexagonal in shape, approximately fifteen feet across, and with a ceiling that was much lower than the laboratory area, just ten feet above the flooring. Like the rest of the strange headquarters, the walls to the room appeared to be constructed of ice, but it was much darker than the other areas that Kane and his companions had visited, reminding Kane of snow turned to slush. Light came from overhead in a single beam that lit the center of the room. There, standing in the center on a pedestal, stood a glass cabinet, similar in construction to those that the Cerberus team had encountered in the room they had originally broken into. This one, however, had reinforced wooden struts along its edges. The cabinet held a single item—a knife. Kane guessed that the knife was fifteen inches in length, including the handle, and it appeared to be carved from stone. Even from this distance, Kane could see the writing along its blade, though he didn't recognize the language itself. To one side of the blade, trapped within the glass cabinet like a fly in amber, a streak of darkness like a smear of paint seemed to hover in the air. As Kane moved his head, he saw the darkness glitter, like stars in the night sky.

There were people in the room, too, a dozen of them. Although none of them wore a specific uniform, they all seemed to be of a type to Kane's eyes. There were eight men and four women milling hurriedly about the room. One man was running a handheld scanning device over the glass display case, and several people were consulting laptop displays, running diagnostics as the information was fed to them. A tall woman was pacing the room impatiently, barking orders, while a broad-shouldered man watched her, shaking his head. Several armed guards stood to the edges of the room, looking uninterested in the whole affair, doubtless having already scanned the buried headquarters and found no one within.

Kane realized with a start that these people had arrived here before the Cerberus team, and had either used or created a different entrance. Given the size of the Laboratory of the Incredible, and the snowstorm raging outside, it would have been easy to remain utterly unaware of any other intruders unless they actually crossed paths.

"What about if we just break the cabinet, then?" the woman was saying, an irritated edge to her voice. She was tall—exceptionally so for a woman, almost certainly over six feet in height—with dark hair cut to fall just below her shoulders. She wore a formfitting outfit finished in matte-black leather, with red piping that accentuated her lithe frame. Kane could see a small pistol held in a holster at the rounded swell of her hip.

"We'll unlock it, Simona," the broad-shouldered man said in a placating tone. He was dressed in a similar black outfit, and sported a holstered gun hanging low to his hip. His hair was almost entirely shaved, with just the dark hint of stubble across his scalp along with two plaits that trailed down behind his right ear, falling over his shoulder where their ends were clamped with two metal beads. "Calm yourself, there's no rush."

"I just want to get out of here, Carver," she said, stopping before him with her back to Kane and the doorway. "This place is…abnormal."

Standing this close, Kane saw that, like many tall women, Simona was strangely shapeless, with small breasts and only a slight curvature at her hips in the otherwise flat line leading from shoulder to ankle. It made her seem that much taller, and somehow more graceful as she moved, like a person designed by aeronautic engineers to reduce drag.

"Heck, I didn't think you'd scare so easy," Carver said, his voice now rumbling with a cheerful tone. "Don't tell me that wacky mirror freaked you out."

"It's not fear," Simona snapped. "Just a healthy desire for efficiency. The sooner we wrap up this op and get back to the Millennial Consortium HQ, the sooner we get paid, fed and off this fucking iceberg."

"You're not really a winter person, are you?" Carver chided.

"I've wasted three months in that damned tent, searching for this hole in the ground," Simona growled. "I just want it to be over. Don't you?"

Reluctantly, Carver agreed.

Standing a little way back from the doorway, Grant looked at Kane and raised his eyebrows as they watched the scene unfold.

"Millennial Consortium," Kane mouthed in response to his partner's unasked question.

Kane, Grant and Brigid had crossed paths with the millennialists on a number of occasions. Twenty-third-century scavengers, they were pirates who profited by salvaging old technology and either selling it to the highest bidder or using it to their own ends. Often, the millennialists would attempt to do both at once. The Millennium Consortium was a vast organization, with branches in several locations and the technology and resources to back up impressive operations the world over. In theory, the millennialists had noble aims: the furthering of humankind and a recovery from the sick days that had followed the downfall of humanity at the end of the nuclear ravages of the twenty-first century. However, in practice, Kane knew, they were a selfish organization, whose only true goal was power, a goal they would readily achieve no matter what—or who—stood in their way.

Reluctantly, Kane stepped away from the doorway and, walking backward, made his way silently along the corridor, leaving Grant in place. At the far end of the corridor, Brigid looked up at Kane hopefully.

"We've located the knife," Kane told her, his voice low, "but there's one hell of a complication."

Brigid raised one perfectly shaped, red-gold eyebrow.

"Millennialists got here first," Kane explained.

"Damn," Brigid spit. "How many?"

Kane shrugged noncommittally. "How important is this thing? Be honest now, Baptiste."

"Why? Do you think you have a chance to snatch it?" Brigid asked.

"I think they're crap odds and we're better off making a tactical withdrawal," Kane growled, "but I'm willing to listen to counterarguments if you have any."

Brigid nodded toward the doorway at the far end of the corridor. "How many?" she asked again.

"Twelve," Kane said, "all of them armed."

Kane watched Brigid for a moment as the slightest crease appeared on her pale forehead while she thought. Then her eyes widened and she reached out to grab his arm, pulling him toward her.

"I think counterarguments will have to wait," Brigid said as the familiar sounds of gunfire shattered the quiet of the laboratory.

Kane turned and looked over his shoulder. Grant was rushing toward him at full sprint, and the Sin Eater had materialized once again in the big man's hand.

"We've been spotted," Grant shouted as he ran from the corridor amid a hail of bullets.

# Chapter 5

*October 31, 1930*
*Isle Terandoa Naval Base, the South Pacific*

"Godkiller." Abraham Flag repeated the word slowly, as though feeling its sharp edges with his tongue. "An ominous name for a weapon."

"Seems pretty weird to me, Professor," Barnaby B. Barnaby said in his cultured New Haven accent.

"It is hardly unprecedented to name a weapon," Flag reminded his archaeologist friend. "Think of Excalibur, or Mjolnir, Thor's hammer. There is a great symbolism to the naming of an item. Ancient people often believed that names were sources of immense power."

Little Ant was still poring over his notes. "But Godkiller, Chief," he chimed in. "Well, it ain't exactly subtle, is it?"

"Nor, I imagine, is being stabbed with a twelve-inch blade of carved stone," Flag pointed out, but there was no hint of malice or superiority in his tone. He turned the knife over once more in his white-gloved hands. "Do you have a workable translation of the text, Little Ant?" he asked.

"I got most of it," Little Ant assured him, "though it ain't nothin' pleasant. There's a lot of lamentations, the destruction of an enemy's family tree and some stuff about being returned to *Tiamat*."

"*Tiamat*," Flag repeated, placing the strange stone knife back on the desk. "She was the great mother of the Annunaki, the family of gods from Mesopotamian and Sumerian mythology. Some myth fragments suggest that she kept her squabbling children in line as they waged their endless battles across heaven and Earth."

"Sounds like a tough old broad," Little Ant remarked jovially as he replaced his modest notebook into his breast pocket.

Abraham Flag's amethyst eyes took on an eerie, distant quality as he turned to look out of the small window of the office. Sunlight streamed through the pane, its golden rays playing along the length of the odd stone knife. Out there, beyond the wire fence that surrounded the naval base, a lush jungle stood poised, brimming with the colorful plant life of Isle Terandoa. "If the stories are accurate," Flag said finally, his voice low, "the Annunaki were beings of immense power, the likes of which have never been seen before or since."

Barnaby shook his head in disbelief, his tousled red hair flopping this way and that. "Gods, Professor?" he scoffed. "They're just stories."

Flag turned back to his companions, his eyes playing across the dark-colored blade. "The artifact before us would suggest otherwise, Barnaby," Flag stated, an ominous edge creeping into his voice.

Both Little Ant and Barnaby B. Barnaby had worked alongside Abraham Flag for many years, racking up a score of adventures across the globe. Neither man had ever seen their de facto leader look as concerned as he did at that moment.

Little Ant shrugged. "You really think a stone knife is gonna do much hurt to anyone, Chief?" he asked.

Flag's gaze met with Little Ant's, and such was its penetrating quality that, even though the little linguist had known the impressive man of science for a dozen years, he found himself shying away. "If this blade belonged to the Annunaki, then we should presume that there is far more to it than meets the eye."

"Like what?" Little Ant asked, a quaver in his voice. "You think it's got one of them death rays or something hidden inside?"

"I held it for less than a minute," Flag considered, "and in that time I could feel that something about it was different. Had you not noticed?"

Flag's companions looked disconcerted. They were familiar with his prodigious powers of observation, but the man was usually so sure of himself that it was a rare day that he would request confirmation from anyone else.

"What kind of a 'something,' Professor?" Barnaby asked.

"Yeah," Little Ant added. "We been with this thing for a coupla days an' I didn't notice no 'somethings.'"

"It is subtle," Flag admitted, "but the knife has a vibrating quality. Infinitesimal, I'll grant you, but it is ever moving, as though in a constant state of flux."

"It looks solid enough," Barnaby stated, "but what you're describing sounds more like it's made of gas."

"It does indeed have the appearance of a solid object," Flag assured him, removing and pocketing his white gloves, "and yet I would wager that your description that it is made of gas is—at the subatomic level—a reasonable analysis."

Then the professor's tanned hand reached forward, the fingers spread widely as they closed in on the knife. But he did not touch the curious weapon. Instead, Abraham Flag held his hand in what appeared to be an open grip, running his widespread fingers along the very edges of the blade, never once touching it. "It has an aura," Flag confirmed. "I would need to perform a full analysis before I can be certain of what that aura is, but I can assure you that it is there."

Flag's companions looked at each other, utterly baffled. Although Flag was renowned as a man of science, he was in fact a polymath, a scholar of many disciplines. In combining the many great bodies of knowledge that he had absorbed, Flag could bring his analytical mind to bear on the most esoteric of subjects. Even so, the words he was speaking now seemed to belong to an utterly different world view from the one to which he subscribed, and that paradigm shift caught his companions off guard for just a second.

Little Ant was the first to speak, voicing his reservations in his famously cheery way. "It sounds like a load of old hooey to me, Chief."

Barnaby's face turned red and he glared at the diminutive linguist. "'There are more things in Heaven and Earth than are dreamt of in your philosophy'," the archaeologist assured him angrily, quoting Shakespeare. "You buffoon," he added, shaking his head.

"Hey, who ya callin' a buffoon, you dust-diggin' goliath?" Little Ant snapped back.

Flag ignored them. He had seen this argument played out a thousand times by his companions, and he knew that, despite appearances, it was an amicable way of letting off steam. Instead, it was the ancient knife that played on Flag's thoughts. It had to have lain at the bottom of the ocean for thousands of years before being brought back to the surface with the shift of the tectonic plates that had revealed Isle Terandoa. Without proper study, Flag couldn't be certain, but his instincts told him that this strange stone knife was incredibly dangerous.

DEMY OCTAVO HURRIED through the dense undergrowth of Isle Terandoa, propelling herself with swift strides of her long, shapely legs. The U.S. Navy clearly considered the island to be secure, she realized as she pushed thick fronds aside and sidled close to the wire fence that surrounded the naval base. There was the occasional sentry patrol, but their movements were languid and unhurried, a sign that it was considered routine rather than a conscious act to protect the base from potential infiltrators. They may well be able to repel a fleet of warships, but they were utterly unprepared for a single interloper.

The beautiful Signorina Octavo brushed aside the heavy leaves of a salmonberry bush, sweeping its rich pink flowers and yellowish fruit from her path. The wire fence stood barely six feet ahead of her now, and just a little beyond that, she could see the window to the small office where Abraham Flag consulted with his companions on the nature of the ancient Annunaki dagger. The window itself was closed, in spite of the heat of the day, and the dark-haired woman sneered with irritation at not being able to hear the discussion within.

No matter. Flag had led her right to the priceless knife, and its acquisition was all that concerned Octavo now. Whatever the nature of that strange stone blade, it could be examined by the fascist scientists of her native Italy as soon as she returned with it.

Her gloved fingers reached down, and Demy Octavo pulled one of the silver-handled Berettas from its resting place at her hip. She flipped the safety catch on the left-hand side, pulling it toward her to engage the weapon.

A thin, heartless smile creased those luscious, falu-red lips as the glamorous Italian special agent aimed the pistol at the tall figure pacing back and forth behind the office window. In a moment, she assured herself, her hated enemy, Abraham Flag, would be no more.

THE AIR WAS BECOMING noticeably warmer in the tiny office as Abraham Flag walked back and forth, weighing thoughts of the Annunaki blade with his razor-keen intellect. The uncomfortable warmth was the effect of three bodies in such an enclosed space, he knew, but that mild discomfort made him conscious of something else: his need for privacy while he studied this queer object from another time.

"I shall take the stone knife to my laboratory," Flag stated, his words cutting into the friendly bickering that was continuing between his two loyal companions.

Even as the words left his mouth, Flag sensed something behind him. He spun on his heel, turning to face the window at the exact instant that its glass pane shattered and a 9 mm bullet raced over his shoulder. Missing Flag by a fraction of an inch, the bullet zipped across the tiny room before embedding itself in the far wall with a dull thud.

"We're under attack!" Flag cried as his companions took cover behind the desk.

As he spoke, Flag saw a familiar figure dressed in a brown leather flight suit moving just beyond the shattered window. It was Demy Octavo, leaping down from the wire fence that marked the border of the naval base. Flag was momentarily distracted as he admired her for a fraction of a second, her lithe, trim body like that of a dancer, her long, dark hair swirling in the island breeze. And then she raised the pistol in her right hand, and another 9 mm slug ripped through the space where the windowpane had been just a moment ago, blasting over Flag's head and rushing onward into the room.

Abraham Flag did not take cover, however. Rather, he was already in motion, a whirling dervish as the glass of the window crunched beneath his booted feet. In a second, Demy Octavo leaped through the window, snapping her heels high in the air and passing through the frame without so much as brushing it, in a feat of incredible muscle control.

While Abraham Flag had been known to kill, he preferred not to arm himself with a gun. He had no objection to the use of ultimate force if it was required; he simply felt that carrying a gun was largely unnecessary when other means existed to halt a foe's progress. As such, the incredible man of science now found himself unarmed and staring down the loaded barrel of a Beretta Model 1915.

"Good afternoon, Professor Flag," the beautiful gun mistress said in English, her throaty voice displaying just the faintest hint of her exotic accent.

Flag saw the slightest hesitation in the woman's eyes, as Octavo went to pull the trigger. He used that momentary hesitation—which could have been no more than an eighth of a second—to shift his head out of the path of the 9 mm slug as it left the barrel and raced through the air toward him. Then, as the bullet clipped past Flag's ear, his hand whipped out and snatched the pistol before Octavo could loose another shot.

Octavo cried out as the pistol left her hand, along with her glove, which was caught up by Flag's swift action. As her glove fell to the floor with a slap, the beautiful Italian turned on Flag, hissing like an enraged cat.

Abraham Flag's eyes never left Octavo's, but his fingers worked in a blur of movement. In less than two seconds, he had deconstructed the Beretta with one hand, dropping the component parts to the hard floor of the tiny office. But that minuscule distraction had been enough. As the barrel, grip and trigger guard tinkered to the wooden floor, Demy Octavo's fist snapped out, connecting with Flag's square jaw.

Caught off guard, Flag took a step backward, reeling from the savage blow. That momentary stumble threatened to cost Flag—and by extension the U.S. government—plenty. Signorina Octavo swooped down at the object resting on the desk like a hawk swooping down on a field mouse, snatching the stone knife in her right hand. She was still moving as Flag recovered, her tall body twisting as she jumped back to the window.

"Look out, Professor!" Barnaby B. Barnaby called from his hiding place behind the desk. "That incorrigible Italian ingenue is escaping. And she's got our knife!"

Octavo leaped once more through the shattered window, an angry snarl marring her flawless features. She had the ancient artifact, but she had lost one of her precious Beretta pistols during the scuffle. Landing on the tarmac beyond the broken window, Demy Octavo took off at a run, the heels of her Italian leather boots clip-clopping against the ground as she made her way past the administration block.

"Where's she goin', Chief?" Little Ant asked as he watched the woman hurry away.

Instantaneously, Flag recalled the layout of the naval base. "She's heading toward the main dock of the base!" he exclaimed. "Signorina Octavo is either planning to steal a boat…or my plane. Come on, let's go." As he said those final words, Flag was at the door to the office, running out into the corridor at a fast clip.

Outside, Demy Octavo had already reached the long airstrip where Flag has landed his experimental aircraft less than an hour before. She was as graceful as a gazelle as her arms pumped, and her long legs strove forward, the ancient knife clutched firmly in her right hand.

Two sailors were refueling Flag's curious air vehicle as Octavo appeared from around the side of the two-story administration building. Nearby, another group of sailors—eight in all—were busy at work refitting a one-man submarine. The sub was still in the testing stages, the parts laid out along the concrete skirt beside the airstrip. All of the naval personnel looked up at the sound of running feet, and were surprised and baffled when they saw the striking form of the Italian special agent sprinting toward them.

Behind Octavo, the door to the administration block crashed open and Professor Flag came running out with his two mismatched partners hot on his heels. "Stop that woman!" Flag bellowed, his powerful voice needing no augmentation to be heard clear across the other side of the sunbaked airstrip.

One of the sailors who had been refueling Flag's aircraft held up his hand, ordering Octavo to stop right where she was. In return, the cruel Italian doyenne brought up her right hand—the one that held the ancient stone knife—and swiped the blade across the unsuspecting sailor's face.

With an agonized cry, the sailor fell to the smooth blacktop strip, a sudden crimson streak marring his youthful features.

Although they were rare, there were times when Abraham

Flag regretted his policy of never carrying a gun. As he watched that brave sailor fall to his knees, the young man's face a ruined mosaic of pouring blood, he felt that pang of regret once more. Despite Flag's years training his body to an incredible level of physical fitness, Octavo had had too much of a head start and Flag's own actions had not been fast enough. Now the young lad would wear that hideous scar for the rest of his life, evidence of the coldhearted cruelty of Mussolini's fascist desires. Armed with the swift justice of a bullet, Flag might have halted Octavo in her tracks, wounded or killed her before she could cause any further damage.

As regrets darkened Abraham Flag's mind, Demy Octavo drew her second Beretta handgun from its holster and began to wave it at the shocked sailors standing along the airstrip.

"Everybody keep back," she warned, her voice as harsh as the ugly punishment she had just doled out to the sailor.

Showing their hands, the sailors backed away, their eyes fixed on the muzzle of that lethal handgun. But Abraham Flag's eyes had been drawn elsewhere. Instead of stopping, he drove himself harder, running at full speed to catch up to the Italian infiltrator, outpacing his companions with his huge strides.

Still holding the sailors at bay with her silver-handled Beretta, Demy Octavo turned at the sound of Flag's running feet. "Stop right where you are, Professor," she ordered, "or their blood will be on your hands."

As if to prove the seriousness of her threat, Octavo pulled the trigger, and a bullet spit from her gun, spearing through the air over the heads of the wary sailors.

Now twenty feet from Octavo, Flag stopped, his eyes fixed on the scene before him. "Demy, no!" Flag cried, and it seemed that there was the slightest trace of fear in the great man's voice. "Stop!"

Octavo laughed, a vicious, ugly sound from such a beautiful face. "I'll be leaving now, Professor, and no one will dare stop me," she assured him, taking a step toward his waiting aircraft.

Abraham Flag fixed the woman with his stare, his incredible amethyst eyes exerting an almost hypnotic power. "Please, Demy," he said, his voice calm once more. "Look at the knife."

Suspicious of a trick, Demy Octavo glanced at the stone knife in her hand. Its strange, dark surface rippled with sunlight, and yet the glow seemed somehow unnatural, as though it didn't really belong. Across from Octavo, still kneeling on the airstrip with his bloody face in his hands, the wounded sailor was clearly going into shock. But there was something else about him, something different. From beneath the sailor's hands, Octavo saw that selfsame glow, tinged with red and pulsing like something organic. As the man lowered his hands, he revealed a rent in his face that was so unnatural as to defy description.

Flag had sensed as much as seen the nightmarish change to the young sailor's face. It wasn't simply a cut, the way a knife would cut. It seemed almost as though that ancient blade had burned him like acid, eating into the flesh and sinews that hid beneath his fragile skin. But there was more to it than that. The young man was wounded at a cellular level; the very fiber that made up his being had been damaged in a manner that utterly defied human comprehension.

For an awful moment, the name of the stone blade bubbled to the surface of Flag's thoughts once more: Godkiller.

But it wasn't just the young sailor's face that had been altered. Demy Octavo was changing, too, as she clutched the knife in her elegant hand. She stood there looking at it, holding the blade in front of her as though transfixed.

"Demy," Flag urged, his voice firm, "Miss Octavo? Please, put down the knife."

For a moment, Octavo did nothing. She just stood, as still as a statue, as the Pacific sun beat down on the thin black line of the naval airstrip. And then, in a movement that seemed eerily inhuman, her head turned and she looked at Abraham Flag with a fierce anger in her eyes. Those deep brown eyes seemed darker now, but that was not the most remarkable thing that struck Flag as he stared into the orbs; it was their whites. For their whites were no longer white at all—they had taken on a crimson aspect as the blood bubbled within them.

"Put the knife down, Demy," Flag urged once again. "It's not safe."

In response, Demy Octavo's lips pulled back in an animal's sneer.

# Chapter 6

*Early twenty-third century*
*Laboratory of the Incredible, Antarctica*

Seven armed troops came rushing from the corridor after Grant, and a moment later the clattering of feet from the far end of the vast laboratory area revealed more had been skulking in the distant shadows.

Kane and Brigid were already running, weaving between work surfaces covered with electrical coils, vacuum tubes, microscopes and a dense forest of other scientific equipment. As he ran, Kane tensed his wrist tendons and the Sin Eater shot into his grip. He could already feel the angry determination welling inside as a hail of bullets whipped past him and Brigid.

A little behind his colleagues, Grant leaped over a desk, sliding across it on his buttocks and back, blasting a burst of fire behind him from the muzzle of his own Sin Eater. His shots peppered the doorway around the corridor, felling two of the millennialists and driving the others to cover.

Smashing beakers and test tubes out of his way, Grant landed on the far side of the desk amid a rain of breaking glass. Righting himself, the huge ex-Mag turned this way and that, searching for Kane and Brigid as gunfire echoed all around him. He spotted his partners crouch-walking between two rows of worktables roughly twelve feet away.

"What happened?" Kane snapped as Grant caught his attention.

"What always happens," Grant replied. "Somebody looked up at the wrong time."

Kane stopped moving for a moment and peered over the desk he had crouched behind, looking across to the corridor. "We should have just ambushed them while we had the chance," he chastised himself as he saw millennialist guards piling out of the exit there.

From the doorway to the corridor, someone shouted, "There's three of them."

A moment later, a cacophony of shots filled the air, shattering glass beakers and monitor screens on the work tops that he and his companions had taken refuge behind. The guards were followed a moment later by the dark-haired woman whom Kane had identified as Simona, striding through the open doorway, her high-heeled boots clattering against the hard floor with the pounding of a jackhammer. Kane saw her face properly for the first time, and not just the profile. It looked aristocratic, long with a pleasing curve to the chin. Kane noticed something else about it—something dark was marring the whole left-hand side of the woman's face. Before he could ponder any further on this, the woman raised her voice, shouting instructions in an authoritative tone.

"Don't damage anything," she ordered. "The material in this laboratory could be invaluable to our cause."

Invaluable was good, Kane thought. It gave them a chance to do more than dodge bullets. He switched on his Commtact and began to outline his plan, subvocalizing his instructions to Grant as he ushered Brigid toward the double-helix staircase at the far end of the vast laboratory room. "These ice rats have got us outgunned and outnumbered," he said, "and it sounds like the only thing stopping them from shooting us where we stand is the equipment in this lab. Let's use that to our advantage and get ourselves out of here while we still can."

Brigid turned to Kane as they rushed through the lab. "You're crazy," she spit. "We can't just leave—"

"Kane's right," Grant's voice stated over their linked Commtacts. "I don't much want to get shot in the head today, so let's just get back to the Mantas and call this one a bust."

"But the Annunaki blade—" Brigid began.

Kane silenced her with a look. "This isn't the time," he growled, and Brigid saw that steely determination in his gray-blue eyes.

As if in response, Brigid's arm snapped up and she thrust the TP-9 handgun at Kane's face. "Get down," she yelled.

Kane didn't stop to think. He was already dropping to the floor in a forward roll as Brigid's semiautomatic weapon spit a burst of bullets where his head had been just a second before. Still rolling, Kane spun, tracking Brigid's arc of fire with his own weapon. He saw three millennialist guards there, sprinting to keep pace with himself and his red-haired companion. One of the millennialists dropped as Brigid sprayed his head and torso with 9 mm bullets.

Fast runners, Kane thought with irritation as he righted himself and snapped off a quick burst from his crouching position on the shiny floor of the laboratory. The remaining Millennial Consortium men continued running, bearing down on Brigid as Kane's bullets cut the air all about them. Several bullets clipped the guards, but only slowed them momentarily, their kinetic armor diffusing the impact of the blasts.

Then the two remaining guards were on Brigid, weaving past the worktables as they turned on her.

A little farther back, Grant was trading shots with another group of guards. The millennialists were wary, careful not to hit any of the potentially invaluable equipment in the lab. Grant used that to his advantage, peppering the lab with bullets and punishing any of his foes who broke cover.

The two millennialists who had chased down Brigid and Kane split up. Brigid fired another blast from her TP-9 at the nearer guard, but he rolled sideways just fractionally quicker than Brigid's aim. A second later, the same guard sprung up from the work surface he had rolled behind, and his left leg whipped out in a snap kick. The guard's foot slammed into Brigid's stomach, and she flailed backward, a burst of fire from the TP-9 going wild, the bullets zipping into the air before disappearing with a staccato echo into the rafters of the vast room.

As Brigid recovered from that first, savage blow, the millennialist swung his right fist at her face, a small pistol clutched in his fingers blasting bullets through the air. Brigid stepped backward just quickly enough to avoid the shots, and, gun in hand, her foe's fist whipped through the air just beside her.

Brigid's reply was swift and deadly. Her right arm zipped up and her index finger locked on the trigger of the semiautomatic pistol she held, lacing her foe's body with a stream of bullets that drew a continuous line from groin to face. The millennialist rocked backward with the bullets' impacts as they smashed into his kinetic armor, and then he was toppling into the array of distillation equipment on a desk behind him.

As blood spurted from his lips, the Millennial Consortium footman fell into the distillation tubes, smashing the fragile glass equipment to little more than a mosaic of shattered glass.

Just two desks over, Kane was having his own problems with another of the guardsmen. Kane's initial observation had been spot-on—his opponent was a fast runner. So fast that Kane suspected he had some kind of augmentation under his baggy winter clothing—perhaps a cybernetic upgrade, something like one of the mechanical suits his field team had encountered in Greece just months before.

Through luck or skill, the millennialist remained on his feet as Kane's Sin Eater spit bullets at him. Then, in a blur, the man lunged at Kane, leaving the ground in a jump that took him several feet into the air. There was no time for Kane to react as his opponent's pointed right foot snapped out and drilled him in the side of the head.

For several seconds Kane's head reeled, and he felt as though he was falling. Even as he recovered his wits, Kane received the guard's follow-up blow—a brutal kick that caught him in the ribs, rolling him across the floor.

As Kane reeled from the blow, he squeezed his eyes shut and sought his focus, stilling his mind and ignoring the stab of pain in his side.

A flurry of movement, and the millennialist was lining up a spinning kick with Kane's head as its ultimate destination. Instinctively, Kane sent his Sin Eater back to its holster and reached above him with both hands. His hands grasped that approaching foot, which seemed nothing more than a blur, grabbing the ankle and snapping it backward. The attacker shrieked as he toppled back, his trapped ankle acting as the fulcrum to his plunge. The millennialist struck the floor solidly with the back of his head, and Kane released his leg and scurried forward, scrambling over his foe's fallen body.

Kane's right fist pumped forward, smashing the millennialist across the face, caving his nose in a burst of blood. As the guard's head reeled from Kane's first blow, the powerful ex-Mag pulled his right arm back as though for another swing. As he did so, Kane unclenched his fist and commanded the Sin Eater back from where it had retreated in his wrist holster just seconds earlier.

His eyes blurred in double vision from Kane's first, thunderclap blow, the Millennial Consortium guard saw Kane's fist approach his face a second time and saw the hard, black shape of the pistol forming within it like a butterfly emerging from a chrysalis. Then Kane's hand seemed to flash in explosion as he unleashed the full extent of the Sin Eater's unforgiving fury at his opponent's head.

Kane leaped back from the bloodied corpse, turning to see how his partners were faring. Brigid came running toward him as her own foe lolled against the shattered distillation equipment. Behind her, Kane could see Grant scrambling between worktables as more of the millennialist soldiers spewed from the far corners of the stadium-sized laboratory.

"There could be a thousand treats on that hard drive," Kane told Brigid through gritted teeth. "We can't nab all of them. Now, let's get up the stairs and make sure we're alive long enough to grab the next one."

Brigid continued running toward the staircase. She was annoyed, but she knew that Kane was right. Besides, there was every chance that Cerberus could acquire the blade from the Millennial Consortium at a later date—albeit at a high price. Reluctantly, Brigid led the way up the spiralling stairs toward the upper level. Kane scrambled after her, and a moment later Grant joined them as they hurried up the circling staircase.

"They've stopped shooting," Grant said over the Commtact, relieved.

Kane peered over the high, icelike banister as he ran up the stairs, taking them two at a time. "But they are following," he said.

"Guess they want to make sure we stay away," Grant proposed as the Cerberus trio reached the top of the strange stairwell. "You know we could pick them off from up here," he added, glancing back down at the scrambling figures who were fanning out across the lab, checking every area with grim efficiency.

Simona was bellowing fierce instructions, ordering her men to check everywhere to ensure that there were no other intruders in the buried laboratory.

Shaking his head, Kane jogged along the balcony toward the doorway of the trophy room. "Let's just keep moving before we run into their backup," he advised.

Ahead of Kane, Brigid was passing through the open doorway into the room at the apex of the buried Laboratory of the Incredible, heading back to the point through which the three of them had entered. As she moved into the trophy area, Kane's words from just a moment before proved horribly prophetic. An arm snapped out from off to the side of the open doorway, grabbing Brigid around the throat and wrenching her off her feet before she knew what was happening. She swung the TP-9 pistol around and her finger jammed against the trigger, unleashing a spray of 9 mm, 158-gram subsonic bullets that sputtered around the brightly lit trophy room.

Kane bolted through the doorway after their companion,

and saw Brigid move so swiftly to one side that he thought she had fallen.

"What the—?" Kane began as he heard the TP-9 spitting fire and saw Brigid being yanked backward, her heels sliding along the floor.

Brigid had been grabbed by a large man dressed in a thick coat with a fur lining, Kane saw. The man was over six feet tall, built like a grizzly bear and wearing a scarf and goggles that obscured his face. A Calico M-960 subgun hung from a strap over his shoulder. The long-barreled automatic rifle featured two handgrips for better control of the field of fire, and it was the preferred weapon of the Millennial Consortium. Kane took it for a sure sign that this man was with the other people they had encountered in the glacial fortress. And that could mean something else, too, Kane realized, his heart sinking—there may be even more millennialists just waiting to pounce on them.

TRAPPED IN THE huge man's grasp, Brigid was struggling to find her footing, her boot heels scraping across the white floor as she was dragged backward away from the doorway. She finally unhooked her finger from the TP-9's trigger, and the weapon went silent. She tried to gain purchase on the hard floor, but found that she was being pulled back so quickly that she couldn't even regain her balance for a second.

Kane raised his Sin Eater, stilling his mind as he took aim at the man pulling his companion across the floor.

The huge millennialist dragged Brigid between the glass display cabinets of the room, swinging her this way and that, using her as a human shield to prevent Kane taking his shot. "Try it," he growled, "and you'll execute your girlfriend, chum."

Kane held still, the Sin Eater tracking the man's movements as he continued yanking Brigid to and fro.

"Now, why don't you put your gun down," the millennialist suggested, reaching for his swinging Calico subgun with his free hand.

"Better yet," Kane snapped back, "why don't you put my friend down and we'll settle this like men."

Just entering the doorway to the huge trophy hall, Grant's voice came to Kane, urgency in its tone. "Kane, they're coming up the stairs. Boxing us in."

Kane's eyes flicked around the room, taking in the curiosities that stood silent vigil in their glass boxes. Trinkets and tablets that glistened beneath the miraculous lighting from overhead: bones and stones; here a chunk of masonry shaped like a wing, there a frayed rope wrapped around itself in a knot as thick as a person's torso.

Behind him, Kane heard the familiar sound of a Sin Eater as Grant blasted shots at the approaching enemies.

"Kane," Grant urged as the first of the millennialists reached the top of the double-helix staircase and dived against the far wall for cover. "Time's run out."

"Not yet it hasn't," Kane growled, and the Sin Eater bucked in his hand as he fired a single shot at the millennialist holding Brigid.

The bullet cut through the distance between Kane and his foe, slicing three long strands from Brigid's red hair as it passed her and smashed into the face of the man holding her. Immediately, the guard staggered backward, his grip faltering around Brigid's neck. Brigid didn't need any further opening than that. She was already regaining and shifting her balance, struggling forward and flipping her assailant over her shoulders. The man crashed to the floor in a heap of furs and trailing scarf.

"I'm fine, Kane," Brigid called across the trophy room. "Let's go." Without waiting for an answer, she turned and began rushing across the trophy-filled room.

Kane and Grant were already moving, racing down the walkway between the huge glass cabinets. Brigid was sprinting toward the far wall, where the icelike shelves had formed the makeshift steps for their entry into Abraham Flag's buried laboratory of wonder. Kane and Grant weaved between the cabinets that held the carved throne and the single bullet, making their way swiftly toward the far wall to join their redhaired companion.

Though knocked off his feet, the millennialist guard who had grabbed Brigid was not dead. He reached for his Calico M-960 as he lay on the floor beside a glass cabinet holding a single clay tablet. Kane's bullet had indeed hit him; it had slammed into the goggles that he wore, impacting against the hard plastic of the right eyepiece, leaving a scar across its surface like a spiderweb. Beneath the goggles, the guard's cheek ached, and he would have a black eye inside of an hour. But, other than disorienting him for five seconds, the bullet hadn't created any lasting damage. Now he turned his subgun in the direction of the fleeing figures and pumped the trigger. A stream of flat-nosed 9 mm bullets spit from the muzzle of the Calico, spraying out over the trophy room. Automatically, Kane, Grant and Brigid dived for cover as the bullets raced toward them.

As his team ducked behind the tall glass cabinets of the room, the string of flat-nosed, wadcutter bullets smashed through the cabinet at Kane's back, shattering the panes of glass and embedding themselves into the eerie, carved throne that waited silently within.

*Guatemala, May 19, 1926*

IT TOOK A FEW MOMENTS for his eyes to adjust when the sack-cloth bag was removed from Abraham Flag's head. Warily, he looked around at his new surroundings. He was in a small, windowless room that appeared to be barely eight feet square. Lit by a single, flaming torch, the room held the distinct smells of dust and decrepitude.

When Flag tried to move, he found that his wrists were held in place. He looked down and saw the large wooden clips that had been placed over them like some tribal woman's bracelet, clamping them to the arms of the solid wooden throne that he now sat upon. As hard as amethysts, his purple gaze played over the chair itself, examining the strange markings he saw there. The chair was covered in carvings, pictograms that Flag immediately recognized as the ancient written language of that dead race called the Aztecs.

Flag's lightning-quick mind worked overtime, swiftly translating the words that he could see, ascertaining their meaning as swiftly as he was able. The meaning of those symbols was clear: it was a throne of execution.

Suddenly, Flag became aware of movements behind him, and then a sinister voice came from close to his shoulder. "I see you are awake, Professor Flag," a man's voice stated. The man spoke in heavily accented English, and Flag recognized almost immediately that the speaker was from the Latino region of Central America.

"You have me at a disadvantage, friend," Flag replied. "I don't believe we've been introduced."

"'A disadvantage' would be a more than fair analysis, Professor," the man said, stepping from the shadows. Flag saw that he was a short man, carrying a little extra weight and dressed entirely in white. A vicious-looking scar ran down the right-hand side of his face, ending several inches into the man's hairline. The man's hair was hidden by a magnificent headdress of feathers, each of them dyed a vivid, bloodred. "You may call me Mr. Hidalgo. I am the man who will kill you before this day is out."

Abraham Flag had heard that same threat in numerous forms over the length of his career, and he felt no trepidation at facing death once again. Instead, he merely smiled at the irony of the man's name, for *hidalgo* meant *noble* in Spanish, the strangely garbed man's native tongue. This hidden threat had been close by ever since Flag had journeyed down to Guatemala to help with Michael Brand's construction project and encountered that first hideous corpse. Only now had that threat finally been given a face. The terrible, twisted and scarred visage owned by Mr. Hidalgo, the revived priest of the bloodthirsty Aztecs.

"The chair that you now sit in," Hidalgo explained, "has lain beneath this pyramid since its construction over three thousand years ago. It is a throne for the dead, and all who sit in it must surely die."

As Hidalgo spoke, Flag could feel a cold shiver wrenching at his spine. There was something about this chair, some uncanny ability that could affect a man in ways almost beyond comprehension. The ideographs were more than simple representations of its purpose—they acted in some way to channel a person's will, forcing them to die, their heart to cease beating.

"You feel it already, Professor Flag," Hidalgo said, wide teeth showing in a sickening smile. "You feel the dreaded march of death's approach."

This strange throne was the primitive equivalent of an electric chair, Flag realized, but one that was powered solely through the will of the executioner himself. Flag's only means of survival was to outthink Hidalgo before the dreams of death overcame him.

Flag narrowed his eyes and concentrated, his muscles tensing as his arms wrenched at the bonds that held them in place.

"You are a fool, Professor," Hidalgo mocked as he saw Flag struggling at his restraints. "You cannot break those shackles—no man can. And, in a few moments, you shall be dead."

Flag ignored the man's ranting, concentrating on his inner strength, the nobility of purpose that had served him through the most dire of situations. He could feel Hidalgo's thoughts in his mind now, sifting through them as a man's hands will sift through sand. Suddenly, that terrible, invisible hand clawed within Flag's skull, and the great man of science let loose a desperate gasp.

Hidalgo, that resurrected priest of a blood-soaked civilization of the ancient past, laughed as he tightened his mental grip on his victim, feeding all of his terrible hate through the strange and mystical chair through his thoughts alone. Trapped in that seat of doom, Abraham Flag fixed his fierce stare on the man in the abominable headdress, feeling the pressure bearing down upon his mind. His skull felt as though it might explode like some rotted fruit, but still Flag clung to life, recalling the miraculous things that he had discovered, thinking of all the sights he still had to see. And in that moment, something else flashed through his exceptional brain.

$$u \times d + (c \times s) - (t \times b)$$

It was the incredible equation he had been developing at his hidden Laboratory of the Incredible in the Antarctic, the equation that proposed to hold the key to life itself. He concentrated all of his thoughts on the equation, on life itself.

$$Up \times Down + (Charm \times Strange) - (Top \times Bottom)$$

As the equation raced through Flag's thoughts, the ideographs on the chair began to glow and, incredibly, to alter their shape. The parable of death that had been written there just moments before changed, the millennia-old carvings shifting their lines subtly as their meaning altered forever at Flag's command.

At first the priest, Hidalgo, failed to notice the extraordinary change that was occurring before his eyes. He stood in that tiny death chamber, grinning at Flag's plight as he focused his thoughts to power that incredible, ancient machine. And then, like an old sheet finally wearing through, something in Hidalgo's mind seemed to tear, ripping apart. The whites of his eyes took on an aspect of crimson as all of the capillaries burst, and blood trickled from his nose before he fell to the flagstone floor.

With a final strain of superhuman effort, Abraham Flag snapped the two shackles that held his wrists to the chair, their wood shattering into a thousand splinters as he leaped from that terrible throne of death....

KANE HELD HIS HAND over his face to protect his eyes as glass crashed down all around where he crouched on the trophy room's floor. Swiftly, he ran his hand through his hair, and twinkling slivers of glass tinkered to the floor. "Son of a bitch," he snarled, scrambling behind another cabinet and reeling off a burst of gunfire from his Sin Eater.

Kane's bullets cleaved the air all around the Millennial Consortium guard, but the man rolled behind another cabinet, this one containing a carved stone wing from some long-forgotten statue.

"Kane," Grant called from his own hiding place. When Kane looked, Grant was nodding toward the doorway. "More company."

Kane glanced up and saw more millennialist guards rushing through the open doorway. Grant and Brigid peppered the doorway with a sustained burst, and one of the newcomers fell to the floor amid a spray of blood as his companions rushed to find cover.

"There's no way we can get up top while they're here," Brigid said over the Commtact, her voice sounding frantic. "Any ideas?"

Kane's eyes narrowed as he assessed the scene before him. They were trapped in a room full of pointless crap as a dozen armed men closed in on them. Reluctantly, he engaged his Commtact's microphone. "I guess we play a game of Last Man Standing," he growled.

# Chapter 7

Sin Eater in hand, Kane backed up against a glass cabinet displaying nothing more than one lone bullet, its silver casing ringed with a single line of gold like a wedding band—a marriage of violence.

All around the brightly lit storage room, a dozen foot soldiers of the Millennial Consortium were finding their own cover as they hemmed in Kane and his companions. Both Grant and Brigid were somewhere off to Kane's right, closer to the ladderlike shelves than he was, but neither they nor he could get out of the room without moving out into the open and risking execution.

As Kane tried to track all the enemies in his mind's eye, his Commtact burst to life once more. It was Grant.

"Not that I'm complaining," Grant said, "but we're outnumbered here, partner."

"I noticed," Kane sourly acknowledged. "Looks like they had reinforcements tucked away."

"These see-through cabinets are no cover at all," Brigid added over the hidden Commtact unit.

"What are you suggesting?" Kane asked, his eyes fixed on the sentry who had grabbed Brigid. The man was busy reloading his Calico subgun. Kane saw now that the sentry had entered via a smaller chamber set to the rear of the trophy room.

They had to have walked straight past the inset door when they had originally entered the complex.

"A bloodbath might not be our best avenue of attack," Brigid mused.

"Ever the diplomat, Baptiste," Kane growled in response, but under the circumstances he tended to agree.

Though Kane had absorbed Brigid's words, his mind was focused on the guard by the cabinet containing the stone wing. The man had already shown himself to be dangerous, with a quick temper and an itchy trigger finger. What's more, he was deadly fast—a lethal combination to face in any armed man. Worse yet, Kane thought as he peered at the spent shells at his feet, the lunatic was using wadcutters, nasty, flat-nosed rounds that did more and bloodier damage than a standard bullet. Any of Kane's crew hit by one of those, even a glancing blow, would likely be incapacitated if not outright killed. The carved throne at Kane's back had great rents across its upright section now, and thick wooden splinters carpeted the floor around the busted display case where the wadcutters had torn the arcane piece of furniture apart. With fortune on his side, a man could take a bullet and remain standing; wadcutters just ripped apart anything they made contact with, and could easily go straight through the shadow suits the Cerberus team wore.

Kane turned his mind back to the conversation of strategy. "I'm gonna go make friends," he stated over the Commtact.

HIS SUBGUN RELOADED, the guard with the wadcutter bullets inched around the cabinet, the light glinting from his shattered goggle lens. Holding it solidly by its twin-handled grip, the man poked the Calico's long muzzle in Kane's direction, his cheek burning from the bullet his goggles had deflected.

RELUCTANTLY, KANE sent the Sin Eater back to its hiding place in his wrist sheath and stood to his full height, hands held in the air above him. "Salutations, millennial guys. Wonder if we can—" he began.

The itchy-triggered guard in the furs didn't wait for the rest. His finger pressed down on the firing stud of the Calico, blasting a round of wadcutters across the brightly lit room. Kane dived for cover as the formidable stream of hot lead cut through the air toward him.

Across from Kane, Grant located the assailant, placed the firing millennialist in his sights and returned fire, bullets spitting from the nose of his Sin Eater. Lightning quick, the millennialist ducked back behind cabinet cover as a dozen high-density, 9 mm bullets raced at him. Grant's leading bullet slammed through the front pane of the cabinet, shattering the glass and drilling into the worn stone wing that rested within. The bullet's lethal siblings followed a split second after, peppering the mossy surface of that strange hunk of masonry.

*Paris, France, September 3, 1928*

ONLY THE KEENEST of eyes would have noticed, but then Abraham Flag did have the keenest of eyes. One of the grotesque gargoyles that was perched atop the medieval church was not quite as worn, as decayed and moss-covered, as its companions. It was a well-disguised replica, but Flag could tell instantly that it was newly crafted. So, where was the original that this imperfect impostor had replaced? And why had someone gone to so much trouble to cover up the switch? Flag's formidable mind was immediately intrigued.

However, before Flag could even begin to process this information, a dark shadow loomed overhead and suddenly swooped down toward him. Flag dived for cover behind the nearest gravestone, and whatever had attacked flew back up into the gray sky, but not before Flag had glimpsed it.

Now Flag knew why there was a new stone gargoyle watching over the tower—because the old one was no longer made of stone. Gargoyles were meant to watch over, guard and protect their church from evil spirits and so this rogue had to be stopped, and fast. Professor Flag had been in many tricky, even dangerous, situations, but this was unlike any other he had encountered. It would take all his skill to put this right.

There was not much time to think, as the demonic creature dived at him again. This time Flag didn't get out of the way, but instead stood his ground. His bravery seemed to confuse the gargoyle, and it pulled itself up short directly in front of Flag. They were now face to evil face. Flag's mind was in motion, drawing quickly to the surface everything he knew about gargoyles and medieval beliefs.

Flag recalled a popular prayer from medieval times, for protection against evil. It was a prayer to Saint Michael the Archangel. Well, he certainly needed protection from evil now, and he had nothing to lose. Without ever taking his eyes off the hovering gargoyle, Flag began to recite:

"As smoke vanisheth, so let them vanish away: as wax melteth before the fire, so let the wicked perish at the Presence of God. Judge Thou, O' Lord, them that wrong me: overthrow them that fight against me."

Instantly, in midflight, the live gargoyle turned back into stone and came crashing down to the ground. As Flag leaped out of the way of that falling chunk of lifeless masonry, his fierce eyes spotted a motionless figure watching from high up in the bell tower—a human figure. As their eyes met, Flag heard the flapping of leathery wings, felt the coldness of a shadow from overhead as another stone demon bore down upon him....

THE CACOPHONY of gunfire echoed all around the trophy-filled chamber as the millennialists traded shots with the Cerberus trio. Bullets zinged back and forth as the battle continued. The gargoyle's wing that, moments ago, had sat safely behind glass for almost three hundred years toppled from its mounting and crashed to the floor as Grant's bullets peppered it. The millennialist guard who had been using its cabinet for cover was already on his feet, hurrying across the room, to the next piece of available cover—a glass cabinet holding a signet ring with a crimson gemstone. The ruby twinkled as it caught the light of gunfire and explosions all around it.

Then a woman's voice, authoritative and loud, cut through the noise of the firefight. "Everybody stand down." It had issued from a niche near the open doorway entrance, and Kane recognized it as the Consortium woman whom he had already tagged as Simona.

Peering from behind another glass-walled cabinet, Kane scanned the room as he waited to see what would unfold. The gunmen from the Millennial Consortium stopped blasting and, after a moment, Kane's team did the same. The room fell into an eerie silence as the echoes of gunfire ceased. No one moved. Kane's eyes fixed on where he thought Simona's voice had come from. After a moment, he saw a shadow moving by the wall. She was back there; he was sure of it.

The woman spoke again, her firm voice carrying effortlessly across the large, ice-white room. "Do you wish to negotiate?" she asked, her words echoing in the eerie stillness.

And then silence once more, just nervous shuffling from the edges of the room where the millennialists waited, poised.

Kane's mind raced. They were outnumbered and these modern-day pirates had no love for outsiders, unless they could work them over for a fast profit. Was he about to walk into a trap or, worse, an execution? Or had he just averted one?

Standing a little way across the room, Sin Eater held ready, Grant activated his Commtact. "It's your play, Kane," he said quietly.

Kane glanced over to the towering ex-Mag. Across from Grant, Brigid Baptiste crouched behind a glass box containing what appeared to be a propeller of a huge steamship, taking the pause in action to reload her TP-9 semiautomatic. She nodded once to Kane as he caught her eye, assuring him that she would back his decision.

After a moment's consideration, Kane let out a slow breath and stepped out into the open once again, his hands spread wide to demonstrate that they were empty. "My people are standing down, too," he announced. "Let's negotiate."

A few seconds passed, and Kane felt that the eyes—and guns—of almost everyone in that room were trained on him. Then the tall and lissome figure of the woman called Simona walked out into the open, pacing several steps forward in her black leather boots, stiletto heels tapping against the icelike surface of the floor. She stopped a few paces from the wall and rested her hands on her hips, openly assessing Kane from a distance. Kane could see now that the dark marring on the left-hand side of her face was a tattoo of a cobra, its triangular head lunging from around her eye socket in a blend of black-and-bloodred stripes. It ruined an otherwise flawless face.

"Introductions, if you please," the tattooed woman urged, fixing Kane with her penetrating, dark gaze, one-half of it emerging from that snake's hideous visage.

"Kane," Kane stated shortly. "My partners, Grant and Baptiste. We're here for the same reason you guys are, I suspect."

"Which is?" the woman asked, not hiding her contempt for him from her fierce expression.

She was someone used to having orders obeyed and getting exactly what she wanted, Kane guessed. *Like I wouldn't recognize that trait from every other woman I've tangled with,* he thought bitterly. "Scavenger hunt," Kane replied, raising one eyebrow as though it might be a question rather than a statement.

Dressed in her black formfitting outfit with the red piping that accentuated her frame, the tall, graceful woman nodded to herself, her deep brown eyes flicking across the vast trophy room, taking in every treasure. "Well, Kane and partners Grant and Baptiste," she said, "my name is Simona Jurist of the Millennial Consortium. We have scavenger rights here by prior claim. Do you wish to contest them?"

"No, ma'am," Kane assured her, uncomfortably aware of the number of armed millennialist guards in the room. There would be time enough to "contest" those rights when he didn't have a dozen or so guns pointed at his head.

"Presumably, you didn't stumble upon this cache by chance," Simona Jurist surmised. "How did you come to be here, Kane and partners? What do you know of where you are?"

It was a typical pumping for information disguised as a

friendly—albeit not very friendly—query. However, with guns fixed on him from every side, now was not the time to start playing dumb, Kane reasoned.

"We're traders," Kane lied. "We came across details of this place by chance. Heard it belonged to some old scientist from way, way back, prenukecaust. Figured it maybe had some stuff we could use."

"Any particular item?" Jurist pressed.

Kane smiled uncomfortably, thinking of the way this woman and her squad had been clustered around the stone knife when he'd stumbled upon them. "This and that," he answered.

"And yet," Simona Jurist observed, "you didn't take anything from this room. Presumably, any one of these trinkets would have been of interest to a trader…." She left the sentence dangling, as though it was a question.

Kane shrugged. "Well, you know how the market can be," he ventured.

Simona Jurist's hand slid down her body, tracing along the curve of her hip before stroking the handle of the pistol she had holstered there. "I think you can do better than that, Trader Kane," she said.

Kane's eyes flicked from Jurist's holstered pistol to her dark, impenetrable eyes. "Let's not play that game," he warned her. "You draw down on me and we'll be right back where we started. And I can't guarantee your safety if that happens."

Jurist smiled haughtily. "So you fancy yourself as a quick draw?"

Kane ignored her. "Ask your questions, Jurist," he growled.

"Then answer them, Kane," Jurist snapped back. "You didn't just stumble on this place. It's out of the way, too much so for an independent trader. Which means you're either looking for something specific, or you planned to ransack the whole place. Either way, it's a prohibitively costly operation, too much so for an indie. So, why don't we try again, and you can tell me *exactly* what it is you came searching for."

"We're looking for a weapon," Kane admitted, feeling his grip on this conversation slipping. "How about you guys?"

"A weapon?" Jurist echoed, ignoring Kane's question. "That's a term that can cover a multitude of sins, Kane. Which specific weapon were you looking for?"

Kane ground his teeth before he answered the consortium woman. "Same one as you," he told her.

A thin smile lit across Jurist's aristocratic face at that. "Can you open it?" she asked. "Do you know what it does?"

Kane made a show of ticking off his answers on his fingers. "Perhaps…and maybe," he said, with no short degree of irony.

"We understand that it is old and powerful," Jurist explained, "but we don't know exactly what the knife does." Her bangs brushed over her eyes as she fixed Kane with her dark stare, encouraging him to explain.

"Well, since only one of us is going to walk out of here with it," Kane said, "I don't see much point in telling you stuff you don't know. What's in it for me and my people?"

Jurist turned, and Kane found himself admiring her exceptionally tall, thin figure as the overhead light glinted from the lean curves of her leather-sheathed body. "Look around you," she instructed. "You're outnumbered four to one. I have sixteen more troops in this redoubt, and another ten men at ground level in a fully equipped mobile base." She turned back to Kane, fixing him with her stare once more, her left eye peering from the blood-and-charcoal stripes of the snake tattoo. "You can either assist us and live, or you can—what's a term you'd understand? I wonder—have your ass handed to you."

Kane snorted. "My ass…?"

Jurist snapped her fingers, and in less than a second every millennialist gun in the room blasted a shot at Kane. Bullets cleaved the air all around him, leaving a circle of damage just inches ahead of the toes of his boots and shattering the glass-fronted cabinet he stood beside. Inside the shattered cabinet, the single, gold-banded bullet shook on its plinth.

*Manhattan Island, January 17, 1924*

SMILING, ABRAHAM Flag, Barnaby B. Barnaby and Little Ant left Commissioner Allen at the top of the steps to deal with the gentlemen of the press alone. The commissioner could decide how best to explain that his job had been reinstated—whether he chose to mention the deception played on the Museum of Natural History by the so-called specters was of no concern to Flag. The most trusted man in New York City was back in his position, his untarnished record clean once more, and he would remain a strong ally should the extraordinary man of science ever require his aid again.

Striding beside his companions, Flag made for his sleek roadster where they had left it at the side of the curb, and, as he did so, something caught his eye. A tiny flash of light played on a rooftop across the street as the sun's rays hit upon a metallic object there. Where another man might have ignored or dismissed such an occurrence, Flag's sharpened senses went on immediate alert, and he was already turning back toward the stone steps of the police station where Allen continued to field questions from the reporters crowded there.

"Commissioner," Flag cried as he ran, "get down!"

Even as the warning left Flag's mouth, his exceptional hearing picked up the subtle sound of the sniper's rifle as its bullet left the silenced barrel on a certain, deadly path toward the commissioner's head.

Abraham Flag turned, a graceful movement despite the size of his powerful body, and his right arm snapped out, reaching into the air. It was a remarkable thing to witness, as Flag enacted that astonishing feat of agility before the assembled men of the press. A split second later, he was rolling to the sidewalk, dragged down by his own arm as though his hand had suddenly become impossibly heavy. It was not weight that dragged him down, however; it was the kinetic energy of momentum.

Commissioner Allen's words came back to Flag as the incredible adventurer righted himself. "What is it, Abe? What's going on?"

Abraham Flag held up his right hand and revealed the tiny metal cylinder that he held there, poised between thumb and forefinger. It was a bullet from the sniper's gun, snatched from midair. "This bullet was meant for you, Commissioner," Flag announced, "and I intend to stop at nothing to find the culprit."

With those fateful words, Flag and his allies took off at a run, weaving through the afternoon traffic as Commissioner Allen hurried the gentlemen of the press through the police station doors to safety. "Godspeed, Professor Flag," he said. "Godspeed."

*Early twenty-third century*
*Antarctica*

KANE LEAPED BACK as glass shattered all about him. Across the room, Simona Jurist was smiling smugly as her soldiers aimed their weapons at Kane and readied to fire another round. Behind him, Kane knew that Grant and Brigid were preparing to return fire.

Eyeing Kane, Jurist grinned. "I'm sorry, Kane, but I have a very low boredom threshold," she informed him.

"Yeah," Kane growled, "I'm getting that. Look, enough of the pissing contest, Jurist. If we don't figure some way to resolve this, we're all going to end up dead."

"And what would you propose?" Jurist asked.

"You let us out of here and we won't bother you," Kane said, shaking his head with annoyance. "Everything that your men haven't shot to shit is yours, no contest."

Jurist's face broke into an amused grin. "Everything here is mine already," she announced, "which makes your offer redundant. No, you'll have to do better than that."

Kane cursed himself for a rookie. Jurist was calling the shots, and she knew it. The best thing to do now—the only smart thing, in fact—was to play along until an opportunity presented itself that Kane's team could turn to their advantage. He leaned back against a glass cabinet holding a fob watch and let out a long sigh. "Okay," he said at last, "what do you want?"

"Tell your partners to disarm," Jurist responded, the triumph clear in her supercilious tone. "You, too," she added.

"Now, why don't you give me a good reason why I'm likely to do that?" Kane growled.

"You have nothing to fear," Jurist assured him. "The Millennial Consortium are seekers of knowledge, Kane. *I* am a seeker of knowledge. When I have a resource in my hands I use it to my best advantage."

I ain't in your hands yet, you arrogant bitch, Kane thought, but he reached for his sleeve and, securing his weapon inside, unstrapped the Sin Eater's holster. Once he was done, he waved the holstered blaster out before him, like some perverse flag of surrender.

Jurist nodded. "And now your friends," she encouraged, a gleam of satisfaction playing in her coffee-rich eyes.

Within three minutes, Kane, Grant and Brigid had been stripped of their weapons and other potentially questionable equipment, including Kane's pocket toolkit and a host of tiny explosives geared to a variety of effects. Kane accepted this with irritation, but he consoled himself that their subdermal Commtacts were hidden from view; if need be they would still be able to communicate if they were to be split up.

Seeing his irritation, Jurist stepped close to Kane and whispered, her lips almost touching his ear, "See, life's so much nicer when we just try to get along."

Kane glared at her.

IN A SHOW OF supposed friendship, the Cerberus team was taken back to the adjunct room of the main lab where the stone knife was held in its solid display box. When they entered, the black-garbed man, with his shaved head and twin plaits of hair, was instructing a squad as they carefully unscrewed the cabinet from its base in preparation for moving it. The shaved-headed man wore a set of electronic goggles around his neck, and he looked up at their approach.

"We caught up with the intruders," Jurist explained as her guards positioned themselves at the door. "They've agreed to assist us."

*Agreed* seemed a bit too strong a word, Kane thought irritably, but he let it pass.

"Hi," the man offered as his men continued at their pains-taking work. "Name's Carver."

"Kane," Kane responded, "and my partners, Baptiste and—"

"Grant," the man called Carver finished, looking at the broad ex-Mag.

Grant frowned. "Do I know you?"

"Cobaltville, right?" Carver said wistfully. "You graduated the year above me as a full-fledged Magistrate."

Grant thought back to his days in Cobaltville, the thou-sands of people he had interacted with as a Mag. "Carver, Carver," he repeated to himself. "Man, yeah—you had one of the best scores for research detail. I'd almost forgotten you."

Carver's plaits bounced as he laughed. "Not surprised," he said. "I quit pretty much the day I graduated."

"You were a Mag?" Kane asked.

"For about two months," Carver said. "You?"

Kane nodded. "Why'd you leave?"

"A better opportunity presented itself," Carver said. "You?"

Kane chuckled. "Something like that."

It was not unheard-of for a Magistrate to go rogue, strike out on his own, but it was rare. The admission told Kane one thing—this man was a highly trained killer, despite his affable nature.

"Enough of the school reunion," Jurist snapped. "Show them what we have and let's get moving."

Carver stepped aside from the stone knife in the holding box to allow Kane's team a closer look as his crew continued dismantling the holding plinth. The plinth appeared to have been riveted to the floor with what could best be described as extreme overcautiousness.

"This is it," Carver said, tapping at the reinforced glass. "The records we found say this is an ancient weapon belonging to a group called Annunaki, if that means anything to you. Reportedly, these Annunaki were gods, their battles would rage across the skies—all that crazy myth shit."

"So we've heard," Grant said. In actuality, the Cerberus team hadn't simply heard of the Annunaki—they had faced them in savage combat, and much of the team's ongoing efforts were dedicated to repelling the Annunaki's insidious control of humankind.

"Pulled some details off an old military database out in old Dakota," Carver continued. "The info's fuzzy, but it suggests this little baby has a lot of kick to it."

"How much 'kick'?" Brigid asked, already knowing the answer.

"Encrypted military file," Carver told her, "says it sunk an island out in the Pacific."

"Isle Terandoa," Brigid stated, recalling the report she had read.

Carver looked at her, his eyes widening in surprise. "I guess we read the same reports," he said.

Smiling back, Brigid raised one of her thin, fiery red eyebrows. "Small world. Who'd have thought it?"

"Wait a minute," Simona Jurist spit, "this knife sunk an island?"

"On October 31, 1930," Brigid Baptiste confirmed, fixing the taller woman with her emerald stare.

# Chapter 8

*October 31, 1930*
*Isle Terandoa Naval Base*

"'Tyger, tyger, burning bright,'" Barnaby B. Barnaby muttered as he halted in his tracks, staring down the length of the airstrip at Demy Octavo.

In Octavo's hand, that awful stone blade flashed in the sun's rays, and yet there seemed something uncanny about the way the sun was playing off its sleek lines. In her sneering face, her eyes continued to alter, the crimson behind them bubbling like boiling water in a pan.

"Quit yer yappin', mud sifter," Little Ant shouted as he grabbed Barnaby by the arm and pulled him to the ground. "Something real rum is going on here, and I just know the chief wouldn't want us getting in his way."

Barnaby agreed, but for once he was at a loss for words.

The man that Little Ant called the chief—Professor Abraham Flag—was standing on the airstrip, legs widely spaced, his center of balance low as he spoke to the glamorous fascist insurrectionist holding the ancient knife. "This has gone on for long enough, Demy," Flag said, his voice calm and commanding. "You need to relinquish the Annunaki blade before anyone else gets hurt."

Sneering, Octavo ignored Flag's words. Instead, she swung the fearsome length of the knife dubbed Godkiller through the air, as though to keep Flag at bay.

Still eight feet from the Italian secret agent, Flag stood his ground as the blade cleaved the air before him. Even at that distance, he heard the sound of the blade as it sliced toward him. To Flag's acutely sensitive ears the knife's passage sounded like rippling water, a sloshing, bubbling noise. Despite the grim source of that strange sound, it seemed almost musical, reminding Flag of the tranquil gardens he had visited in Japan, with their water sculptures granting a background sound so natural that it encouraged the occupant to a state of sublime meditation.

Suddenly, the mesmeric spell that the blade was weaving ended as a gunshot broke into the tranquil song of its passage. Flag saw the flash of propellant as a bullet blasted from the group of watching sailors. One of them had seized the opportunity to halt Octavo in her tracks, and Flag knew that man would get a medal if his desperate actions succeeded.

Even Flag's unrivaled mind struggled to absorb everything he witnessed in the next fraction of a second. The bullet sped through the air toward its intended victim, but Demy Octavo's lithe form appeared to move so fast as to not move at all; she was standing facing Abraham Flag and at the same time she had turned to face her attacker, thrusting the curious stone knife before her.

Flag heard the ricochet as the sailor's bullet struck the polished length of that ancient blade. Incredibly, the blade held true, and the bullet bounced off into the waiting jungle beyond the wire fence.

Even as Flag took in the information that his amethyst eyes fed to his brain, Demy Octavo was moving forward, a runaway juggernaut of fury, a lightning streak in human form as she charged across the tarmac airstrip.

Flag watched, helpless, as the scene unfolded. The stone blade was swinging through the air, held in the elegant, long fingers of Demy Octavo and yet, somehow, no longer controlled by her. As he had just moments before, Flag heard that enlivening rippling as the blade moved through the air, a sound so beautiful that the blade's passage threatened to hypnotize the unwary.

Demy Octavo was moving, and her motions were so fast that they defied comprehension. Flag could only watch as she powered toward the watching sailors, swinging that terrible blade and butchering those brave young men as they tried frantically to withstand her onslaught. Bullets were fired, and several seemed destined to reach their target, but each one that got close was flicked aside by Demy's knife hand with such casualness that it seemed to be as nothing.

Flag ran as never before, his powerful strides eating up the dozen or so feet that now separated him from Octavo and her victims. In his mind, he prayed that she would forgive him for what he was about to do. Shoulder down, Flag barged into the blur of incredible motion that had replaced Demy Octavo, felling her the way a linebacker will level a blocking back. In all honesty, Flag could not see Demy Octavo; he could just see the dark shape where she spun and twirled, engaged in her deadly dance of death. It was like watching a fly's wings in motion.

Abraham Flag grunted as his shoulder connected with the something that was Demy Octavo, and both of them rolled to the hard-packed soil at the side of the airstrip. Something cracked in Flag's shoulder, and he wondered if he had broken it, for hitting the svelte form of Demy Octavo felt like running into a solid wall. And yet his ploy had worked. Octavo tumbled to the ground, and that incredible burst of speed left her as the knife flew from her hand.

Flag ignored the ache in his shoulder. instead his keen eyes were on the stone blade as it skittered across the tarmac of the airstrip. Flag's peerless brain raced, considering a dozen different options and discarding each in rapid succession as he ran for the deadly discarded dagger. There was something about it, he realized, something unutterably beyond human understanding.

Abraham Flag had faced the apparently supernatural before now, although he had always been able to present a rational explanation for it once he had studied it fully. However, the proceeding that he had just witnessed, with fascist temptress Demy Octavo's metamorphosis into some primal being of incredible speed, belied rational thought. It was as if she had been possessed, Flag realized, feeling sick to the pit of his stomach at the very word. However, if the knife had somehow exerted control over Octavo, Flag needed to know how and why before he could proceed any further. Even as the thought hit him, Flag's grasping hand reached for the knife…

And stopped.

Skin contact? Could that be it? In Kinver's office, Flag had handled the millennia-old blade with gloved hands, and he might presume his allies had, too. Octavo had lost one of her gloves during their brief clash in the office, and had subsequently clutched the knife in her bare palm.

But there had to be more to it than that, Flag knew. If skin contact was the trigger, then the weapon would be utterly impractical for any human to use.

The whole discourse had taken Flag less than two seconds to consider, but he became suddenly aware of movements behind him. Crouched over the knife, careful not to touch it with his bare skin, Abraham Flag peered back to where he had left the fallen figure of Octavo. And what he saw chilled him to the very marrow.

Demy Octavo was pulling herself upright, and yet it seemed like a movement no human had ever made. Her limbs were held at angles, like the legs of a bug, and her beautiful face was tilted so that she peered at Flag from close to her left shoulder, her mouth fixed in a hideous grin. Her eyes burned with a red swirling behind her dark irises, a bubbling crimson fury where the whites of those eyes had once been, raging like a twister on the horizon. She stood balanced, that much was true, but nothing about her manner recalled anything that Flag would associate with human movement. Something in the way Demy Octavo now stood made her seem not taller so much as longer, thinner. Overall, it was a chilling sight for any man, and even Abraham Flag, that globe-trotting man of action whose eyes had witnessed many strange and fantastical sights, felt a shiver run down his spine.

Worse still was what Flag saw behind the rising body of Demy Octavo. Lying there was the fallen sailor, still pawing the surging, pulsing rent in his head, which had opened like some perverse window looking into a whole other place. And the other sailors were different now, too. They also had been touched by that devastating blade, spattered by the blood of their wounded comrades. Those cuts, those tears, those splashes of blood were changing, altering into things that glowed red as the setting sun. That awful red glow was so powerful that it hurt Flag to look at it, and yet he knew instinctively that the pain was not in his eyes; it was something more fundamental. The pain was an inability to truly comprehend what his eyes were seeing, as though this panorama was somehow too large to digest.

The creature that was Demy Octavo, or was building upon her like some *favela* shack—Flag could no longer tell—stood in the red glow and oozed from the wounds and blood behind her, pulsing and popping like a volcano in full fury.

Flag's skull felt small, his brain large. There was an aching behind his forehead the like of which defied description. Here was something not meant for human eyes. Here was something that he had to look away from or be forever seared by.

Somewhere deep inside, Abraham Flag felt his heart skip, his breathing cease and restart, as though his autonomic functions were failing. It was his brain, he knew, the burning of the brain eating through him like a raging forest fire. Octavo's stance reminded him of a puppet as she staggered slowly, deliberately forward, step by agonizing step. Behind her, the redness—the bleed—swirled and churned, an angry tide of blood.

With a supreme effort of will, Flag urged himself to turn away, to close his eyes against that hideous, dazzling visage that threatened to overwhelm his every thought. The last thing he saw were the lights reaching out from the bleed, emerging from the rip that had been made by the carving of human flesh. And those lights, may Flag be forever cursed, looked beautiful. As beautiful as angels.

Kneeling on the airstrip, hunched over the stone knife, Abraham Flag turned away, closing his mind to everything that he had just witnessed.

In his mind's eye, Flag saw the swirling crimson of the bleed, assaulting his senses. And the blood was clotting around his thoughts, adhering to them, scabbing over and sealing them forever from his conscious brain.

And that blood was no longer red, he saw now; it was black.

As black as night.

As black as death.

The clawing, inky hands of the grave.

The black blood had spread, drop by aching drop, on the whiteness of the sheet, settling into blocks and clumps, regular patterns. And each of the dark clumps was bordered by the whiteness of the beyond, that untouched curtain waiting for the blood to be spilt, to come defile it evermore.

History—Flag's history—was the black blood staining the white sheet in constant repetition, a hundred thousand inky marks on the page.

AND THEN HE WAS awake again, someone shaking him frantically by the shoulders.

"Wake up, Chief, we gotta get outta here," a voice urged.

Abraham Flag's amethyst eyes flickered open, and he stared into the familiar visage of Little Ant. The petite linguist was bending over him, shaking him by the shoulders over and over.

"What happened?" Flag asked, his voice sounding raw to his own ears.

Barnaby B. Barnaby stood behind Little Ant, his ruddy face set in a baffled frown. "You blacked out, Professor," he explained. "We didn't want to move you, but Ant's right—we really have to go. Something's tearing the island apart."

Flag sat up, staring around to get his bearings. He was still on the airstrip, his experimental plane waiting just a few feet away, its refueling complete. As Flag looked around him, he saw that there were holes in the tarmac of the airstrip, and several large cracks had ripped across the soil of the naval base. It was as though they were experiencing an earthquake, and yet Flag could not recall the start of this occurrence. Hadn't he been battling with Demy Octavo just moments before?

"How long was I unconscious?" Flag asked, slowly rising from the shaking ground.

"Had to be four minutes, Chief," Little Ant told him. "Man, you missed some real crazy—"

Flag ignored him; he had more pressing matters to attend. "Where's the blade?" he snapped.

"The blade?" Little Ant repeated.

"The stone knife," Flag clarified, his eyes searching the ground. Then he spotted it, just a foot from where he had woken. Barnaby was leaning over to pick it up. "Don't touch that," Flag warned him, and the archaeologist stopped dead in his tracks.

"What's going on, Professor?" the red-haired archaeologist asked.

"Did you see the lights?" Flag asked as he reached into his jacket and produced his white cotton gloves once again. "Where are the sailors? Where is Demy Octavo?"

"They just disappeared," Little Ant said. "I can't explain—"

Flag stopped him. "Everyone on this island is in an exceptional amount of danger," he stated, reaching for the stone blade with his now gloved hands, "including us. I need you two to evacuate whatever personnel remain. Find General Kinver, tell him to get his fleet out of here as soon as humanly possible."

Barnaby B. Barnaby looked at Professor Flag in confusion as the ground beneath them shook once again. "What is it, Professor? What's happening?"

"If my calculations are correct," Flag said, his words coming in a rush, "this whole island—and everyone on it—is about to sink back into the Pacific Ocean. And it's all because of this stone knife."

"But how?" Barnaby asked.

"There's no time to explain," Flag told him. "I need to get this weapon into secure storage before it can wreak any further damage."

Flag's mind was already unraveling the problem, calculating the speed he would need to travel to get to his Laboratory of the Incredible in the Antarctic. Even using the prototype flyer it would be a close shave. Once there, he at least had a chance of containing the knife, just as long as it had no further contact with blood or skin.

"Are you going to be all right?" Barnaby asked.

"Everything will be fine," Flag reassured his companions, as he had so many times during their adventures. "I'm going to take this item to my laboratory, but we shall rendezvous at my New York apartment in three days' time, 10:00 a.m. Agreed?"

Barnaby and Little Ant agreed, and then they set about evacuating the Pacific paradise of Isle Terandoa. Abraham Flag smiled grimly as he watched them rush to the main buildings of the naval base, for he knew that they could be depended on in any crisis.

As Little Ant and Barnaby B. Barnaby hurried about their business, Professor Flag took to the skies in his single-seater airplane, the stone blade wrapped in a rag and secured in his tiny luggage compartment.

# Chapter 9

*Early twenty-third century*
*Laboratory of the Incredible, Antarctica*

Kane knew that the situation was spiraling out of control. In the space of a half hour, his field team had gone from locating and entering the hidden base to being surrounded, disarmed and forced to barter for the continuance of their lives based on how much knowledge they brought to their captors. Though Simona Jurist had agreed to release them once this operation was over, Kane was under no illusions—the Millennial Consortium didn't let resources out of their grasp willingly, especially living ones.

Right now Kane found himself, along with Grant and Brigid, striding through the vast laboratory area in the company of Jurist, ex-Mag Carver and a dozen armed guards as the millennialists carted the stone knife out of the complex. The knife remained in its sealed box, which, as Kane understood it, had proved surprisingly durable against possible interference.

When he had been questioned about it, Carver looked at Kane's team and sniffed. "We can't get it open," he growled, clearly irritated.

"No key?" Kane asked.

"Our men have searched all over," Carver explained with a shrug. "Whoever sealed this thing wanted it to stay shut."

That fact struck Kane as strange. The box had the appearance of a wooden display cabinet, with glass panels so that the item within could be admired without being damaged. But apparently the glass was very resistant to pressure and had refused to break.

For most of the long walk through the huge lab, Carver had been chatting to Grant, catching up on the events in Cobaltville and all that had happened since. From what Kane overheard, it seemed that Carver had been with the Millennial Consortium or similar outfits for over a decade, trekking the globe, unearthing forgotten treasures from the past. In many ways, Carver's life mirrored their own, Kane realized. The simple difference was that while Cerberus struggled for the salvation of humankind, the Millennial Consortium cared only about itself.

Carver's team had been drawn to Abraham Flag's hidden laboratory after decrypting a military file discovered in the Grand Forks base in North Dakota several months previously. Grant had kept his poker face when he heard that. He had been at the same base with Kane and Brigid, where they had fenced with the local millennialist contingent and escaped with a single hard drive that had ultimately produced the exact same data. As Brigid had observed earlier, theirs really did appear to be a small world. Once again, this wasn't the first time that the consortium's agenda had overlapped with that of Cerberus, Grant reminded himself.

"Through here," Carver instructed, pointing to a wide doorway at the farthest end of the lab.

Carver and Jurist led the way through the wide doorway, which had several burn marks at the edges where it had been forced open with an explosive charge. Through the door, the group found itself in a hangar with a low ceiling, all of it finished in that icy white. There were a variety of antique vehicles on display, including a one-man gyro, an aircraft of a design Kane had never seen before and a clutch of land vehicles specifically designed for use on snow and ice. There were also several modern wags, including two Scorpinauts, near the exit, which Kane presumed belonged to the millennialists. Several Millennial Consortium guards waited at strategic points around the room, standing to attention when they saw Carver and Jurist enter.

"What is all this stuff?" Grant asked, peering at the gyro.

"This?" Carver asked. "We found it all here, just like this. Seems this Flag guy was quite an inventor. He probably scratch-built that and the plane."

Grant whistled as he admired the sleek lines of the dartlike aircraft that rested beside the gyro. "That's one pretty bird," he said.

"We have our own wags over here," Carver explained as they walked past the prototype aircraft.

Two Scorpinauts were waiting where Carver indicated at the far side of the room. The preferred land vehicle of the millennialists, a Scorpinaut was a sturdily armored, low-slung, boxlike vehicle that moved on eight heavily tread wheels. The shell was dotted with numerous rocket pods and weapons ports, and twin .50-caliber, swivel-mounted machine guns stuck out from two armatures at the front of the vehicle like a pair of foreclaws. To the rear, the ten-foot-long snout of a 40 mm cannon protruded on a huge swiveling arm, docking in a resting position at the back of the vehicle, which looked like a scorpion's stinger-tipped tail.

"How did you get these down here?" Kane asked, impressed.

"We used a burrower to locate the entrance," Carver told him proudly. "Found a reinforced tunnel. Must have been here for centuries. Tunnel stretches almost three miles." The ex-Mag indicated the wide double doors at the end of the room.

"So this would have been the way that Flag entered his Laboratory of the Incredible all those years ago," Brigid mused. "And the exit's three miles away, you said? No wonder we didn't find it. We must be under one hundred feet of snow here."

"I suspect that's how he wanted it," Carver told her. "The guy liked his privacy."

Jurist's ice-cool voice cut through the companionable nature of the conversation. "Perhaps he had a lot to hide," she mused.

BOARDING THE Scorpinauts as two parties, along with the Annunaki knife in its display box, the group followed the low-ceilinged, wide tunnel to the surface. The tunnel was roughly three miles in length, its walls carved straight from the hard-packed snow. Some form of fluorescent lighting appeared to have been installed along the ceiling at wide intervals, but when Kane peered at it he realized that it didn't contain any bulbs, nor any power source that he could perceive.

Kane estimated that they had traveled over two and a half miles before they saw the tunnel's exit in the distance, and he wondered at the accuracy of Jurist's observation. If, way back when it had been in use, this had been the only route into and out of the Laboratory of the Incredible, then Flag had indeed believed in keeping the place private. The strange cloaking tricks that had been played on Brigid's scanner certainly lent weight to that suspicion. But if this was the sole access route, it would have taken an exceptional pilot to maneuver that single-seater aircraft that he had seen in the hangar.

Kane considered himself to be an exceptionally competent pilot, having been rigorously trained during his time as a

Magistrate, but even he balked at the prospect of guiding an aircraft along the length of such a tight tunnel. As Kane pondered this, Brigid's description of Professor Flag came back to him: "The man was extraordinarily intelligent. 'Genius' doesn't even begin to scratch the surface." Would being something more than genius somehow mean a man could perform the impossible? More likely, Kane thought, the aircraft had been built in the hangar and never removed.

*October 31, 1930*
*Antarctica*

THE ARROWHEAD aircraft cut through the skies over the frozen continent of Antarctica. Sitting at the controls, Abraham Flag urged more power from the air-pulse engine—a design of his own creation that switched between fossil fuel and pressurized air for maximum efficiency.

Professor Flag gritted his teeth as the freezing winds buffeted the shell of his tiny, single-seater aircraft. It had been almost seven hours since he had evacuated Isle Terandoa, and he could feel the hands of the clock ticking ever closer toward doom. Doom, that was, unless he could halt the damage that the weird stone knife was causing. He could feel the blade waiting, lurking like a living thing in the side compartment, bundled in rags lest it make contact with the air or, worse still, Flag's skin.

A light winked to life on the control board of the aircraft, indicating the high-frequency locator beam that emitted from Flag's Laboratory of the Incredible. Flag pulled at the control yoke, and his amazing airplane banked, swooping toward the hidden entrance to his remarkable lab.

To a casual observer, had there been such a person watching on that lifeless terrain, it would have seemed that Flag's aircraft hurtled straight into the ground, where it would doubtless crash and burn. However, that observer would have been surprised to see that Flag's maneuver resulted in no explosion. Rather, the vehicle swooped to the ground at high speed and weaved into the hidden portal that waited in the snow, disappearing under the snow-covered ground. Barely as wide as the airplane was long, the portal was perfectly camouflaged against the blue-white snow. Despite the breakneck speed with which his craft had entered the portal, Abraham Flag used no autopilot to accomplish this fantastical feat; his perfect hand-eye coordination was instrument enough to perform what might appear to another man to be impossible.

The aircraft zipped into the underground tunnel and raced along its vast length. The tunnel was lit by overhead strips that appeared to be glass tubes. These tubes, another of Flag's incredible designs, reflected sunlight from the surface above via a series of mirrors, much like the principle of the periscope used in submarines. As such, the lights required no actual power source, merely that it be daytime or a cloudless evening when the moon was bright.

The tunnel itself had been built to an exacting specification, running 3.0000060273 miles, which was precisely one league. Flag had chosen this length out of his uncanny desire to keep things perfectly ordered. In actuality, it had no further meaning than that it pleased him and, in so doing, freed his exceptional mind to concern itself with matters of greater import.

Flag flipped a switch on the control panel as a set of wide double doors came into view at the far end of the tunnel, and his aircraft emitted a radio pulse, commanding those doors to open. Abraham Flag cut back on the thrust as the doors opened on their curved tracks, and a moment later he pulled the dart-like airplane to a halt, the landing gear's rubber tires shrieking against the snow-dappled surface of the tunnel floor.

Once the strangely shaped aircraft had come to a stop, Flag shoved back the blister-style canopy atop the fuselage and rushed down the side ladder, clasping the bundle of rags containing the stone blade. The prototype aircraft had come to a halt in the hangar of his magnificent Laboratory of the Incredible, where a dozen other vehicles were prepped for Flag's private use. A roadster with steel chains around the tires skulked like a jungle cat in the shadows, and beside it a one-man motorcycle with twin skis in place of the back wheel. Other vehicles waited in the room, as well, many of them fresh from Flag's own drawing board, including an experimental one-man gyro that the United States Army Air Corps would dearly wish to examine if only they knew that he had constructed it.

The soles of Flag's booted feet slammed against the floor as he rushed from the hangar and into the main laboratory area of his polar headquarters. As he ran, his free hand snapped out, punching the button that closed and sealed the hangar. It was crucial now that the whole of this secret base remain utterly secure. Should his plan to incarcerate the paranormal knife fail, the hard-packed walls of this building would be the only thing standing in the way of the bleed running over and destroying the world.

Sprinting through his marvelous headquarters, Professor Flag recalled the strange sight of the bleed as that eerie rift opened about the seaman's face. The bubbling redness with sparks of firefly light within it still haunted him, even a full seven hours away from the experience. An ancient quote popped into Flag's mind as he hurried past the living quarters and on to the Shadow Room, that point of ultimate security within his exceptional laboratory: "Those whom the gods wish to destroy they first make mad."

Flag ran past the scientific equipment of the high-ceilinged lab, dashing past numerous experiments that had progressed without him while, at the U.S. Navy's request, he had been drawn away from his studies. Jars bubbled and crystals grew, but Flag ignored them all in his single-minded quest to house that ancient lethal blade. When he reached the end of the short hallway leading to his Shadow Room, Flag pulled himself to an abrupt stop. A seven-inch-thick steel door was pulled closed over the doorway, like the door of a bank vault. Tendons like steel cables tensed in Flag's arm as he wrenched that door open, undeterred by its colossal weight.

The door swung open at his back and Abraham Flag stepped into the room beyond. The room was roughly fifteen feet across, hexagonal in shape with a ceiling far lower than the three-story open area of the main laboratory. The walls here were much darker, too, like black ice, and the lighting came from just a single spot in the center of the six-sided room. The spotlight lit upon a lone pedestal, atop which, open like a flower, rested the four sides of a glass cube. Flag had constructed this cube almost four years ago, as an experiment into the possibility of a self-reinforcing pressure chamber. Once closed, like some devilish logic puzzle from the Orient, the pressure chamber would suck into itself, a mild form of implosion that would hold its sides rigid with exceptional force. Without the proper opening protocols, that sealed cube could never be unlocked, and anything placed inside would remain utterly in stasis, held in a fashion that, Flag theorized, might actually stand outside of time's entropic passage.

Flag had constructed the cube out of curiosity, with some vague inkling of applying its principles to perfect storage of materials outside Earth's atmosphere. Once completed, he had begun to consider the security applications that such a device would present. It could serve as an impregnable containment area for the sorts of evildoers that he regularly faced. It had been an idle consideration and one that Flag had never fully explored.

Now Flag silently chastised himself as he examined the condition of the plates of reinforced glass that would close inward to form a two-foot-tall box of exceptional durability. If only he had devoted more time to this experiment, then he might be assured of its success.

# Chapter 10

*Early twenty-third century*
*Antarctica*

After a full six minutes in the tunnel, the Scorpinauts reached the exit and powered onward across the snow-blanketed ground beyond. The sky above was heavy with dark clouds, and the snowflakes swirled around on the wind, creating a dappled effect to the vista visible through the windshields of the vehicles.

Kane turned to Brigid and smiled. "Monotonous, isn't it?" he said.

Brigid laughed.

The Scorpinauts continued charging over the icy terrain as the howling sounds of the wind rose and fell, buffeting their metal flanks. They were a long way from the spires that Kane's team had discovered out in this frigid wilderness. It was little wonder, Kane thought, that they hadn't been able to locate this entryway.

The convoy trundled on through the bleak conditions, the wipers battling to keep snow from their windshields.

As they bumped across the snowy ridges, Grant turned to Carver and asked him where they were headed.

"We have a mobile base out this way," Carver explained.

"Well stocked, and we have five techs on tap there, as well as a complete communications array. Once we get there we can figure out how to open the box."

"Sounds impressive," Grant acknowledged. "You been out here long?"

"Over a month," Carver said. "Took us a while to locate the entrance to this place, and the main doors didn't open straightaway, either. Took some pushing and shoving."

"Seems like the box is going to take the same," Grant said with a grim smile.

"Yeah," Carver said, nodding thoughtfully. He leaned closer to Grant then, keeping his voice low so that it was barely audible over the growl of the engines. "The wait didn't do nothing for Simona's patience—know what I mean?"

"Yeah, I got that," Grant muttered. "She's not exactly the social type, is she?"

"Not exactly," Carver agreed.

IT TOOK ANOTHER five minutes for the Scorpinauts to reach the mobile headquarters of the Millennial Consortium. Its cloaking device was shut down at their approach so that it flickered in and out of vision as they neared.

The base looked like a metal sphere, three hundred yards across and buried to below its midpoint in the snow. The domed surface was rough, made up of curved plates that had been slotted together under the harsh conditions of the unforgiving environment. Even though it was, presumably, less than two months old, Kane could already see spots of rust forming, and there were several places where the outer shell had clearly been patched up with whatever had been to hand.

At the zenith of the dome were a half-dozen antennas and

boosters, pointing ramrod straight into the sky. These had to be part of the communications system that Carver had spoken of, Grant realized.

A wide awning stuck out to one side of the buried sphere, its flat surface piled with snow, the underside of which sparkled with shining icicles. The drivers pulled the two Scorpinauts to a halt under this awning, beside a third vehicle that had already been stashed there. A few moments later, the wags' doors were opened—accompanied by a swell in the furious symphony of the howling winds—and everybody stepped from the vehicles.

With the consortium guards watching them, Kane, Grant and Brigid were escorted into the mobile base by Simona Jurist and Carver, while the stone blade in its containment unit was retrieved from the other Scorpinaut.

Inside, the base had the atmosphere of a submarine, all low ceilings and narrow corridors. The interior walls appeared to be constructed of some metal-plastic hybrid that radiated a chill, making the whole place feel cold. In fact, as they walked into the base, the Cerberus exiles found that they could still see their breath misting like fog before them when they exhaled.

The noise of a generator echoed through the corridors and, while not loud, it sounded like a busy steelworks in the middle distance. Kane brushed his hand against one of the corridor walls and felt a steady thrumming vibration, shaking the structure in time with that pounding echo of the jenny.

Small, rectangular rooms could be seen to the sides of the corridor, and Kane, Grant and Brigid took a sly peek inside them, recognizing them instantly as cramped living quarters. The narrow corridors themselves appeared to have been constructed in a radial pattern that led to a large room at the cen-

ter. This room had a much higher ceiling, domed and rising
to almost two stories. The room was circular, with curving
walls and eight doors that fed off to the corridors that speared
through the temporary structure. This was the main hub of the
mobile base, and it reminded the Cerberus warriors of their
own control room back in the Montana mountains.

Along with a bank of six computers, there were several
large pieces of equipment in the room, including a tomograph
scanner and a medical laser mounted before a steel vise.

Over to one corner of the room, a separate area had been
partitioned off with shoulder-high screens. As they strolled
past this area, Grant peered over the screens and saw a fully
functional communications desk and monitoring equipment
being overseen by one of the Millennial Consortium people,
a young female with blond hair and small, round-framed
spectacles on her freckled nose. She looked cold, even bundled up as she was in multiple layers of clothing, including
two scarves around her throat. Besides the communications
sergeant, there were five intellectual types, two of them
women, who peered up from their work at the computer
banks, acknowledging the newcomers before going back to
their screens.

Jurist's loyal squad brought the impenetrable display cabinet, less plinth, into the room on a low flatbed trolley. Jurist
left the others as she went to discuss matters with one of the
half dozen techs at the monitor screens.

Brigid appeared casual as she listened in on the conversation for a moment. The lab tech was giving Jurist an update
on something he had been studying. The scientist was in his
thirties, with thinning hair and a little paunch. He wore a
maroon shirt over thermals, and had placed a thick sable

jacket over this to keep warm in the icy coolness of the room. At the end of his nose, the man wore a pair of half-moon spectacles. Although he wasn't an especially short man, the scientist appeared small as he stood before the Amazonian figure of Simona Jurist, who appeared that much taller thanks to her heeled boots and the thin, red vertical piping that decorated her black leather outfit. The scientist appeared to cringe a little before the fierce woman with the tattooed face.

From what Brigid heard, it sounded as if some sort of a bomb or explosive device had been extricated from Flag's laboratory on their first recon. Whatever it was, it seemed that the device had proved unusable, having rotted over the intervening years. Simona Jurist nodded once, and went on to explain in a low voice what they had brought with them.

"Nice setup," Kane remarked as he peered around the gloomy circular room. "Good for entertaining."

Carver eyed him. "It serves its purpose."

"Study area, right?" Grant asked.

"Yeah." Carver nodded, pulling at the electronic goggles he wore around his neck. "Come over here." He led the three Cerberus warriors to where the stone knife waited in its box. "Look at that—what do you see?"

Kane and the others peered closely at the box, examining the knife and the strange sliver of sparkling blackness that seemed to float in the transparent container beside it.

"A knife," Brigid told him, "most probably carved from volcanic rock, judging by the smoothness and the sheen."

"You seem to know more than these guys about its origins, Brigid," Carver said. "Care to explain?"

"I just read the report," Brigid explained, glaring at Kane and Grant, "which is more than some people here."

Carver followed Brigid's eyes. "Really? You surprise me. In my day, Mags were supposed to digest as much information as possible before entering a situation," he said, holding Grant's gaze. "*Any* situation," he added.

"Nah," Grant assured him. "The smart ones find someone to do that for them so they can get on with their jobs. Guess that's why you washed out so quick, huh, Carver?"

Carver snorted with laughter, shaking his head. Then he removed the goggles from his head and handed them to Grant. "Take a closer look at it, Grant," he encouraged.

Grant took the goggles and placed them over his head. When he looked through them, he saw a heads-up display, with various iris-activated functions, including magnification, spectrogram and infrared. The motors of the goggles whirred close to his left ear as he checked through the settings.

Under magnification, the stone knife didn't look much different. It appeared to be carved from volcanic rock, as Brigid had said, a shining obsidian that glinted even under the dull lighting of the room. The other settings were generally unremarkable, as far as Grant could divine, until he reached the infrared.

With the goggles on their infrared setting, Grant found himself staring at what appeared to be a white-hot object, glowing like a star. The object still had the distinct knife shape, its sleek lines absolutely rigid. The rest of the display box, both the glass and the wooden struts at its sides, were dark, radiating no heat whatsoever. Grant stepped back from the cabinet and peered around the room through the goggles. The people in the room glowed a volcanic red, as he had expected, and a very dull glow radiated from the walls and other surfaces, as would be natural. He turned his attention back to the knife in the display box, looking once more at the vertical blazing white line that cut through the vision. "It's hot," he concluded.

"No, it's not," Carver said from behind him. "Look again."

Still using the infrared, Grant looked at the knife once more. It burned a fierce white streak across the sensor display, so bright it stayed with Grant after he had closed his eyes. "No, that is definitely—"

"Look around it," Carver instructed, "at the glass and the things it's touching."

Grant did so. They were dark, showing up in a mixture of dull greens and lifeless grays.

"Something that hot should be radiating heat like there's no tomorrow," Carver explained, "but it's just there, utterly contained by the blade."

Grant pushed the goggles from his face and passed them to Brigid so that she could look. Once she had done so, she handed the goggles on to Kane, who peered through them and let out a low whistle.

Brigid touched one of the glass panels of the box containing the Annunaki knife, pushing her palm flat against it after a moment. "It's cold," she confirmed, turning to the others.

Carver nodded. "Something that hot should have been blasting heat at us, even through the walls of the cabinet. This may be reinforced glass," he said, rapping the side of the box with his knuckles, "but it shouldn't dampen heat to that extent. Nothing should."

Kane handed the goggles back to the ex-Mag. "Maybe your equipment's screwy," he suggested.

Carver nodded thoughtfully, idly running the strap of the goggles through his fingers. "Something's not working right, that's for certain."

"Could be special glass," Grant mused. "Containing the heat pattern, maybe?"

Carver shook his head. "If that were the case, then the whole interior of the box would still appear hot, and, as you have seen, it doesn't. It's just the knife that glows under examination."

"What if," Brigid proposed, "the infrared sensor is reading something that it can't translate? Not heat at all."

"Like what?" Carver asked.

"Molecular vibration generates heat," Brigid proposed. "Maybe it's…moving."

"Doesn't look like it's moving," Kane said as he peered through the strengthened glass. He found his eyes drawn once more to that dark smear that seemed to float off of the edge of the blade itself. "You have any idea what that is?" he asked, pointing at the strange smear. It looked to Kane like the night sky seen through a hole in the roof—a slice of the sky with stars twinkling within.

"None whatsoever," Carver admitted. "We ran tests from outside the box but…" He shrugged, at a loss to explain.

"So, you're pretty much in the dark until you get this crate open," Kane surmised, still peering at the strange ebony streak that appeared to float beside the stone knife.

Carver nodded.

"What about the legend written on the blade itself?" Brigid asked. "Seems to be pretty deep stuff."

Carver looked pleasantly surprised. "You can read that?" he asked.

Brigid rolled her eyes with embarrassment. "Well, some of it." She crouched on her haunches and peered through the glass box once again, scanning the ideograms carved into the side of the twelve-inch blade. There was further writing scored across the handle, she saw now, running in a circular pattern so that, from this angle, she could only see snatches.

Carver watched Brigid as her eyes played across the surface of the strange object in fascination. "Well?" he encouraged.

"It's ancient Sumerian. There's no one definitive translation for these kind of symbols," Brigid explained. "You have to interpret the words and their meaning, piecing it together and creating the context. But…" She stopped.

"But?" Carver asked, clearly fascinated.

With Carver's attention distracted, and Jurist off liaising with the tech, Kane and Grant stepped away from the blade and took a longer look around the control room. They fanned out, and Kane made his way across to where the communications desk stood, his eyes taking in the equipment there.

The consortium woman at the controls glanced up at him, pursing her lips with irritation. "You need something, ice-pop?"

"Kane." The Cerberus warrior offered the communications officer his hand. "You look cold sitting there."

The woman brushed her palm briefly with Kane's and nodded. "Lacea," she said quietly, "and, yeah, I'm frozen. I tell you, Kane, this whole setup sucks."

"Really?" Kane said encouragingly as his eyes roved across the communications system, taking in the details of the setup. In his mind he was already working out the swiftest way to disrupt it so that it couldn't be used when he and his crew made their inevitable break for it.

Grant, meanwhile, stepped across to the tomograph under the watchful eyes of the millennialist guards. The tomograph was a heavy piece of tech, roughly eight feet long with a cluster of scanning equipment around its far end. An item could be pushed inside using a manually operated conveyor belt, where a CAT scan would then be administered. The machine had to have been hell to transport, Grant realized, and would eat up juice like there was no tomorrow; in fact, he saw now that it had its own portable generator attached, which stood at roughly knee-height to him at the side of the device itself.

Across the room, Brigid was slowly translating the ideograms that had been carved on the surface of the blade. "'Beware!'" she read. "'I am the bringer of Death, the Destroyer of Souls, the alpha and the omega, the end point.' Or maybe 'vanishing point,'" Brigid said, glancing up at Carver as he listened intently to her words. "You look pale. Are you okay?"

"I'm fine," Carver said. "Just wondering what it is we're about to open. Please, go on."

Brigid read the whole chant that had been written onto the knife, drawing from her incredible memory to interpret the ancient symbols as best she could.

"'Beware! I am the bringer of Death, the Destroyer of Souls, the alpha and the omega, the vanishing point. Mourn now the end of your life's journey, for all shall fall before my power, their family line expunged from all histories, their bodies returned to *Tiamat*. I am the blade Godkiller. Gaze upon my bloodwork and lament.'"

Around the hilt, Brigid saw a symbol that she took a moment to register. "This is the symbol for Enlil," she explained as Kane and Grant returned to the discussion at the display cabinet, "but it's been altered."

"Altered how?" Kane asked. He knew Enlil, that mad would-be god of the Annunaki. Enlil had been involved in the subjugation of humankind from the very earliest days, and had been the instigator of several terrible plots to cull the species

once it had displeased him. The most notable of Enlil's plots
to eradicate humankind had been the Great Flood, which had
been recorded in many religious texts, including the Bible.
That plot had revealed a rift between the Annunaki family
members, with Enlil's own brother, Enki, showing compas-
sion for humankind, helping it to survive that terrible deluge.
More recently, Overlord Enlil and his allies had orchestrated
the nukecaust and taken advantage of the postapocalyptic
conditions that followed.

Still crouching before the glass-sided display cube, Brigid
pointed to the knife's hilt before looking up at Kane and
Grant. There was clear concern in her emerald eyes. "It's the
name of the knife's owner," she explained. "I think it means
'Son of Enlil.'"

"Enlil had a son?" Kane said, unable to keep the surprise
from his tone. "That's just a great stinking dog's crap of ter-
rific." Offering his hand, Kane helped Brigid up from the
floor. "You have a name?"

Brigid shook her head. "That's his symbol," she said,
"there on the blade. I'm pretty sure of it, but I'd need to check
into it to find an actual name."

Kane ground his teeth, irritated at this new revelation. The
Annunaki had been a fearsome threat for so long, that stum-
bling across one of their artifacts with the revelation that there
may be more of the durable, lizardlike bastards waiting in the
shadows was not truly a surprise.

Seeing his frustration, Brigid placed her hand on Kane's
arm and looked in his eyes. "You okay?" she gently prodded.

"This son of Enlil is dead, right?" Kane growled.

"Probably," Brigid said. "For at least five thousand years.
I don't think he's coming back anytime soon. Just left us his
cutlery."

Simona Jurist snapped her fingers, attracting everyone's attention. "They are here to help us," she reminded Carver, "not vice versa. Now, get it open so we can conclude this operation and get out of here."

"What now?" Brigid muttered.

"This is Dr. Winterslow," Jurist explained as she introduced the scientist she had been speaking to for the past few minutes. "Doctor, these are the guests I told you about. They have some thoughts about the weapon."

Winterslow nodded wearily, his breath misting like a cloud of fog before him in the ice-cool air. "Did I just hear you reading the writing along the side of the blade?" he asked, and Brigid nodded.

"It's called Godkiller," she said, "and we think it belonged to the son of, well, a god. Kind of."

"Interesting," Winterslow mused as his eyes flicked to the display box and back to Brigid. "These ancient peoples believed in a lot of mumbo-jumbo."

"I'm not so sure it is mumbo-jumbo," Carver said, an edge creeping into his voice.

"Godkiller?" The scientist laughed. "It's a pretty preposterous boast, isn't it?"

Kane fixed the man with his gunmetal eyes. "Let's hope that's all it is," he said.

# Chapter 11

*October 31, 1930*
*Isle Terandoa, the South Pacific*

The redness had gone from her vision, like the dissipation of some terrible rage. In its absence, Demy Octavo's head throbbed, as it had after her nights in gay Paris, when she had gracefully glided her lithe figure through the ambassadorial balls, turning the heads and hearts of the foolish old men who saw her.

Now the dark-haired Italian agent found herself, much to her astonishment, bobbing in the sea, with no memory of how she had come to be there. She thought back, trying to piece things together, but it was as though she had been given a difficult math problem with too many missing digits. The last she remembered, she had been in a tiny office, thrusting one of her beautiful Beretta pistols in the face of her nemesis—Professor Abraham Flag. She had come through the window, following the path of her bullets, with the intention of taking the ancient knife that lay atop the desk. A foolhardy plan, perhaps, but she had seen that Flag's unique aircraft was being refueled and if she could take that off the island, no vehicle on Earth had a chance of catching up with her. It would hardly have been the most audacious escape that she had ever made in her incredible career.

Octavo smiled, the falu-red corners of her full-lipped mouth turning up in a pleasing curve, as she recalled her father's motto: Life is risk. Her father had been a high-ranking member of the Italian secret service until he had met with his untimely end during a secret mission in far-flung Africa. Octavo had readily followed in his footsteps, accepting the most terrifying of missions in the service of the great leader, Mussolini.

Demy Octavo turned her thoughts back to the matter at hand as she swirled amid the swelling waves of the Pacific Ocean. After she had entered the office, Flag had executed a maneuver that had disarmed her, snagging her glove in the process. And then she had grabbed the knife, too fast for Flag himself to follow, and rushed from the office at lightning-quick speed. Flag would have followed, she felt sure, and yet she couldn't remember anything after that.

There were colors—that was all. Orange, black, red—the colors one would associate with a volcano, perhaps with the fires of hell itself.

Demy Octavo spun there like a spindle in a knitting machine, a pendulum in the azure ocean, her feet far below the waves, her head bobbing above, making the slightest movements with hands and feet to keep herself afloat as the current pulled her in a wide arc around and to the east. Her dark hair clung to her neck in wet clumps, irritating her for a moment as she peered all around.

Over to one side she saw a landmass—a small island off in the distance. And above it, a plane angled into the sky, taking off from the island itself as high waves churned all about it.

Terandoa, she recalled. That was the name of the island,

named for the seaman who had discovered it just a few years before. It seemed so small from here, as though she might reach forward and pick it up, a tiny little thing floating in the bathtub ocean as the high waves lapped against it.

As Agent Octavo watched the island, something floated past her. It was the figure of a man. Octavo watched him hurry onward, heading toward the island, pulled along by the current. He wore an American sailor's uniform and lay flat on his stomach, face in the water. The man was dead, Octavo realized with a start, and as the thought struck her, something sinister whispered in the back of her mind, a dark memory being jogged.

There had been sailors, she remembered, American naval personnel. And she had been threatening them, and yet it had not seemed to be her. It had been something she held, speaking in her mind, directing her body's actions, craving blood.

*The vampire knife.*

She saw it then, for a fraction of a second, that great red mass that called from another world. Demy Octavo had only had the briefest glance at it, but she knew just what it was. She closed her eyes, letting the sun play across her eyelids, seeing the patterns the bright rays formed beneath. That thing, that redness that she had seen, was everything that a person was, a surge of blood being sent running around the body. It was the bleed.

The surface of the sea was churning faster now, and Demy Octavo opened her eyes to see what was causing it. Isle Terandoa was closer than it had been a few moments before, and she could feel the current pulling her nearer. All around, the dead bodies of U.S. sailors washed past her, hurrying to the island like farmers to market.

As she looked, a clawing horror clutched at Demy Octavo's dark heart, and she realized that the island was not simply closer. It was lower, too, for she could see the tops of its highest points, as though she were in an airplane flying overhead, while the shore seemed to be disappearing as the waves lashed against it.

She looked behind her, peering over the graceful curve of her brown-sheathed shoulder, and her bottomless, dark brown eyes widened at what she saw. A wave roared toward her, threatening to topple upon her, to engulf her. That enormous breaker loomed over Octavo's fragile form, and she was pushed helplessly ahead of it.

Agent Octavo looked about her, and a final grim realization dawned. She was not on the surface of the ocean, as she had first believed. She was swirling, spinning, turning around and around in a whirlpool, trapped as though in some gigantic basin full of water with the stopper removed, being drawn inevitably toward the drain. At the center of that whirlpool, she realized, stood the tiny landmass of Isle Terandoa, its orange-brown soil shining amid the tumbling wash of the sea. The island was—incredibly—sinking, returning to the sea it had emerged from less than a decade earlier.

Demy Octavo's arms flailed as she struggled to free herself from that raging whirlpool, all the while knowing in her heart that her attempts were futile. She screamed as she was pulled beneath the waves, feeling the pressure of the water pushing at her nostrils, her eyes, washing inside the canals of her delicate ears. She closed her eyes, wishing that there was something she could do, some solution she might meet, wishing that the American Abraham Flag might appear just one more time and come to her rescue, as he had before, reaching for her with a powerful hand, his nobility rising above petty notions of country and politics when he saw a woman in trouble. But there was nothing. No hand came to grab her, no submersible opened beneath her, no net plucked her out of the furious, unforgiving sea.

As the waters of the Pacific washed all about her, Demy Octavo opened her eyes once more, and she watched as the island plunged beneath the waves, sinking into the vastness of the ocean. As it did so, she saw something else, and she recognized it instantly, her eyes drawn to its spiteful glow. There, at the center of the sinking island, was the bleed, that awful redness that she had seen inside her eyes, on the airstrip. That awful scarlet that seemed to be the redness of life itself, yet a mockery far removed from all the good things that a life might bring—the horrors of life, perhaps.

Signorina Octavo felt compelled to watch as that red mass throbbed and pulsed, expanding and contracting, an organ from another world. The bleed seemed to grow before her, and she watched as it grew, fascinated and repelled by whatever it truly was.

There were black streaks within that awful crimson wound, as dark as the Grim Reaper's cloak. Octavo watched their inky swirl, recalling them now from the island airstrip, from that moment when her vision had become something not of this world.

As Demy Octavo was drawn down into that churning whirlpool, water above and beneath her, trying urgently to find a way to free herself as the redness of the bleed loomed closer, she saw something else in that awful rent. There was the scarlet streaked with black, but there were things there, too, flashing within its churning patterns. Tiny lights like distant stars played across the red, floating within that awful, organic mass.

She had been under the water for too long, Octavo knew, and she needed to draw breath without taking in water. She was being inescapably drowned in that rampaging swirl as the island sank back into the depths of the ocean. No one was coming to save her from that vertiginous fate, she knew. All she had was herself.

She opened her eyes once again, watched as the sinking island appeared to rotate closer, and all the while she was turning in the roaring torrent, being sucked to a watery grave.

Demy Octavo watched the uncanny streak of red that cut into the island, saw the dark streaks and the white spots that moved within it. The white specks moved, creating streaks across Octavo's vision, like the aftereffect of a lightning flash. They raced this way and that, and the Italian femme fatale counted seven of them in all.

She was breathing water now, swallowing it down with each frantic breath, feeling its weight drag heavily at her lungs. The wash crashed about her ears, whirling her around and around. A figure moved past her in the racing ocean, a naval officer dressed in his smart white dress uniform. Demy reached out for the man, her hand clutching at his ankle as he was dragged away. Hanging on, she was dragged with him, clambering up his body in her desperate bid to clutch on to something solid.

Octavo coughed and spluttered then, bringing up great foamy gouts of seawater. Her body heaved, shaking as she coughed up more of the salty water, shuddering with the urgent battle between expelling water and retrieving air.

"You must help me," Octavo pleaded, her hands on the sailor's chest.

The sailor whom she clung to was dead, Octavo realized then, his face pale. He had a cut across his belly, a crimson swash of blood staining at his uniform. Horrified, she let go of the corpse of the young man, letting it float free, wanting desperately to scream.

She was closer to the center of the whirlpool now, being dragged toward the outcropping that sat at its eye, all that remained of the sinking island. Water batted at her from every side, tossing her soaked hair across her vision, filling her mouth with its salty tang.

As her body shook once more in a last frantic attempt to expel the water from her lungs, Demy Octavo peered toward the red rift that had opened beneath the ocean, the window that looked into the bleed. The seven white sparks had become larger now, as though they had moved closer to the facing edge of that tear in reality. They were working there, Octavo realized, dancing around the rip.

As Demy Octavo took one last lungful of seawater, the final victim of the cataclysm that destroyed Isle Terandoa, she saw those seven sparkling white lights whir around inside the red wound. The largest of the lights—the nearest, Octavo realized—turned and looked at her. It looked at her *with a face*. A face so beautiful it made Demy Octavo begin to cry, her salty tears mingling with the seawater that overwhelmed her.

The face of perfection emblazoned on her thoughts, Demy Octavo disappeared beneath the surface of the Pacific for one final time.

# Chapter 12

*Early twenty-third century*
*Antarctica*

"We'll scan the box first," Dr. Winterslow announced, indicating the tomograph, "and work from there."

The Cerberus team watched as Jurist's men placed the box on the manually operated conveyor belt of the tomograph, and it was shunted inside. The generator at the side of the tomograph burbled as it came to life, chugging contentedly in the shadows of the room, the smell of burning dust wafting from its mechanics.

The scan lasted a full fifteen minutes, but finally the tech gave up.

Impatiently, Simona Jurist pushed Winterslow aside and looked at the screen herself. A three-dimensional rendition of a rock-solid block rotated on the monitor.

The scan showed very little of interest, other than that the box couldn't be scanned. It resisted any attempts at study, appearing as a solid black square in the display, rather than the layered scan one would normally associate with a tomogram.

"Nothing," Winterslow concluded, removing his spectacles and tapping their arm against his teeth nervously. "Whatever it is, we can't scan it."

"Fine," Simona Jurist barked with impatience. "Just open the damn thing. Then you and your brainiacs can scan the fucking knife to your heart's content."

"Yes, ma'am," Winterslow agreed, placing his glasses atop his nose once more. His wide brow was furrowed with deep worry lines.

Brigid shot Kane a look, and Kane could see that she was concerned, too. In response, he held up his open hands, indicating he didn't know what to do.

"I don't think that this is such a good idea," Brigid said, stepping forward and addressing her comment to Jurist, clearly the leader of the operation.

The tattooed woman shot Brigid a withering look of contempt. "What are you afraid of, Baptiste?" she asked. "It's a million-year-old rock."

"Which has been carved into a knife and threatens to kill gods," Brigid reminded her.

Jurist crossed her arms and glared down at the shorter woman. "So, you're scared of what exactly? Ancient graffiti?"

"I'm not scared," Brigid corrected. "I'm just urging you to proceed with caution. That writing was placed there for a reason."

"Bragging rights," Carver suggested from over Brigid's shoulder, though he didn't look as confident as he sounded. "That's all."

Brigid looked around her, addressing the enemies who surrounded her in the circular control room. "Words can be powerful, when they're used in the right combinations," she said levelly. "I can read the symbols. What I can't do is guarantee how literally they need to be taken."

The guards securing the display box containing the stone

knife before the medical laser had stopped their work, and they looked at Simona Jurist for advice. "You want for us to move it somewhere else, Miss Jurist?" one of them asked, his voice rough with an accent Kane couldn't place.

Jurist closed her eyes in thought. "No," she said. "I'm not afraid of ancient fairy stories. Let's get it opened."

Dr. Winterslow visibly swallowed when he heard Jurist say that. But he obeyed her instruction, helping the millennialist footmen clamp the cube of glass and wood in the vise before the medical laser. Under his instruction, the guards angled the box to ensure that the laser would have maximum effectiveness.

"You may want to shield your eyes for a moment," one of the other techs told everyone as he and his colleagues placed tinted goggles over their eyes. "And I'd recommend you not look directly at the beam during this operation."

Everyone in the room turned away and the medical laser came to life, firing a narrow beam of light—as thin as a pin—at the glass front of the holding cabinet. The tiny laser beam glowed red against the front panel of the glass cube. Nothing happened; the beam just seemed to splash against the glass, having no notable effect.

"Hmf," Winterslow muttered as he checked at his computer monitor. "This is going to take a few minutes before it breaks through."

Simona Jurist tapped her foot impatiently.

*November 1, 1930*
*Antarctica*

STANDING IN the hexagonal Shadow Room, Abraham Flag steeled himself before he unwound the cloth from the stone knife. As he stripped away the rag covering, the darkly gleaming surface of that unholy knife shimmered, reflecting the single overhead light source.

Flag felt the breath catch in his throat as the knife was fully revealed, its twelve-inch blade and three-inch hilt carved from blackest obsidian. The eerie language of the ancients was glimmering across the surface of the dirk, and now it appeared to have been written there in the fiery lava of a volcano.

Beware! it read. I am the bringer of Death.

But there was something else now, too, something that Flag had not noticed until that moment—a sliver of darkness beaded on the blade's edge like water, just a quarter of an inch in length. Automatically, Flag brushed at it with his gloved hand, and the curious smudge grew infinitesimally, still attached to the blade's side. It was almost as though the dark blade itself were ebbing away, a flowing part of that dark stone pouring off the sleek line of the knife. The streak of dark liquid turned with the knife, holding its position in a way that liquid should not.

His curiosity was piqued, and now Professor Flag yearned to study that tiny smudge of blackness, but he reminded himself of the urgency of his task. Almost unconsciously, he checked his wristwatch and saw the hands tick past midnight. Halloween was over; it was All Saints' Day at last. Had Flag been anything less than the implacably scientific man that he was, he may have taken this for a good omen. As was, however, he simply continued in his endeavors, bending to his thankless task. There was not a moment to spare; he had to contain this frightful weapon under the glass of his self-reinforcing pressure chamber.

Flag placed the knife within the open portal of the box and swiftly folded the sides in upon themselves. The strange cube slotted together like some three-dimensional jigsaw puzzle, and Flag's deft hands felt at its edges until he was certain that it would hold. The knife was held in stasis now, contained within the scientific marvel of that tiny, self-strengthening chamber. For now, however, it might still be opened at any time. That was an eventuality for which Flag could not allow; it could only be him or one of his trusted allies who might ever obtain access to that terrible knife, lest the weapon create more destruction than it had on Isle Terandoa.

Flag left the hexagonal Shadow Room and paced the length of the corridor that connected to his main laboratory area. The professor swept past the many desks and surfaces that contained his numerous fantastical experiments, hurrying to a specific creation he had developed a few years previously and had been using for various minor tasks ever since. He reached the appropriate cabinet and, opening the wooden door there, withdrew a small dish containing a pool of blended cyanoacrylate liquid.

As he made his way back to the Shadow Room, Flag became aware of a light blinking on the surface of his communications array. The light was insistent but unobtrusive, and the unit on which it blinked was one of several similar arrays held in the vast complex of this Laboratory of the Incredible.

Toggling a button marked with the word *engage,* Professor Flag picked up the microphone unit and spoke into its pickup grille. "This is Professor Flag," he acknowledged with brusqueness. "Speak."

"Chief, it's me," the familiar voice of Little Ant came over the crackling speaker of the wireless device. "We've got huge trouble here."

"I'm busy right now, Little Ant," Flag said testily. "Is it

something you and Barnaby can deal with or will you require my assistance?"

"Oh, we've got it covered," Ant announced. "Just thought you'd want to know that the whole blamed island sunk under the waves. You wouldn't even know it had ever been there no more."

"Unfortunate," Flag mused, his amethyst eyes taking on a distant quality, "but hardly unexpected. How did the evacuation go?"

"That's just the thing, Chief," Flag's linguist colleague explained, a concerned whine in his tone. "General Kinver and the brave boys on Terandoa—they all started acting weird, and it was like they didn't hear us no more."

"What about Barnaby?" Flag prompted.

"Barn was seeing stuff for a while, but he says he's feeling better now," Little Ant replied. "I mean, we were both seeing some things for a while. I was lucky to nab that bird and take off in time."

"What sort of things?" Flag urged. Even now, his prodigious brain was racing as he tried to place all the pieces of the puzzle together.

"Like…paint," Little Ant responded. "Like paint in the eyes, all reds and blacks. I can still see it a little."

"And what about Octavo?" Flag queried. "Did she make it off the island?"

Flag's companion was silent for a long time at the other end of the wireless connection, and for a moment Flag wondered if their remarkable communication device had failed. "Ant?" he asked.

"A lot of people were caught up in the backwash when that island sunk, Chief. Pulled under," the diminutive linguist finally replied. "I don't know if Demy Octavo was among them or not. Most of them were lookin' as good as dead anyway, if you saw them."

The mighty figure of Abraham Flag turned away from the radio set for a moment as he collected his thoughts. Then, with steely determination in his purple eyes, he engaged the microphone pickup once more and spoke in his most solemn tone. "Ant, I need you and Barnaby to confine yourselves to your apartments, or to a hotel, as soon as possible. I need you to remain there until such time as the paintlike visions pass. You must have no further contact with a living soul, not even an optometrist, until such time as the visions have entirely and completely left you. Do you understand?"

"What about our ten-o'clock rendezvous in a coupla days?" Little Ant asked.

"I shall understand if you are unable to attend," Flag stated, though his thoughts were now contemplating the likelihood of his own nonattendance. The ancient stone knife had done something truly terrible to all who had been in its proximity when it had triggered, and he realized now that Kinver's men had shared close quarters with it even before it had tasted Demy Octavo's blood. Engaging the knife had been like dropping a bomb, a bomb whose impact would keep expanding unless Flag could contain its awful power.

Flag switched off the radio unit and strode back to the Shadow Room, the container of cyanoacrylate in his hand.

With the application of heat, Professor Flag used the cyanoacrylate compound to augment the seals of the pressure box, locking the stone dagger within. Then he placed wooden strips along each corner, sealing them on with the gluey substance of the heated cyanoacrylate, and secured the cube atop the plinth that stood in the center of the room. The stone knife waited ominously within that glass chamber, its eerie blackness shimmering in the overhead light, the strange smudge of black bleed glimmering on its surface.

Once the knife was safely sealed away, Flag took the used dish and the heating equipment and left the room, locking the seven-inch-thick steel door behind him.

He paced across his wondrous laboratory, pondering what to do now. The blade was secure, locked away from contact with the world. Theoretically freed from the passage of time, its horrifying effects should diminish. Barnaby and Little Ant should begin to revert to their normal selves, and the ruins of Isle Terandoa would lie beneath the ocean with whatever victims they had claimed this day.

Satisfied, albeit warily, the incredible man of science stripped the cotton gloves from his hands and brought his right hand up to brush at his hair and massage the tired muscles of his face. As he did so, he saw something unexpected— a tiny cut, just a sliver like a paper cut, where his index finger met with his palm. The cut appeared to be shifting, pulsating as he watched the tiny red line on the surface of his skin.

Irritated, Flag reached for the gloves he had stripped off just moments before, and examined the one that he had used to cover his right hand. There was a rip, a snag in the cotton where something had torn the weave.

Abraham Flag had never been a man given to panic. Even now, despite the emotions that rushed through him, his face remained stoic, a mask of control. The only indication of his concern could be seen in his fierce purple eyes, and that might only be recognized by the closest of his friends.

With long, determined strides, Professor Flag made his

way swiftly through the Laboratory of the Incredible toward a tall cylindrical unit that waited close by the double helix staircase. The unit was about eight feet in height, and several thick, snakelike tubes fed into its apex. Flag had been working on a theory of cryogenics—the science of freezing living tissue so that it could be thawed months or even years later—in his spare moments in his Antarctic laboratory. But he had never expected to use the device on himself.

He stared at the towering tube that waited beneath the high balcony of the upper levels, his reflection wrapping around its glass front like some mocking funhouse mirror. There were problems with the system, he knew, issues to do with the wake-up protocols that he had simply been unable to master, foolishly believing he had all the time in the world to iron out such kinks. Flag reached for his notebook where it lay at the control board that operated the cryogenic tube and gazed regretfully at the tiny cut on his hand.

"What I do now," Flag told himself, his voice echoing in the vast chamber of scientific marvels, "I do for the good of mankind."

Then Abraham Flag picked up his pen and added a new note to his log, dating it clearly in his neat, controlled hand. "It is with regret that I now find myself in a situation where I must use this untested equipment upon myself," he wrote, "with ill preparation on my part. I am aware that I have been unable to finalize the wake-up protocols. However, under such circumstances as those I face today, it seems that this will be for the best. My body must be frozen, a timeless thing, that the monster lurking in my blood not be set free to enact its apocalyptic rampage."

Initialing the passage he had just written, Abraham Flag

replaced the cap on his pen and triggered the initiation sequence on the cryogenic chamber.

"Okay, old girl," he muttered as the pump system chugged to life and began mixing the freezing elements, "let's you and me see what you've got."

A moment later, Abraham Flag, two-fisted adventurer scientist, stepped into the freezing chamber of the cryogenic device.

*Early twenty-third century*
*Antarctica*

THE NARROW RED line of laser light burned against the front panel of the glass box containing the stone knife Godkiller. For a long time there was no sign of movement, but finally a tiny trail of smoke began to spume from the point where the laser met with the sealed cube. The smoke smelled faintly of something sweet, sickly even, and everyone in the room covered their noses as the operation continued.

Dr. Winterslow leaned close, examining the point where the laser was drilling a hole in the box. "It's getting through," he said, turning to Simona Jurist, her tattooed face reflecting on the dark lenses of the goggles he now wore. "It's being a little slow about it. What did you say this thing was made of?"

"We think it's glass," Carver piped up.

"Glass would melt quicker than this," Winterslow told him.

"Maybe it's been toughened somehow," Carver suggested.

Winterslow leaned close to the laser beam once more, peering through the tinted lenses of his goggles at the mark it was making in the glass box. "If that's toughened glass, it's like nothing I've ever come across before," he admitted.

Simona Jurist glared at the scientist, looking irritated with the whole discourse. "Are you going to open it or not?" she asked.

"It's coming," Winterslow assured her.

Kane smirked at the woman's obvious impatience. "Just try to contain your excitement there, sweetheart," he goaded.

In response, Simona shot him a foul look. "You would do well to remember that you are a guest here, Kane," she said, "and *guest* is just another word for *prisoner.*"

Kane was still smiling when he replied. "Thanks for clarifying that," he said.

Then there was a cracking noise from the box, and they saw the laser's tip spark as it cut through the foremost glass plate. The spark turned to a little flame in an instant, burning at the side of the cube.

"Turn it off!" Jurist snapped, and the tech hurried to obey.

Once the laser shut down, Carver slapped at the single flame licking up the side of the box until it was dowsed.

When they examined the box, they found a tiny pinprick hole in the front panel, proving at last that it could be penetrated.

"We'll hook something in there," Carver proposed, "use it as a lever to crack the glass. Now it's been busted, it won't be too difficult a job."

Jurist nodded and instructed the man to do so.

It took another forty minutes of pushing and pulling with various implements until finally the glass box cracked under the pressure exerted upon it, and the front plate fell to the floor of the control room with a clatter, breaking in two.

As the front plate fell away, the stone knife seemed to glow, catching the measly light of the room. That strange slice of blackness beside it, the thing that had reminded Kane of the night sky, shimmered like a coin spun on a tabletop, the light playing on its surface. And yet, without the panel of glass separating them from it, it no longer appeared to be a thing so much as a nothing. A hole, where there should be something, just hanging there in the air.

Fascinated, Simona edged closer, peering at the stone knife and the thing that adhered to it. "It's beautiful," she whispered as her hand reached out and clasped the hilt.

Kane wasn't so sure. In his experience, beautiful and deadly tended to go hand in hand.

# Chapter 13

The control room of the temporary base was utterly silent as Simona Jurist plucked Godkiller from the glass-fronted display box where it had remained untouched for almost three hundred years. She stood transfixed, holding the ancient Annunaki blade in her hand, staring at it as it glided through the air. The dark lines of the weapon glinted as the lights played across its sleek edges.

"It's beautiful," Jurist whispered again, unable to take her eyes off the carved stone.

Kane and the others watched as the tall woman swept the Annunaki knife through the air, over and over, assessing its weight, its heft. Still attached, almost like syrup, the gelatinous black streak followed each move of the blade through the air. The streak glittered with pinpricks of light, and had the illusion of depth despite, they saw now, only being paper thin.

Concerned, Dr. Winterslow took a step toward Jurist, his eyes on the knife in her hand. "Miss Jurist," he began timidly, "I think we should do more tests to assess the nature of the acquisition."

Simona Jurist simply ignored him.

Then the ex-Mag, Carver, stepped forward, gently pushing Winterslow to one side as he stood before his partner. "Simona?" he asked. "You want to maybe think about putting that thing down now? Letting it go?"

For ten seconds or more, Jurist continued playing the stone knife through the air before her, and it seemed that she was not going to respond. Then her dark eyes flickered and she peered at Carver as if seeing him for the first time. "You need to feel this treasure," she told him, a smile creeping across her lips. "It's…so invigorating."

Gently, showing infinite patience, Carver spoke to Jurist, bringing her down from the strange high she was experiencing.

Kane, Brigid and Grant watched the proceedings without comment, but all three of them were thinking the same thing. There was clearly more to this strange, stone knife than met the eye. It was a weapon from the original days of the Annunaki, perhaps even predating humankind, and it clearly held some pervasive power that could stun a mind into something akin to submission. Only recently, Kane's team had encountered a similar problem, albeit in a different form, when an amalgamation of ancient Annunaki slaves had invaded Brigid Baptiste's mind, threatening to overwhelm her. That problem had only been conquered through use of the uncanny bond that Kane and Brigid shared as *anam-charas,* or "soul friends."

Now, deep in the icy wilds of the Antarctic, they were presented with a weapon that seemed to have a similarly devastating effect on its bearer. Such an item wasn't beyond the realm of comprehension—the Annunaki race had perfected the melding of organics and technology in such a manner that a weapon of this sort certainly wasn't impossible. Furthermore, Kane realized, the Sin Eater pistols that he and Grant carried as a standard weapon from their Magistrate days operated using the tendon flinch, in its own way a synergy of organics and technology, albeit a simple one.

However, the question that was foremost in Kane's mind—and that of his companions—as Jurist continued to move the knife slowly through the air was whether the blade could be controlled by its wielder, or whether it would control them. If the weapon guided the mind of its bearer, then it posed an unprecedented threat—for a weapon only had one function, and that was to destroy.

Furthermore, if a battle was instigated by that weapon's desire, then who would be the ultimate victor? At what point would a weapon cease performing its primary function? At what point would a weapon choose to stop killing? Kane thought back to the stories he had heard of the global conspiracy that had led to the outbreak of nuclear hostilities in January 2001. Earth's population had been pushed to the brink of annihilation by the nukecaust, and even now its future was far from guaranteed. Ultimately, the nukecaust had resulted in just one clear victor, and that had been the weapons themselves that had acted in the Grim Reaper's stead.

Unarmed and surrounded by enemies on all sides, Kane wondered how he might contain such destruction if the blade Godkiller fulfilled its promise.

Simona Jurist reluctantly gave up the knife, and it was taken aside for study, where Dr. Winterslow's team ran it through a gamut of tests. Despite Jurist's initial reaction, the blade seemed surprisingly ordinary, registering simply as a hunk of carved stone, nothing more. Winterslow was unsure of where the stone had originated, however, and he was reticent when questioned on the subject. "It's not obsidian," he assured Jurist and the others, "I can tell you that much. But what it is…? Your guess is as good as mine."

"But it *is* stone…?" Carver probed.

"Definitely." Winterslow nodded. "It's been carved from an igneous rock with very slight porosity."

Kane looked at Brigid. "Slight porosity?" he asked.

"Godkiller's a holey rock," Brigid clarified with a chuckle.

As Winterslow's team continued studying the blade, Kane spoke to Brigid and Grant in a low voice.

"This thing's dangerous," Kane began. "Did you see Jurist's eyes? It was like she was under some kind of spell."

"The incantation and age of the blade suggest it was used between feuding Annunaki," Brigid stated, "at a time when those evil lizards were the most advanced thing on our planet."

"Hmm," Grant snorted bitterly, "like that's ever changed." When Kane and Brigid both glared at Grant, he expanded on his point. "We know from experience that the Annunaki outgun us in every way, and they're next to impossible to kill for certain. Even with their mother ship, *Tiamat,* damaged they've still displayed a nasty habit of cropping up when you least expect them. Sheesh, I don't have to tell you two this."

Kane nodded. "You're right. The Annunaki have proved to be able to outclass us at every turn, and we all know we've used up our quota of luck holding them at bay."

"Meaning?" Brigid prompted.

"This knife is going to kill someone," Kane said. "Maybe not the way we think, but the damn thing is crazy-ass dangerous. What did it say on the side? 'Mourn now your life's journey'?"

"If this Godkiller is as powerful as you think," Brigid reasoned, "then we may be able to use it against them, Kane."

Kane gazed warily around the circular room, checking on the guards and making sure they weren't drawing any unnecessary attention. "Okay," he said sotto voce. "Let's pretend for a moment that we're not surrounded by these millennialist goons, that we can get to our weapons and can exit this base with the knife. You saw what it was doing to Jurist. How do we carry it?"

"Put it back in the box," Grant said.

"Fine," Kane accepted. "We repair the box and use that as a carryall. Problem—when do we take it out and how could we ever use it?"

Grant pondered that, looking increasingly frustrated with the knotty problem.

"So," Brigid suggested, "we destroy it, then. Is that the best option?"

"I don't know, Baptiste," Kane admitted. "What I do know is that I'm sure as hell not ready to 'mourn my life's journey' just yet."

At that moment, Winterslow's voice became louder from the other side of the room, and the Cerberus field team turned to see what was going on.

"No, you don't understand, Simona," the scientist was saying. "This blade exists at a vibrational frequency that is beyond our ability to measure with the equipment here."

Simona Jurist looked imperiously down her nose at the shorter man, holding him with her harsh stare. "What exactly are you babbling about, Doctor?"

Cowering before Jurist's imposing height, Winterslow shook his head, struggling to find the answer to her question. "I think it perhaps exists," he stuttered, "in more than one reality. It is a multidimensional object, and what we see here is just one angle of the whole."

Urgently, Kane stepped across to join the discussion, with Brigid and Grant following. "What does that mean, Dr. Winterslow?"

"That thing you see here," Winterslow explained, pointing to the weird smudge of blackness that was attached to the knife like a vapor trail, "that's a hole into elsewhere. It's a break in the fabric of reality."

Kane's eyes flicked to the inky smudge for a second, before turning to Brigid with a querulous look on his face.

"The Annunaki are multidimensional beings," she reminded Kane. "Without getting heavily into the mechanics of super-string theory, we have established before now that we are only seeing one of their facets."

Carver was intrigued when he heard that. "You've met these gods, then? These Annunaki?"

Grant nodded. "Now and again," he confirmed. "Nothing good came out of it."

Carver looked poised to ask further questions, when Simona Jurist snatched the blade from the desktop where it was being probed.

"What would happen, do you think, if we were to plunge this multidimensional blade into something solid?" Jurist asked, looking around the room. "Would it cut through the wall, say?"

"I couldn't begin to guess without further study," Winterslow admitted.

Stone knife in hand, Jurist turned and fixed her dark gaze on the scientist. "With science," she explained patiently, "you sometimes have to take risks to find the truth."

Winterslow was nodding uncomfortably in agreement at Simona's statement, but even as he did so, she drew back the knife and thrust it ahead of her, driving it through his chest, up under the ribs and into his heart.

"Simona! No!" Carver cried, reaching to stop her. He was a fraction of a second too late.

Simona Jurist yanked the blade from Winterslow's torso, and a sound rang around the room, as light and pretty as birdsong. The sound emanated from the blade.

Winterslow swayed on his feet for a moment, and a trail of blood oozed between his clenched teeth as his body rocked. Then, horribly slowly, he sagged to the floor, dropping to his knees with a clang against the metal plating, before keeling over to where he finally lay still.

Everyone in the room was stunned, standing in shocked silence as the lifeless body of Winterslow settled on the floor.

"You didn't need to..." Carver spit angrily. "Shouldn't have..."

The tattooed woman smiled, her eyes alight with desire. In her hand, the blade seemed to change, the carved words on its edge taking on a fiery glow, witch fire playing across its gleaming darkness. "Look at him," she said, indicating the fallen body of Dr. Winterslow. "Look at what *we've* done."

Whether Jurist meant her and Carver, through their partnership, discovering the hidden Laboratory of the Incredible, or whether she, in fact, referred to some strange partnership she now felt with the knife, Carver wasn't sure. Still in shock, he turned to look where Jurist was pointing, and he saw the man's body lying there. There was a terrible, bloody wound stemming from his chest, the blood pumping out to darken the many layers of clothing he wore. But there was something else, far less expected. Where Simona had stabbed the man, literally the point where her blade had entered when he stood, was an impossible split, hovering in midair. The split was the black-and-white smudge that they had noticed floating from the blade, for it had finally broken free. The eerie starlight twinkled within, but even now the inky smudge was changing before their eyes.

A moment before, it had been a black starfield hovering, unaided and perfectly still, in the air. Before that it had been attached to the knife itself, like a strand from a spiderweb. Now it was looming in the air above Winterslow's fallen body, its thin line slowly expanding to twice, then three times its length until it was an eighteen-inch streak suspended by nothingness. As it pulsed, like sides pulling back, the line—the wound—opened. It opened in utter silence, yet with each pulse it opened farther, its length increasing, like lips parting, splitting in a vertical streak.

Within the rent, it was no longer blackness with flecks of light. It was a churning, swirling, angry redness. The lights fizzed within that redness still, sparkling and glowing, fireflies in blood.

It looked like a wound, Kane realized, a bloody gash across the skin. Except there was no skin, just that hideous slit hovering in midair, like some horrible, toothless mouth. It was almost three feet in height already, expanding to fill the space, an eerie obstacle in the circular chamber. And it pulsated, the split opening a little wider, then reverting to the size it had been a moment before, on and on.

"What is it?" Carver asked, his voice little more than a whisper.

"Some kind of hole," Grant decided.

Simona Jurist was staring at it, looking at the stone blade in her hand, the fallen body of Winterslow as blood stained the man's clothes. "This knife did this," she said, an ecstatic smile across her face. "It cut that…thing."

As the consortium guards edged around the room, taking up positions, pointing their Calico subguns at the tear, Kane paced around the bloodred rent, examining it from all sides.

It had lengthened to where it was now over five feet in height, expanding with each eerie pulse.

"This would be a good time to give us back our blasters," Kane told Jurist, fixing her with his no-nonsense stare, the one that he had used to such great effect during his time as a Magistrate in Cobaltville.

Jurist's reply was mocking laughter. "And quite how do you reach that conclusion?" she asked.

Angrily, Kane grabbed Simona by the back of her head and thrust her toward the throbbing redness that loomed in the middle of the room. "Look at it," he snapped. "Look at what it is you've opened up with that knife."

Jurist shook, struggling to free herself from Kane's grip as her guards surrounded them, their weapons aimed at Kane. "Get your hands off me, Kane," she shouted. "I'll have you executed for this."

"Good," Kane snarled back. "Because a quick death might just be preferable to whatever the fuck that thing's going to do to us. You understand?"

Irked, Simona Jurist glared at Kane, her left eye peering from that ugly snake design tattooed on her face. "What? And you know what it is?" she asked, her voice raised.

Kane shook his head. "I just know I'll be a lot happier exploring it with a gun in my hand."

Before the argument could continue, Grant spoke in an urgent voice. "Kane, the rift. It's expanding."

Kane turned and looked once more at the bloody gash in the air. Grant was right. The crimson line was now nine feet or so tall, and it was pulling apart, wider by the second. Each pulse split those strange lips apart, so wide that a person might step into it at its fullest extent. Inside, Kane—and the other occupants of the control room—saw a swirling, glowing mass of red, corpuscles and sinew, moving to its own unhurried beat. This was the bleed.

Beside Brigid, Carver was cycling through the view options on his goggles as he peered into the breach. "Sweet heavens!" he spit, turning to Simona and glaring at the Annunaki knife. "Do you realize what you've done, Simona?"

Jurist's eyes were wide, and she struggled to turn away from the throbbing red line of the bleed as it parted like an oyster shell. "What?" she asked vacantly.

"Here, look through the goggles," Carver shouted, shoving them into her hand. "That's a hole in space, a thing that cannot be. This blade we've found—this is the knife that cut God. You've fucking cut the body of God." He was ranting now, his words bellowed out in a rush.

"Calm down," Jurist said, though she seemed too distracted to lend her words any weight. She was transfixed by the bleed now, watching that swirling red as it pulsed before everyone's eyes.

Around Jurist and Kane, the guards were backing away, fearful of the impossible line that floated before them, a doorway into the body of the cosmos.

Standing beside Jurist, Kane reached down and took the knife from her grip. She seemed barely to be holding it now, transfixed as she was by the red bleed, and she showed no resistance when he pulled the blade away.

All around the room, the other millennialists were watching the opening rift, that eerie breach in reality, the cut on God's skin, as Carver had described it.

Brigid Baptiste watched the rift with her emerald eyes, but she also felt the bleed echoing in her mind, like a clock, its ticking painfully loud. "This is what Professor Flag was try-ing to stop," she said to herself, her voice quiet.

"I have the knife," Kane said, stepping beside Brigid. "What did you just say?"

"This is why Abraham Flag locked the blade Godkiller away," Brigid explained, still watching the throbbing, bloody hole in space, "and this is why he froze himself. He said it in his notes, Kane, how there wasn't enough time to perfect the wake-up protocols. He needed to seal himself away before this thing devoured him and everything around him. Maybe even the world itself. And now we've set it loose again and fed it blood. We've charged it with blood."

Kane stood before Brigid and placed his hand on her shoulder, forcing her to look away from the bleed. "I've got the knife now," he said. "It's okay."

Brigid's emerald eyes were wide with terror. "No, it's not," she said. "Now is the time to be scared."

"Not yet it's not," Kane growled, his mind discarding op-tion after option in a fraction of a second. There had to be some way to stop what had been started, he knew, if he could just work out how. Abraham Flag had cryogenically frozen himself because of this thing. Did that mean that freezing worked as a weapon against it? If so, if coldness worked, could they somehow lead this unearthly thing out-side into the subzero temperatures of the Antarctic and let nature freeze it in place? And if it couldn't be led, then break the temporary base apart, bringing the outside inside, as it were?

Standing beside Brigid, Grant was looking decidedly ill, rocking in place on his heels. "What is that thing?" he asked, the words slurring as he spoke them.

"A breach in infinity," Brigid replied, choosing her words carefully.

"And what does that mean?" Grant asked.

Kane answered before Brigid could. "It means we should step away, *right now*."

Under Kane's guidance the three Cerberus teammates backed away from the rent in space as it continued to swell, becoming wider with every pulse. The millennialists were still watching, transfixed by the eerie sight in the same way that Abraham Flag and the unfortunate people on Isle Terandoa had been almost three hundred years before.

And then a most incredible thing happened, in a day of incredible things—the most magical thing that Kane's team had witnessed in a lifetime of magical things. The infinity breach opened to an even greater width and a glowing human figure stepped out.

An angel was walking the Earth for the first time in countless millennia.

# Chapter 14

Everyone in the ice-cool room stared, mouths agape, eyes wide, as the angel stepped out of the bloodred breach in the infinite. Neither clearly male nor female, the figure glowed pure white with such intensity that it lit the dingy, circular room like an explosion. It was an explosion held in stasis, molded into humanoid form.

Kane's left hand opened without him noticing, and the Annunaki blade fell to the floor. He was tensing the wrist tendons in his right forearm automatically, muscle memory kicking in, commanding the Sin Eater to his hand. It took him a moment to realize that the Sin Eater was missing, and longer yet to remember that he had been disarmed several hours before. The opening of the rift and the pulsating bleed had threatened to overwhelm his thoughts, burn through his brain like wildfire, dismissing every thought he held there. Only now, as he acknowledged his empty palm, did he begin to recall the moments leading up to this moment.

The glowing figure hovered before them, several inches above the ground, as tall and thin as a shadow at sunset, a willowy specter in purest white. It—he or she?—turned, head rotating on a beautiful, swanlike neck, examining the scene before it, surveying with unutterable superiority.

Before the angel, the room waited in silence, its audience hushed.

Behind, clambering from the breach, another white figure appeared, and then another, until there were three of them, emerging from the bloody rent in the air like babies plunging from the womb. Angels being born into the world, fully grown and at an absolute oneness with the cosmic flow.

Kane's eyes were adjusting now, picking out details in the first one's face. For it had a face, he saw now, thin and gaunt, like everything else about it, stretched like a badly reproduced image, a piece of avant-garde art. Its eyes—*her* eyes, Kane decided—were white, like her skin, her body, her robes. And yet the eyes were darker somehow, a blue that wasn't there, that could only be seen if you stopped looking at it. There was a mouth, too, with lips. The creature—the angel— had lips, full, luscious lips carved into an elegant pout beneath a perfectly straight Greek nose. She was like a statue of alabaster, the only details created by the shadows that the carving threw upon itself. Yet she was brighter than marble, a fierce, virginal whiteness to her burning glow.

The other white ones stepped forward, and more arrived, parting the lips of the breach, dragging themselves out into the real world. Each one of them burned with that unnatural whiteness, a spectral glow so bright that it dazzled and ached, hurting the eyes yet calling to them like siren song.

It had been seven minutes since the breach had opened and began spewing the figures. There were seven of them in all— seven minutes and seven figures, Heaven's number. In all that time, the occupants of the room, fourteen representatives of the Millennial Consortium along with the Cerberus trio, had stood in awed silence. All except for Winterslow, who bled out on the metal floor where the knife had sliced across and through him, the very wound that had somehow caused the formation of the infinity breach by reacting with the inky wisp on the blade.

Now, precisely seven minutes after the first of the angels had stepped from the rift in the cosmos, Grant spoke up, his voice seeming strangely faraway after such an extended break in all noise.

"What do we do?" he asked, voicing the question on everyone's mind, all eyes still fixed on the marvelous beings who had emerged before them.

Kane didn't have an answer. He stood there, watching the eerily beautiful creatures move, traveling through the air like fish in water, and all he could think about was how naked he felt without a gun. Here was a spectacle, a marvel, a miracle, and all that Kane could think was how he had been forced to witness it unarmed. A part of him hated what he was then, what he had always been. Killer Kane.

Brigid Baptiste watched the seven glowing figures, the pillars of Heaven, stepping out of the bleed, gliding across the cool metal of the floor, and she did something she had never done before: she told herself to remember this moment, to lock it in place in her memory. Brigid Baptiste, whose eidetic memory retained every single scrap of data that it had ever been fed, who remembered things to such a degree of detail that it seemed impossible to a lesser mind, found herself fearing that she might forget this one beautiful instant when she had seen angels walk the Earth.

Standing close to Kane, Simona Jurist watched the Coming with her dark eyes. The glowing creatures burned into her consciousness, their blue-white eyes on their pure white faces penetrating through her, gazing into her soul. And as they looked, she felt the darkness there, the black cloud looming over her heart, drenching everything in its rottenness. Turned against herself, gazing into the abyss, Simona Jurist struggled to look away.

And Carver, the other ex-Mag in the room, watched the proceedings as dumbstruck as everyone else. His analytical mind began to piece together what he was seeing, realized that these creatures had stepped out of the infinite for a reason. The breach was open, the blood was flowing, and these things had come from the beyond, reaching out from elsewhere to here, from their world to his.

"What do we do?" It was Grant's question that broke the silence seven minutes after it had begun.

"We let them work," Carver said intuitively, suddenly seeing the angels for what they truly were.

With that, like the scales being lifted from his eyes, Carver seemed to awaken from the hypnosis that had taken hold of everyone in the room. He shook his head and stepped away from the throbbing hole of blood. With muscular arms, Carver reached behind him, patting the others in their sides, against their chests, waking them as he had woken. "We have to leave here," he stated, curiously sure of himself.

"What are you squawking about, Carver?" Kane spit, his thoughts running at normal speed once more, his eyes turning away from the mesmeric sight of the creatures of light hovering above the metal floor.

"Those things, we have to leave them, let them work," Carver replied. "You know what they are?"

"Angels," Kane stated automatically, unsure of how the word had formed. He felt that he should be embarrassed by using the term, and yet three others in the room had muttered the same word in response, in sync with his own vocalization, and still others had thought it.

"They're here to fix it," Carver said, breathless. "To fix the breach in infinity."

Kane looked up and saw the truth of the man's words. The seven angels were gliding around one another in a swirl of glowing robes. They were like bees twirling around one another as they spiraled around the bloodred hole in space to the unheard sound of the *musica universalis.* The throbbing, glowing, brain-burning rift itself was stable now, no longer pulsating, no longer angry, no longer threatening to rip entirely apart. Whatever the angels were doing, whatever their dance meant, it appeared to be holding the tear in place, halting the primal onslaught of the bleed.

The humans in the circular control room pulled themselves away, shuffling out through the eight exits. The communications tech, Lacea, rushed over to Carver, asking him what had just happened.

"I heard them in my head," Carver explained. "They came to help, to… I don't know how to explain."

Brigid Baptiste nodded in agreement. "They're antibodies," she stated, realization dawning, but slowly. "The angels are the antibodies of the universe. That weapon, the Godkiller knife, it cut an impossible hole."

"Because it's multidimensional," Kane realized, catching on as he hurried the others through the door.

"This is what Abraham Flag saw on that island in the Pacific," Brigid surmised. "This is why he hid the knife in that vault, so that no one else would ever use it. This is why no one ever saw him again."

"Guess we should have left well alone, huh?" Grant rumbled. "You said this knife sunk an island, right?"

Brigid looked at Grant, then at Kane, with a look of childlike fascination on her beautiful features. "We just saw angels," she said.

Kane looked nonplussed. "I don't like it," he growled.

"Kane, they're—" Brigid began, but Kane stopped her.

"Angels," he said. "I heard. And, in fact, I already had them pegged as such. But every time we come up against something good—which, no lie, isn't very often—it somehow ends up in a massacre."

"Angels don't massacre people," Lacea stated, looking up from where she stood beside Simona Jurist, who appeared to still be in shock.

Kane fixed the blonde communications officer with his cold stare. "Everything massacres everything eventually," he stated. "Spiders kill flies, cats kill birds and people kill anything that gets too close. It's the way of the world."

As though awakening from a trance, Simona Jurist shook herself and addressed Kane in a solemn voice. "No, they're here to help us. They wouldn't harm anyone. Can't you hear them speaking to you?"

"They've haven't said anything to me yet," Kane told her, although he could not truly tell how he knew that they were angels if they hadn't told him.

"You have to listen," Jurist told him in a patronizing tone. "They speak in your head as they dance to the *musica universalis.*"

"The music of the spheres," Brigid translated automatically. "An old concept for how the cosmos was ordered."

"Well, I'll tell you what," Kane said, glaring at Jurist. "You give us back our weapons, and I'll listen to all the damn sphere music you want."

"Are you scared of them?" Jurist asked, astounded.

Kane didn't answer immediately. Instead, he peered back into the control room, watching the beautiful specters as they spun their mesmeric dance around the cut in space–time. Remarkably, the rift was closing, and its length had diminished to barely an eighth of its greatest size.

"They're closing it," Kane said at last.

A minute later the breach was sealed. A moment before, the tiny red scar had hung in the air as the angels danced around and around, their robes flowing, their willowy arms waving. Then, impossibly, it vanished as if it hadn't been there at all, and the angels' dance slowed.

The Cerberus exiles and the millennialists watched as the angels ceased in their beautiful dance and peered about the room, heads turning on those exquisite, long necks. As one, they spied the ancient stone knife where Kane had dropped it on the floor in his initial moments of shock, and one of them spoke.

"Impurity discovered," it said, its voice like birdsong.

The other angels took up the chant, like a choir bursting into song. Then they circled it, seven luminescent beings, spinning a single spot in the floor, dancing around the circular room.

The Godkiller blade sparkled with inner power, the volcanic lines of the runes wavering along its edge. Abruptly the dance stopped, and one of the angels reached down, bending with its whole body, arching its back yet never touching the floor as it snatched up the blade. In the angel's hand, the blade glowed brighter, and then it seemed to disintegrate, turning to ash, which in turn became nothing at all as the angel's long fingers clutched empty space.

"That's solved that problem," Grant muttered to himself.

As if hearing Grant's words, the angels turned—their movements like flocking birds, heads moving as one unit— to look at the doorway where the humans watched. The lead angel, the one whom Kane had tagged as a female, smiled, such benevolence pouring from her like a physical force, lapping against the onlookers like a wave.

"The children," the angel said, her beautiful mouth opening but the lips never moving in that shining white face. "Welcome." Then her mouth closed and she smiled again, and behind her the other angels smiled, too.

Simona Jurist left the others, stepping forward, transfixed by what she saw. She walked back into the room, striding up to the angels on her long, sapling legs. "You're real," was all she could think to say.

"This garden is yours," one of the other angels said. The voice sounded more masculine, though the features seemed androgynous. "Child."

Jurist reached for the lead angel then, her hand touching the fiercely glowing robes that she wore. The angel's smile grew wider, and she looked upon the tattooed woman with loving eyes, a mother to its infant. Then, with no warning, the angel's smile disappeared, and a look of horror crossed her beauteous face.

"Impurity discovered," the angel said, and the others repeated the words like a choir.

It was the work of only an instant then, a second, perhaps two. The seven angels, Heaven's number, circled Simona Jurist, their dazzling bright robes swishing in their wake. Jurist turned this way and that, wondering what was happening as the angels closed in around her.

"What is it?" Jurist asked. "I don't understand…"

Ignoring her pleas, the angels reached out to her, placing the glowing white palms of seven white hands upon her, their eyes fixed on their subject.

Simona Jurist began to scream.

# Chapter 15

"What th—?" Carver spit, hurrying back through the doorway and into the circular control room as Simona Jurist began to shriek in agony.

Kane grabbed the man, pulling him back from the open doorway.

"What the hell do you think you're doing?" Carver snapped at Kane.

"Could ask you the same question," Kane shot back, barring the way into the room as he glared at Carver.

Behind Kane, through the open doorway, Carver could see the seven angels swirling around Jurist's form in their eerie dance, their outstretched palms brushing against her. Even as he watched, Jurist's eyes rolled up into her skull while her mouth remained open in a hideous scream that just went on and on and on.

"We have to help her," Carver told Kane, struggling to push the ex-Mag aside. When Kane didn't move, Carver raised his hand, balling it into a fist. "I'm warning you…"

Grant stepped in then, grabbing Carver's wrist as the ex-Mag swung the first blow. "Carver, we need our weapons," Grant told him, his voice level and calm. "We need them *now*."

"I can't authorize that," Carver began, but the words

seemed to tail off as his attention was drawn to the control-room doorway once more.

Within, Simona Jurist was glowing a bright, bloody red like an angry volcano, her scream wailing forth from a mouth held so wide it looked as if it might tear open. The fight drained from Carver's body, and Kane peered over his shoulder to observe what happened next. Jurist screamed as the angels' snow-white hands played across her, and her body seemed to flake away, starting from her booted feet and working upward through her long, black-clad legs.

Kane had never heard anyone scream for so long without taking breath. In fact, none of them had. But Jurist held that shrill, painful note as her body broke apart as easily as gossamer, disappearing like spume on the waves. It was as if her body had become stuck screaming, like the key of some hideous, poorly tuned musical instrument being held down, jammed in place. The burning, or whatever it really was, made Jurist half a person, then less, as it worked over her hips and up through her torso, disintegrating her chest. And still she screamed relentlessly, far beyond anything a human breath could achieve, the sound like something artificially looped. The disintegration reached Jurist's shoulders, then the beautiful curve of her long, fine neck. Beneath her head there was nothing now, and yet her mouth continued screeching that impossible shriek.

Kane watched in horror as Simona Jurist's neck swirled to nothingness, her lower jaw burned away, and then upward through her nose, her eyes, destroying any evidence of that foreboding cobra tattoo that she wore over her equine face. Then just the scalp remained, the roots where her hair connected to her skin. The hair itself bleached to white, then be-

# Get FREE BOOKS and a FREE GIFT when you play the...

# LAS VEGAS GAME

*Just scratch off the gold box with a coin. Then check below to see the gifts you get!*

## YES!
I have scratched off the gold box. Please send me my **2 FREE BOOKS** and **gift for which I qualify.** I understand that I am under no obligation to purchase any books as explained on the back of this card.

## 366 ADL E373          166 ADL E373

|  |  |
|---|---|

FIRST NAME                           LAST NAME

ADDRESS

APT.#          CITY

STATE/PROV.      ZIP/POSTAL CODE

**7 7 7** Worth TWO FREE BOOKS plus a BONUS Mystery Gift!

Worth TWO FREE BOOKS!

TRY AGAIN!

Offer limited to one per household and not valid to current subscribers of Gold Eagle® books. All orders subject to approval. Please allow 4 to 6 weeks for delivery.

**Your Privacy**—Worldwide Library is committed to protecting your privacy. Our privacy policy is available online at www.ReaderService.com or upon request from the Reader Service. From time to time we make our lists of customers available to reputable third parties who may have a product or service of interest to you. If you would prefer us not to share your name and address, please check here ☐. **Help us get it right**—We strive for accurate, respectful and relevant communications. To clarify or modify your communication preferences, visit us at www.ReaderService.com/consumerschoice.

▼ **DETACH AND MAIL CARD TODAY!** ▼

© 2009 WORLDWIDE LIBRARY. Printed in Canada. ® and TM are trademarks owned and used by the trademark owner and/or its licensee.

If offer card is missing write to: The Reader Service, P.O. Box 1867, Buffalo NY 14240-1867

**BUSINESS REPLY MAIL**

FIRST-CLASS MAIL    PERMIT NO. 717    BUFFALO, NY

POSTAGE WILL BE PAID BY ADDRESSEE

**THE READER SERVICE**
**PO BOX 1867**
**BUFFALO NY 14240-9952**

NO POSTAGE
NECESSARY
IF MAILED
IN THE
UNITED STATES

came nothing. For a moment more, Jurist's pained scream continued, echoing throughout the Antarctic complex in sheer terror. Finally, fully seven seconds after Simona Jurist had ceased to exist, her terrible cry ceased, too.

Carver was still looking through the doorway, mouth agog, watching as the glowing angel forms remained in place, circling the empty space where Simona Jurist had stood just seconds before. "You need your weapons," he said in a monotone. Then, still clearly in shock, he turned to Grant. "You'll get them, Grant. I'll see to it now. I want an angel for the consortium."

Grant nodded. "Best we continue this discussion elsewhere, Magistrate," he said, hoping that his use of the man's old title would trigger the disciplined reaction they would need if they were to get out of there alive.

"Right," Carver agreed vacantly. He pawed at his hip holster, pulling out a reconditioned Sin Eater. It was an older version of the weapon that Kane and Grant habitually carried, and it lacked the folding mechanism that was used to store the modern model in the wrist holster.

Kane urged everyone back from the open doorway, hurrying them down the narrow corridor. "Let's get moving, then," he shouted.

Carver shushed Kane for a moment, waving him aside. Then he raised his voice, bellowing an order to everyone within earshot, his voice resounding off of the metal walls of complex. "This is Carver," he shouted. "New plan, people. A bonus and triple wages to anyone who bags me one of those…those glowing things. Dead or alive."

Kane grabbed Carver's arm and hurried the man down the corridor. Was he serious? Had he just put a price on an angel's head?

In the circular control room, the angels stepped away from the spot where Simona Jurist had been, turning as one to look at the fallen body of Dr. Winterslow.

"There were impurities in the child," the first angel said, astounded at the revelation. Her name was Abariel.

"Corrupted," one of the others replied in a voice like a song. His name was Damiel.

Another angel spoke then, the beautiful one called Abariel, her voice like a river glade. "Not all of the children. That cannot be."

"We must test them," Damiel said.

"Judge them," the angel Bateliel agreed. "Each in turn."

One of the glowing angels, this one with a tangle of locks flowing past his shoulders, crouched before the corpse of Dr. Winterslow, touching his hand against the late doctor's face. The angel's name was Domos.

"This one has no spark," Domos stated, the words like the flapping of a bird's feathered wing. "It is not his time, yet his spark is missing. I cannot locate it."

"Is he corrupted?" Damiel asked in his voice of song.

Domos considered the question for a long time, pressing his hand harder against the corpse's cooling flesh. "I cannot tell. There are impurities," he decided. "It is difficult. He has no spark. He should have his spark."

"His spark is gone," Bateliel said, the licking of flame in the sound of his voice. "We shall find others and judge."

"What if they are all impure?" Abariel asked. "What if all of the children have been corrupted?"

"Then we shall cleanse the system," Bateliel stated, "and the cycle shall start anew."

"Cleanse the system," the others agreed.

As the angels were reaching their conclusion, several of the braver Millennial Consortium men edged into the room, their Calico subguns thrust before them.

While most of the consortium men had made their way to safer cover when they had seen Simona Jurist disintegrate, hoping to box in the angels, these three had stayed. Their leader, a man called Irons, had egged them on, encouraging them to return to the control room. "You heard Carver," Irons had growled. "Come on, we can take them."

Irons and his two colleagues, Blythe and Denning, lined up their weapons and began to spray the seven glowing figures with 9 mm bullets.

"Kneecap them," Irons instructed. "Shoot to wound."

The angels watched as the first of the bullets raced across the room toward them. Beautiful Abariel stepped forward, watching the bullets fly through the air, wondering at their purpose. To Abariel, the bullets looked like insects, their shells a lustrous silver. She saw them moving through the air and thought them pretty, shiny, new things. And so Abariel reached out with a chalk-white, glowing hand and plucked the first bullet from the air. It moved so quickly that it stung, burning her fingers as they clasped at it. She had misjudged its speed, having never seen a living thing move so fast as this. To her angel eyes it moved slower or faster depending on how she interpreted it, but it still burned when it was plucked from the air, such was its speed.

Behind Abariel, the other angels were doing similar things, snatching at the silver projectiles flying through the air, gazing at them in abject wonder.

Close to the communications array, his finger clamped on the trigger of his Calico subgun, Irons saw the first angel step forward, a blur of light, straight into the path of his attack like some kind of simpleton. The blur of the moving angel was so fast, and then she stood stock-still as Irons sprayed her with bullets. She stood, holding something between her fingers, gazing at it with such curiosity that it seemed childlike, almost ludicrous.

Irons saw then what it was that this beautiful, magnificent being held: a bullet, impossibly plucked out of the air. Her examination of the bullet concluded, the angel looked up at Irons with those eerie, blue-white eyes, and an indulgent smile crossed the perfect mouth of her white face.

Irons's finger was still clenched down on the trigger of his gun, even as the ammo clip ran dry and the firing mechanism locked in place, waiting to be refilled. He stood there, holding the gun on the angel as that wondrous vision flipped her hand almost languidly, like someone moving through water, and returned Irons's first bullet back to him.

The tossed bullet hurtled through the air, cutting a path back to the nose of the Calico, driving down the barrel and beyond, until it burst the back of the gun and drilled onward, through Irons's shoulder at the far end of the outthrust weapon.

Irons screamed in pain as his shoulder erupted in blood under the impact of the bullet at the same time as the subgun shattered in his grip. He staggered backward on unsteady legs, dropping the useless subgun to the metal plate flooring of the circular control room.

The angel Abariel watched in wonder. She had returned the shiny insect to its nest, its hive, and yet it had not stopped there, had not landed. It had traveled on and damaged one of the children. This was unexpected. This was a new thing. Abariel found it fascinating.

Abariel strode closer to the fallen form of Irons, though her bare feet never touched the floor itself. She watched, fascinated, as the child reached for something at his hip, pulling a short metallic rod from a holder there and waving it toward her. She smiled, for this was also a new thing.

Lying on his back, Irons whipped out the Sigma pistol as the glowing angel—the one who had plucked his bullet from the air and somehow used it to destroy his own gun, and his shoulder in the process—hovered ominously nearer. An insistent voice in his head was urging him not to hurt the angels, for they were angels—reason enough. But they had killed Simona Jurist, he reminded himself, and with that he pulled at the Sigma's trigger, blasting four 9 mm bullets at the approaching form. He watched in horror as the angel's limbs blurred, and she placed her left hand in the path of the racing bullets.

THE ANGEL Abariel saw now that the metal cylinder that the child had produced was another nest, full of fluttering, silver-shelled insects like the first ones the child had tried to give to her. Her eyes could slow time's input, slow it to such a degree that everything would stop or, if she chose to focus on a specific thing, that one event would slow while everything else raced on around her. She slowed the movement of the four silver shells, peering inquisitively, wondering where their wings were. They had none.

Abariel reached forward, remembering the way the first insect had burned her flesh, and she carefully snagged them from behind, hooking them up out of their flight path, grasping them in her palm. Their energy dulled as she grasped them and, disappointed, she brought them closer to study their bland forms. They were long silver things with pointed snouts—perhaps a sting? They had movement but, when she tried to sense them, they had no discernible spark. Perhaps they were not alive after all. Strange, Abariel thought, that children would give these gifts of dead insects. It had to have meaning, though, for all things had meaning.

Abariel dropped the insects to the floor, where they sang against the metal there in pleasing, sweet chirrups as she strode on toward the fallen child with the wounded shoulder. All the while her feet never quite reached the floor.

IRONS WATCHED as the glowing white angel plucked his bullets from the air, peered at them for a second, then tossed them aside. Then, horrified, he saw the angel hover closer, a beatific smile on her perfect face. "I have no insects for you, child," the angel said, sounding apologetic in a voice that ran like sluicing water.

Then the angel Abariel reached for Irons, placing her hand, palm flat, against his forehead where he struggled on the floor. His pulse quickened, his breathing came in ragged gasps and, against his will, Irons felt his bowels vent as the angel touched him. She began her analysis, searching for impurity in the child's shell.

Around the circular room, the screams of Blythe and Denning rent the air as they, too, fell beneath the curiosity of the angels. As the millennialists lay there, wounded by their own bullets, which the angels had sent back to their housings in the Calico subguns, the seven glowing beings moved toward them, preparing to cast judgment.

Their voices echoed around the circular room as the angels touched the three fallen soldiers in unison.

"Impurity discovered."

It sounded like a choir singing of the glory of Heaven.

Once Irons, Blythe and Denning had been judged, the seven angels moved as one, exiting the control room in the same instant via different doors.

Domos hovered out into a narrow corridor to the northeast of the mobile base, his flowing locks swishing behind him. In the metal-walled, low-ceilinged corridor he was immediately accosted by the next wave of Millennial Consortium guardsmen. Their squad leader, a bearded man called Chuck Allen, shouted the order the second the glowing figure passed through the doorway. Behind him, there was a *phut* sound as the compressed air of the launcher was released, blasting a net at the angel Domos.

Domos watched the net flying through the air toward him, perplexed at its purpose. At first he took it for a bird, a strange kind of bird that flew in a clump, its wings spreading as it took off. Then he saw that the netting was insentient, all holes and lines, spreading out through some trick of its launch.

The net fell about Domos then, wrapping around his willowy, glowing form, cinching his arms to his sides as it tautened. Domos smiled uncertainly, wondering at the sensation of the net upon him. It tickled.

Squad leader Allen stepped out from cover, his Calico M-960 held firmly in two hands, trained in the direction of the captured angel, a savage smile on his face. The angel was trapped, and yet he didn't struggle, didn't even appear uncomfortable. He just hovered there, upright as though standing, his skin and clothes exuding that fierce glow, the pure light of Heaven.

Behind Allen, his troops were stepping out of the shadows, their own blasters held at the ready as their leader paced toward the angel.

"We got one," Allen heard one of his men shout excitedly from behind him.

Yeah, that's right, Allen thought. "We got you, you bastard," he snarled, jabbing the muzzle of the Calico against the angel's robed gut.

Domos looked at the child and wondered whether this was a game. Children liked games, he remembered; perhaps they desired to play. "Come closer, child," Domos said in a voice that sounded like the waves lapping against a sandy beach. "I will not hurt you."

Allen looked up at the angel's pale eyes, his pupils narrowing as he peered at the light. The angel had spoken, his mouth open, the words tumbling forward with such beauty but his lips never moving. It was as if the angel spoke to him in his head.

In his eight years working for the Millennial Consortium, Allen had seen a lot of strange sights. He had been part of field teams that had uncovered tombs and missile silos, unearthed dead bodies and gene freaks, creatures that belonged to another time. This luminescent creature, however, hovering before him like a chandelier, exuding beauty from every pore, this was something he had never imagined he might experience. It was like a tune stuck in his head, a wonderful, melodic tune.

"Come, child," Domos repeated in a note of ultimate purity. "Come closer."

The words were in Allen's head, blocking his other thoughts, overriding them. He stepped closer to the angel, his elbow bending to accommodate the length of the Calico subgun that he had shoved against this beautiful creature's torso. The thing—the angel—was trapped in the net. The angel couldn't hurt him, he assured himself. And it wasn't just the voice in his head; he really wanted to get closer to this beautiful creature, to feel his touch.

"It's doing something to Allen," one of the other men in the corridor called. "It's tricking him."

The speaker didn't hesitate. He simply squeezed the trigger of the subgun in his hand, unleashing a stream of bullets at Allen's back, blasting his section leader and the angel in the same burst.

Domos watched as the silver-shelled objects hurtled toward him. He had thought that they were insects at first, but now he had come to recognize them as something else. He didn't have a word for it—nothing like this existed in his world—but he comprehended them as a flying infection. The angels had ever been tasked to deal with the infections to the body of God, and yet the children carried their own tiny versions, things that made rips and holes in their own shapes and the shapes of the things around them in the garden. The silver things were disease.

The bullets sped through the air and pummeled Allen's back, rattling against his body armor and making him rock on his feet. In response, automatically, Allen's trigger finger squeezed and his own weapon started firing—straight into the body of the angel Domos at point-blank range.

Domos simply smiled wider as the bullets blasted from the Calico and into his luminescent body. He was a being of light and, at will, could let objects like the silver shells simply pass through him. Depending on the size and velocity of the projectile, it was simply a matter of choosing the correct frequency. He felt nothing as the stream of 9 mm bullets zipped through his body, like traveling through mist, and out the other side before rattling against the wall behind him in a tarantella of jabbering retorts.

As the bullets continued to drill into the metal-plate wall, Domos shrugged out of the net, bored with the feeling of constriction. Then he reached forward, his palm splayed, and touched Allen on the forehead as the man's body rocked in place. Another stream of bullets, those shiny-shelled disease projectiles whose purpose Domos had still not quite defined, blasted around him, hitting Allen's back and zipping through Domos's body where it remained unshielded by the child. Domos ignored them, allowing them to pass through in their urgent quest for freedom from the metal cylinders the other children held. Dismissing the silvered things, Domos eyed the figure before him, assessing the construct through the palm of his hand.

Then two words emerged from Domos's mouth: "Impurity discovered."

# Chapter 16

Domos was disappointed. He had hoped that this child, his first solo discovery in the garden, would be pure, unlike the others before it. But he was wrong.

Reluctantly, Domos put the child to sleep, squeezing at the sides of the child's head until his skull burst apart. He could not seal the impurity alone, but he could halt it until the others came to assist him.

Bullets split the air all around glowing Domos and the falling figure of Chuck Allen.

THE ANGEL Bateliel now understood that the silver-shelled insects were supposed to damage things. He had admired their swift flight as they exited their metal hives and rushed in their perfectly straight lines toward some destination only they comprehended. But the insects never altered their paths once they had launched, were never distracted by colors the way that insects should be, and there were no flowers around on which they might land. In short, the insects were, by Bateliel's calculations, not very useful at all. As such, he had no qualms about squashing them as another swarm hurried toward him when he exited the circular room where he and his companions had judged Simona Jurist and the three who had followed her.

The children seemed to have a lot of the silver-shelled insects to distribute. Six children waited in the corridor, poking their heads from doorways, edging along the walls, some crouched on the floor. All of them held one of the metallic cylinders that Bateliel had come to identify as nests or hives or mounds. Some of the cylinders were different from the others, and some of the nests dispensed silvery insects of a slightly larger type or at a more rapid rate, but all of them coughed out silver shells in near-continuous streams as Bateliel appeared.

Bateliel slowed time's input through the lenses of his angel eyes, admiring the flying silver things as they hurried toward him. They hung there now, streams of them in straight lines, like droplets of snowmelt, all of them on a path that ended in his luminescent form. With time's input stalled, Bateliel counted the silver-shelled insects, fascinated to see so many swarm at him as though he had been caught stealing their honey. There were over eighty of the insects in the air, with more lined up in the launching mechanisms of the cylindrical hives that the children held. More than Bateliel could catch, even if he held time in stasis while he gathered them.

He let time's input speed up to normal once more in his vision, watched as the flurry of silver shells zipped onward in their deadly straight lines toward him. A being of light, Bateliel shifted his frequency just slightly so that, to an outside observer, he glowed that much more fiercely for the space of a picosecond, and the bullets passed harmlessly through him before thudding against the wall behind.

Bateliel's lips creased in a warm smile as the silver insects hit the wall and were knocked back with funny pinging sounds. He watched momentarily as the insects bounced back, finding new flight paths before they ran out of energy and collapsed to the floor, exhausted.

Then the angel Bateliel turned his attention back to the six children who waited in the corridor, and he took another effortless pace forward, his bare feet three inches above the metal plate floor. The closest of them was crouching by the left wall, the cylindrical metal hive held in a two-handed grip, spitting a steady stream of insects at Bateliel, unaware that the nasty little bugs were passing through him at his current frequency.

Bateliel's hand snapped out, grasping the metal cylinder by its end, whipping it out of the child's grip. The metal nest felt hot where Bateliel's luminescent skin touched it, but it stopped spitting silver shells just as soon as it had been taken from the child's grasp.

Bateliel stood there, his hallowed figure a firework in the narrow confines of the corridor, and stared bemused at the gun he had plucked from the millennialist's hands. The other consortium men in the corridor continued blasting shot after shot at the angel, even though bullets appeared to be having no effect on the fabulous, beautiful entity that glowed before them. Then, as though bored with it, the angel dropped the Calico subgun to the floor.

The angel moved with lightning speed and a beautiful, graceful economy of movement, despite the horrors he was about to unleash upon the men in the narrow confines of the corridor. Bending over himself like an eel diving deeper into a fast flowing river, Bateliel reached down and grasped the consortium man whose gun he had just dismissed. The man's name was Shah, and he hollered a tirade of contempt at the beautiful creature as he was pulled from his knees and lifted higher. A moment later, Shah's feet dangled over the metal surface of the plate floor as Bateliel pulled him close, staring into his dark eyes with his orbs of purest light.

"Get the hell off of me, you freak," Shah howled, struggling in the angel's grip, writhing this way and that.

In silent response, Bateliel studied the struggling man in his hands and shook his head just slightly, an infinitesimal movement of fearsome chastisement.

Bullets were cutting through the air all around the floating forms as the other members of Shah's party tried to bring down the angel. Bullets slapped against Shah's protected body, impacting on the Kevlar vest he wore, cutting through his arms and legs.

Bateliel felt the strange, silver-shelled insects slapping into the body of the child, felt the figure rocking in his hands. The insects were embedding themselves in the child's body, burrowing into him as though seeking new nests.

The silver insects hurt the child, and Bateliel watched distressed as the child cried in pain. There was much anger in the child, he realized—he had ranted at Bateliel, scared of what was happening. Perhaps it was the impurity in their system that made the children angry, Bateliel pondered, unsure of how to respond to hostility. Hostility was a new thing.

Bateliel fixed the child named Shah with his stare, locking eyes. Then he sent pleasant thoughts, allowing his angelic calming influence to pour from him and wash over the child like a warm embrace.

Child Shah smiled at that, and his angry curses ceased. He felt bliss, wafting in potent billows from the angel like incense.

Bateliel readied his hand to connect with the child, to judge him, but he felt more of the silver-shelled insects thud into the figure and then the child's spark left him. Bateliel felt regret then, for the spark was a precious thing and shouldn't be wasted or curtailed before its time. He let go of the body of the child and turned his attention back to the other children in the corridor, the ones who held the metal nests that spit insects at him.

Edward Laine had been with another recovery outfit that had been absorbed by the consortium three years ago, and he had seen many interesting treasures and faced numerous hostile locals. Hidden doors that worked on cantilevers a thousand years old, encrypted computer files that told of devices that could traverse time and space, evidence of races he had never known existed. In short, he thought he had seen it all. Right then, as he hunkered in the open doorway of the facility's bathroom, pumping the trigger of the Calico subgun he gripped in his hand, Edward Laine saw something he could scarcely believe. It wasn't the angels, nor was it the way in which their previous victim, Simona Jurist, had disintegrated before his eyes just minutes before. No, what Edward Laine saw then was so unexpected it made his eyes boggle beneath the scratched snow goggles he wore.

Bateliel the angel had picked up Shah and held him close as the other millennialists continued racking him with bullets. Shah had been caught in the path of some of those shots and, regrettably, had taken more than his armor could withstand, clearly expiring in the angel's hands. As though an infant discarding a rag doll, the angel had let go of Shah then, tossing the man to one side. But Shah hadn't fallen the way that his gun had moments before. Shah had just hung there, floating in the air as though in zero gravity, spinning slowly in space until he crashed against a side wall. Only then, seven seconds after the angel had dismissed his deceased body, did gravity finally take hold of Shah and pull him, reluctantly, to the floor.

It was as if these luminescent beings played with a completely different set of laws of physics.

Laine slapped home a new ammunition clip for his Calico, knowing full well that he was wasting his time.

BATELIEL MOVED with a beauty so absolute that it made his opponents cry. The six men in the corridor had become five since he had discarded the child called Shah, but they still tried to fell him using the little fire-breathing tubes that launched silver shells at him, seemingly oblivious to the lack of effect such actions were having.

Bateliel reached out to the first, that benevolent smile on his lips, and, gripping the end of the gun he held, flipped the man off his feet, tossing him to one side. The man crashed into a wall with a metallic clang, like a clapper hitting a bell, leaving a visible man-shaped dent across the wall's surface as he slid to the floor, his head askew where the bones in his neck had snapped.

The next man, Edward Laine, drummed bullet after bullet into the angel from his subgun. Bateliel ignored the shiny insects as he closed in on Laine, his blue-white eyes penetrating the man's fearful expression. "Calm yourself, child," Bateliel ordered, his voice like the whisper of a velvet curtain.

Hearing the words, more in his head than with his ears, Edward Laine felt a wave of tranquillity flow over him, transcending all the noise and hubbub that surrounded himself and the angel. He eased his finger off the gun's trigger, distantly felt the weapon's rattling cease in his grip. The angel Bateliel moved closer, placing his right palm atop Edward Laine's forehead, generating a subtle tingling like bubbles popping against the skin. Then the angel's blue-white eyes took on a sorrowful aspect, and Bateliel opened his mouth wide, generating the words he regretted saying: "Impurity discovered."

Bateliel cast Laine aside, his palm simply brushing at the man's forehead, but the movement so quick it seared the flesh from the bone. Laine cried out as he spun on the spot, his head whipping around with such speed that it twisted his spinal column.

Broken and twisted, Edward Laine tumbled to the floor, his breathing ragged, his thoughts seared through with agony. He watched through bloody eyes as the angel continued onward, its graceful movements unhurried, closing in on the next member of the defense team, a dark-haired woman called Alison Moran.

Moran pumped shots from a pistol based on a modified Beretta design, the bullets driving into the shining angel's face. The angel Bateliel ignored the blasts, letting the bullets pass through his radiance and out, into the corridor and the walls beyond.

Suddenly the angel's hand reached out and Moran felt a quietness, a calmness, flow over her. The bonus that Carver had promised meant nothing now; all she cared for was that wonderful feeling of completeness that the angel generated inside of her when its gaze fell fully upon her. And then the angel's hand touched Alison Moran, and she felt that beautiful burning across her skin, like a thousand tiny feathers brushing against her.

"Impurity discovered," Bateliel announced, his voice like the embers of a fire.

The two other consortium warriors in the corridor drilled the angel with bullets as Bateliel shoved Moran's limp body into a side wall before moving onward. One of the warriors, a man named Jenson, felt his Calico jam—out of bullets or maybe just overheating, it didn't matter. He tossed it aside and leaped at Bateliel, pulling his long combat blade from its sheath at his belt.

As Jenson dived at the glowing form, Gander—the final consortium man in the corridor—sprayed the narrow area with bullets from his own Calico M-960, ignoring the bodies strewed all about. The shots were going wild, hitting floor and ceiling and peppering the metal walls with a chorus of clangs and pings, but he didn't care now. He just wanted this thing to stay away from him. Gander watched as Jenson drove the knife blade into the angel's neck, shoving it up to the hilt as he grasped the luminescent figure's pure white robes.

Bateliel felt the blade slip into his flesh, and he tuned it out, dismissing it from his thoughts. A being of purest light, his substance was both solid and spectral, a being of two forms, and physical attacks could not wound him unless Bateliel chose to let them. The knife's impact was a sensation, a new thing, but it mattered little to him in any practical sense. He reached out and touched the child who clutched at his robes, brushing the palm of his right hand against Jenson's head.

"Impurity discovered," Bateliel announced, once again disappointed.

The angel's words came to Jenson's ears like the fluttering of wings, the sound of sweeping. Jenson watched as the blade that he had thrust into the angel's neck dropped downward, passing through the shining one's body like a solid through liquid, before clattering on the metal plates of the floor. Then something broke in his head under a savage impact and he was dropping to the floor in imitation of his blade.

Bateliel moved onward, casting the impure child aside, his eyes of palest, whitest blue locating the final child in the corridor. Some still had their sparks, some had lost them in the swiftness of Bateliel's actions, but none had been ascended; there simply was no time. If, later, he and the other angels could dance, then these children would achieve full judgment and leave the garden intact, there to be retooled.

Gander was no longer aiming. Instead, his finger was simply locked on the Calico's trigger, pumping shots at whatever stood in its path. His eyes were wide, watching that graceful, willowy figure approach, closer and closer, its long white feet never quite touching the floor. His friends were dead, Gander knew, or they were lying around him, broken and dying. This thing, this divine creature of such incredible, breathtaking beauty had gone through them all in less than a minute, five trained, armed guards felled in little more than the time it took to recite their names. Worse, the whole exercise had been achieved by some being that wasn't even armed, had just seemed to walk, to move, to *be* and that was enough.

Gander's finger held the trigger down as the angel Bateliel reached out and touched him, judged him and found him wanting. Bateliel killed Gander with the merest movement of his luminescent fingers. And all the while, Gander basked in the angel's glow.

IN ANOTHER CORRIDOR, the angel Vadriel was facing a similar group of Millennial Consortium personnel alone as the angels spread out through the base, looking to cast judgment on the children of the garden.

A consortium man called Houghton ran at the angel, the muzzle of his Calico flashing as he blasted a stream of 9 mm bullets at the heavenly figure before him. Vadriel, who was older and wiser than some of the more inquisitive angels, simply ignored the silver-shelled insects that spewed from the child's device, allowing them to pass through his spectral body with no more than a passing thought.

Vadriel swooped forward, moving at a forty-five-degree angle to the ground, and placed both hands on the chest of Houghton's onrushing form, stopping the man in place.

Houghton's body continued trying to run, unaware that it had been stopped with such absolute certainty, and his insides continued forward, bursting through the fragile skin that encased his frame. Houghton's organs smashed against the sharp prongs of his ribs, and his guts powered forward, a trail of intestines breaking the skin around his gut and flopping outward in gouts of blood.

Vadriel stepped back, feeling the child crumble apart at his touch. It wasn't the speed with which the human had been moving—that had been little more than walking speed—but rather his body's inability to cope with a stop so complete that it defied the laws of physics.

Where Vadriel's hands had touched the child Houghton, he had felt the impurity. Now, sparkless, the child need not be judged.

ELSEWHERE IN THE complex, the same scene was being repeated in different iterations as the angels sought and destroyed the impurities in the garden.

There were six people in the party making its way down the narrow corridor to the southwest. Grant led the way, setting the pace with his long strides. Beside him, Carver ran with his reconditioned Sin Eater in his hand, looking nervously behind him every few steps. One of the millennialist guardsmen, a man called Scriver, ran just behind Carver, wearing black molded Kevlar body armor beneath his winter clothes. Then came Lacea, the communications expert from the control room, her midlength blond hair brushing across her shoulders as she hurried to keep up with the others.

Kane brought up the rear, with Brigid Baptiste just a pace ahead of him, glancing back over her shoulder with a furrowed expression creasing her brow as they heard the gunfire stop and the screaming start.

Kane looked up at his redheaded companion. "I know that look—what is it, Baptiste?" he said, his words coming in fits as his booted feet slammed against the metal plating of the corridor.

"What are they doing?" Brigid asked. "Why would angels kill?"

"So, we're sticking with the 'angels' theory, then?" Kane stated.

Brigid nodded. "We all felt that, somewhere inside us," she said, "some deep memory recognized these beings as angels. We didn't discuss it—we all just *knew*. But why would angels kill?"

"Like I told the girl," Kane growled, "everything massacres everything else."

"I don't believe that," Brigid said as they hurried past another open doorway that led into the crew's meager quarters. "These are angels, Kane. It's just…wrong somehow."

Ahead of Kane and Brigid, Grant had reached the exit and was working the door. The whole corridor was met with a blast of frigid air as he swung the metal door outward on its creaking hinges; the mobile base had been cold, but they had forgotten just how bone-numbing the temperatures were outside.

"Come on, people," Grant urged, his breath clouding around him like steam from a boiling kettle, "let's get out of…" The words trailed off, dying on his lips.

"What is it?" Lacea asked, peering behind her to see what Grant was staring at.

Two more millennialists were running down the narrow corridor after them, and behind them was a third figure. The ghostly white form was hurtling toward them from the far end of the corridor, his mouth closed in a serene expression, his blue-white eyes burning with intensity from his perfect white face.

Kane shoved Lacea forward, and Brigid grabbed the communications officer and helped her to the sheltered area outside where the Scorpinauts had been left.

The angel caught up with the slower of the millennialists, planting a flattened palm against the back of his head, knocking him to the floor. The guard crumpled in a heap against the metal paneling, the loud crack of bones breaking echoing down the corridor, while his colleague turned and rammed his Calico M-960 subgun in the angel's face.

"Eat this!" the millennialist shouted as he pulled the trigger, unleashing a stream of bullets into the angel's face.

Kane recognized the ragged clothing of the millennialist straightaway, and realized it was the guy who had been using wadcutters in the battle back at Flag's souvenir room.

The wadcutter bullets sprayed into the angel's face, and sparks erupted as the bullets impacted with the heavenly being. When the millennialist stopped firing, he saw the angel still hovering over him, undamaged, a look of bliss on his serene features. His pure white hands reached forward, pushing the man to the flooring.

As the angel angled toward the fallen millennialist, Carver's voice came from over Grant's shoulder at the open doorway. "Their weapons are still in the Scorpinauts," Carver called, instructing the guard they had brought with them. "Hurry it up, Scriver."

The angel looked up at the noise, and his beautiful, washed-out eyes met with Kane's.

Standing beside Grant at the open door, Kane watched the angel rushing through the corridor toward them, a burning white streak, his body held horizontal to the ground.

"This," Kane stated, "is not good."

"Yeah, buddy, I'm getting that," Grant agreed as the angel closed in on them and another appeared behind it, a flowing white mane of hair trailing behind his head.

The Cerberus teammates exited the base, and Grant slammed the door closed behind them. Outside, the sky was turning dark, but patterns played across the firmament, greens and reds, the magnetic phenomenon of the Aurora australis. Snow was falling heavily, almost to blizzard levels, the grouped flurries blasting across the white terrain and obscuring everyone's vision.

"You think a door will stop them?" Grant asked as he and Kane ran across the snow-covered ground toward the sheltered area that housed the Scorpinauts, their boots sinking into the snow beneath them.

"They have intelligence, hands with opposable thumbs," Kane observed, "and they can burn things out of existence. I don't think a metal door is going to do jack to stop them if they want to come through, do you?"

Grant shook his head in irritation. "Damn those opposable thumbs."

The two of them reached the shelter where the Scorpinauts were parked.

Brigid was standing at the side of the open door of one of

the Scorpinauts as the millennialist guardsman handed her back her TP-9 pistol from the storage locker where the Cerberus team's weapons had been stashed. She ejected and checked its ammo clip before, satisfied, ramming it back home.

"Do we have a plan?" Kane asked as he joined the others. "Baptiste? Any ideas?"

"They called Simona an impurity," Brigid said as Kane and Grant strapped on the wrist holsters of their Sin Eaters. "What if they sensed the—I don't know—*greed* in her, for instance?"

Kane looked confused. "I don't follow," he admitted.

"We're facing angels, Kane," Brigid stated, "so I figure we have to think like them. Greed is one of the seven deadly sins—*avarita*—in Christian teachings. What if the angels are looking for sinners?"

His eyes on the closed entry door to the mobile base, a dark shape amid the falling snow, Grant strapped on his own Sin Eater by touch alone. "You'll have to remind me what these seven deadly sins are," he admitted, and Kane and the others agreed.

Brigid recalled them swiftly, counting them off on her gloved fingers. "*Luxuria, gula, avarita, acedia, ira, invidia et superbia,*" she stated.

Kane's blue-gray eyes locked with Brigid's. "Once again, and in English," he insisted curtly.

"*Luxuria*—originally extravagance, later amended to lust," Brigid said, "gluttony, greed, sloth, wrath, envy and pride."

"Well, you'd be hard-pressed to find somebody who doesn't have at least one of those," Grant griped.

"It's about degrees," Brigid clarified. "Having pride in a good job is understandable. Being excessively prideful is a sin."

"Degrees," Grant repeated, sounding unsure. "Right."

Suddenly, a noise came from behind them, and everyone turned in time to see the metal door they had just exited shatter into a thousand shining splinters.

Kane shot the Sin Eater into his palm and began pacing across the snow back toward the door. "Who's up for arguing degrees with the nice angels?" he asked.

Brigid and Grant took up their places beside Kane while Carver, Lacea and Scriver followed, each of them now armed.

"They may judge us as free from sin," Brigid proposed.

Kane's eyes were locked on the doorway now as twin glowing, beautiful, angelic forms stepped out into the snow, floating in the air like jellyfish on the ocean's current. "Sure, but don't make book on it, Baptiste," he growled.

# Chapter 17

The angels' names were Damiel and Sazquiel. They had touched the metal square in the artificial construct, making so that it ceased to be, shattering it into one thousand glittering splinters that swam away in all directions, broken into new and perfect shapes as they fell. Outside they saw that rain was falling in the icy, geometric patterns called dendrites: snow.

Sazquiel smiled. It had been millennia since he had last witnessed snow. He had almost forgotten the beauty of those perfectly formed, six-pointed stars, every one of them different, just like the children. He focused his angel eyes, peering at them in their microscopic beauty, marveling at the perfection that each unique snowflake expressed.

Damiel looked through the flurry-curtain of snow, both fascinated and irritated that he could not see straight through it. With but a moment's thought, his angel eyes slowed time's input so that he could peer through the falling snow and at the children who were watching him and Sazquiel exit the metal structure.

There were six of them, two dozen feet away from where the door had shattered outward. They each looked different and colorful. One had bright red hair like fire, while another was big with dark skin as though he had been left too long in the sun.

"They're all different," Damiel said in wonder, "just like the snowflakes."

Sazquiel grinned with satisfaction. "Yes, all the things in the garden are different, Damiel. That's how they were made to be."

Side by side, the angels moved forward, getting closer to the children.

SIN EATER IN HAND, Kane watched as the glowing angels paced slowly through the blizzard toward them. *Paced* wasn't the right word, he realized. The angels remained several inches above the snow-blanketed ground at all times. *Hovered,* then.

"Who feels like being judged?" Grant asked, standing at Kane's side with his own blaster thrust before him.

Kane's mind whirred. "Baptiste," he shouted loud enough to be heard over the sound of howling winds, "are you sure about this judging thing?"

"Not in the slightest," Brigid admitted as the angels took another "step" closer to them.

"Then it's not a risk I want to take," Kane stated as he sighted along the length of his pistol.

Brigid's free hand reached out, and she waved it before Kane's field of vision, a pale blur of porcelain flesh in the whirring snowfall. "Kane, no. We need to be certain."

"Brigid's plan may be our best option right now, Kane," Grant pointed out. "You saw what happened to that consortium guy who tried to shoot them. I'm not so sure that bullets are going to do the job."

"Right now, that's all we have," Kane reminded his partner. "Unless anyone's got anything better in mind."

From behind the trio of Cerberus warriors, ex-Mag Carver spoke in a solemn voice, reminding them of the main gun on the

Scorpinauts. "I've seen its shells knock through redwoods and crumble houses," he explained. "If we can get a good shot in…"

"No," Brigid decided, lowering her pistol. "We must try diplomacy first. Talk to them."

"Diplomacy," Kane repeated, the word coming through clenched teeth. "These things disintegrated Jurist. You saw that, right?"

Brigid turned to Kane, appealing to him with her expressive emerald eyes. "If we shoot them, we'll never know what might have been," she said.

With that, Brigid holstered her TP-9 and stepped out from the covered shelter, walking across the snow to meet with the two beautiful beings of light. Kane and Grant stepped out from cover, too, flanking their colleague, sending their Sin Eaters back to the hidden holsters at their wrists. As they walked out into the blizzard, Kane turned back and instructed Carver, "Get the engines running and the tail guns loaded," he said.

Carver gave an old Magistrate salute, clenched fist to his chest, before turning to instruct his two remaining personnel.

SNOW BILLOWED about the three mismatched warriors as they trekked toward the angels. Damiel and Sazquiel watched, fascinated by the way the children moved, the way that the garden seemed to constrain them, holding them down. They were tied to the Earth with invisible umbilical cords, trapped at ground level. Damiel wondered if they ever dreamed of flying.

The lead child—the female with red hair—stopped to stand eight feet away from Sazquiel and Damiel, looking up at them where they floated in place above the snow.

"My name is Brigid Baptiste," she said, making a show of

how her hands worked that Damiel saw no reason for. He dismissed the movements, powering the energies to his palm, preparing to judge.

Beside Damiel, Sazquiel engaged his own judgment hand.

BRIGID STOOD BEFORE the angels, showing them her empty hands to prove that she was now unarmed, that she meant them no harm. "We don't wish to hurt you," she promised.

To her left, Kane warily watched the angels hovering above them, and he spoke quietly out of the corner of his mouth. "You think they heard you?" he asked.

Brigid ignored him, taking a step forward, her arms still held out to show that she came unarmed.

Then the angels swooped, fluttering toward Brigid like leaves on the wind, their right hands touching her with flattened palms. Kane and Grant watched tensely as the angels felt at Brigid, clearly engaging in some kind of communion.

Brigid rocked back on her heels, her booted feet sinking into the snow as the angels applied pressure upon her. She saw something then, flashing before her mind's eye for less than a second, a blip of information….

*Prehistory*
*Territory subsequently known as Kenya*

IT WAS A TIME when the race that would ultimately become humanity still cowered in trees from saber-toothed tigers.

Anu sat aboard the starship *Tiamat,* surveying the green planet he had named Ki, wondering what games might be played here. He had traveled from the home world Nibiru, compelled by boredom as much as a desire to explore. Ki was filled with life, burgeoning plants and glistening waters, animals that flew and walked and burrowed beneath the rich, fertile soil.

There was one race that intrigued Anu, fascinated him, more than the other wondrous sights he saw. One race above all that drew his attention, again and again, as they hunted and grunted and shunted at one another. Often, the members of this race stood upright on two legs, much like his own people, the Annunaki, though they lacked the Annunaki's strong, scaled skin and graceful sense of self. In other ways, these apelike creatures reminded Anu of the Igigi, his retinue of nameless slaves who adored him with such passion, for they were that much simpler than the Annunaki, that much uglier.

Throwing caution to the winds, knowing that curiosity was getting the better of him, Anu asked his Igigi slaves to capture some of these ape-things, these prototypical human beings, that he might observe them more closely, play with them and study them.

The Annunaki were as ageless as the stars themselves, with knowledge dating back thousands of millennia. Each of them was born possessing the full memories of their ancestors, of every member of their race who had ever been. But here was something new, something no Annunaki had ever seen before. *Yes,* thought Anu, *here is a toy to be played with and shaped.*

The humans had been brought to him, some dressed in furs, others exhibiting no sense of modesty or concern for the changing temperatures of their environment, the dangers to their soft, unarmored skin. Anu had done things to the simple humans, made them run mazes, beg for food, hurt one another, hurt themselves. The humans were interesting at first, but Anu's interest soon waned.

Lord Anu gazed around the glittering interior of the star-ship *Tiamat,* his reptilian eyes studying the vast array of tech-nology there, the blending of organics and mechanics that the Annunaki had perfected thousands of years before. And as he looked, an idea came, unbidden, to Anu's devious mind. The humans might be more durable, and hence more entertaining, if he modified them.

Burdened with the infinite ennui of his race, Anu forced himself to concentrate on his designated task, working within the confines of *Tiamat* to create a simple pocket within the genetic sequencing of humankind where he might add his gift. The gift itself was a tiny thing, a little pep to make the ape-men more exciting, to make them develop into something a little more interesting, to make them more rugged, more hardy.

Anu took his gift and placed it inside the ova of one of the human women, a young and feisty girl who, he had observed, enjoyed the companionship of many males. Once Anu had completed the operation, the Igigi tossed the young woman, scared and confused, from *Tiamat* and watched as she ran back to her tribe in the caves of dust. Once loosed, the gift would spread, subtly altering the DNA of humankind. It was a voracious little creation, and it would attach to every person on the planet in the space of just a few generations.

Anu smiled at his handiwork. Perhaps humans would soon be fun again.

*Early twenty-third Century*
*Antarctica*

As instantly as it had begun, the flash of information had passed, and Brigid saw the angelic forms hovering before her once more.

The angels spoke as one. "Impurity discovered," they said, their words coming like birdsong.

Brigid howled as the judgment came and the burning began. She had seen a flickering of images in her head, a whole story of the Annunaki altering the genetic sequence of humankind, condensed into one single, abbreviated second. This, she realized with horror, was the start of the impurities that the angels were now detecting.

As Brigid began to scream at the passing of the angels' judgment, Grant was already moving, tensing his wrist tendons and recalling the Sin Eater pistol into his hand. A stream of bullets blasted from the pistol's muzzle the very instant it slapped into his palm, drilling against the nearer of the two angels as the pure white being continued to press his hand against Brigid's head in judgment.

Beside Grant, Kane had begun running in great loping strides toward the threesome, his boots squelching against the snowy carpet beneath his feet as he powered his own Sin Eater into his hand.

Caught unawares, the angel Sazquiel drew his hand away from Brigid as Grant's bullets passed through him. Sazquiel turned to face Grant, only to find a second foe coming at him. Kane rushed at the angel, blasting shot after shot at him. Suddenly, Sazquiel didn't know which way to turn, which of the children to face. He slowed time with his angel gaze, watching all of the things that were moving—the snow, the bullets, the running man—but there seemed to be so much that he wondered which needed to be prioritized.

Kane dismissed Sazquiel, trusting Grant to keep him off his back for the precious few seconds he needed to pull Brigid out of the mess she had got herself into.

Damn her, he thought, and her blind trust in archaic knowledge.

Though Sazquiel had been drawn away, Damiel meanwhile continued to touch Brigid. However, the judgment dance was ineffective as a solo, and only truly worked as a group piece. Without Sazquiel or one of the others, its power stuttered and the subject's spark would reject it. Even as he considered that, Damiel became aware of the second child rushing at him and Sazquiel, blasting those silver-shelled insects from one of their strange nests that he gripped in his hand. Damiel slowed the effects of time's input in his angel's eyes, watching the trail of bullets lunging through the falling snow toward him.

To Damiel's eyes, the snow fell like syrup, making its casual way to the ground as the child ran at him. Between the dendrites of snow, the shining insects traveled then stopped, a staggered procession as Damiel considered their trajectory. His free arm, the one not connected with the redheaded child who had just been judged, stretched upward and he caught the insects in his hand, plucking them from the air as though pulling petals from a flower.

As the angel picked the bullets from the air, Kane leaped through the snow, his left arm reaching around Baptiste's waist as he passed her, yanking her free from the awful, corrosive touch of the angel.

Pulling Brigid close, Kane dived through the space between the two hovering angels, sliding across the snow-topped ground on his legs and flank, his pistol spitting bullets behind him.

As Brigid was yanked from his touch, realization dawned on Damiel. He had been distracted by the shiny insects, confused by their whirring and their buzzing. He drew back his hand and looked at the bullets that he held there, wondering at their strange purpose. Insects that distracted? And what of the child that he had touched, what of her impurity? How could these children still live with such impurity rushing through their systems? How had they all been corrupted so? It seemed a travesty and, worse yet, entirely impossible that they should still live with such flaws woven into their beings.

Brigid and Kane fell to the ground, kicking up snow as they rolled. Brigid looked at Kane, her head feeling woozy. What just happened? she asked herself, feeling a million thoughts rushing through her brain, each one vying for attention. Semiconscious, Brigid fell backward into the snow as Kane unleashed a torrent of shots at the angels behind them.

Feeling her slump in his grip, Kane stopped firing and he turned to face Brigid. "Come on, Baptiste," he growled, "this is no time to flake out on me."

Brigid's eyes flickered open again, two emerald orbs in her porcelain face. "It's the Annunaki," she told Kane. "They're what the angels sense."

"Figures," Kane snarled as he slapped a new clip home into the breech of the Sin Eater. He dismissed Brigid's revelation for now, knowing there would be time enough for proper explanations once they were out of immediate danger. "You okay to move?" he asked.

Brigid nodded, but her head felt heavy, as though it might topple free from her neck. "I think I'm going to be sick," she admitted as the air around her seemed to swim in place. A moment later, she tasted bile in her mouth, and a thin stream of yellowish vomit poured over her tongue as she expelled it on the clean white snow.

Kane blasted off another stream of shots as the angels turned toward them. Across the white plain, Grant was keeping up his own assault, trigger locked on the Sin Eater, bullets blasting forth in triple bursts. The glowing beings were flicking the bullets aside, catching them in their hands or simply ignoring them, letting the lethal slugs pass straight through their ethereal bodies.

"We have to get out of here," Kane realized, his eyes flicking to Brigid as she spit more of the watery vomit from her mouth.

"I just need a minute," Brigid said, wiping at her lips, her voice sounding weak.

Sending his Sin Eater back to its wrist sheath, Kane scooped Brigid up in his arms. "We don't have a minute," he told her as he began hurrying across the snow away from the twin glowing forms, the beautiful redhead held in his arms.

As Kane ran, he heard something booming in the distance, and even as he turned he saw a massive 40 mm shell hurtling through the air toward the glowing presence of the angels. Carver had started his attack.

# Chapter 18

The 40 mm shell cut through the freezing Antarctic air, batting snowflakes aside as it hurtled toward its glowing targets.

At the controls of the Scorpinaut, ex-Mag Carver was already ordering a second blast from the tail cannon as he watched the massive shell rush toward the angelic figures before him.

Damiel and Sazquiel saw the shell cleaving the air, and both of them slowed time's input so that they might better appreciate this new phenomenon. It looked like a bird, a small silver bird with a conical head, swooping through the snow-filled air to greet them. Taking it for such, Sazquiel held his arm out straight and encouraged the bird to perch there that they might commune.

In response, the huge projectile slammed into Sazquiel's arm with such force that the angel was shunted backward almost three feet, kicking up a cloud of snow from the ground where his feet scraped across it. Confused, Sazquiel watched as the conical bird crumpled in on itself, flattening out, its point mashing as it met with his pure angel flesh. There was an explosion as it crumpled, and the fiery blossom distracted Sazquiel for a moment as he wondered at its sudden burst of life.

Its fury spent, the massive shell dropped to the ground, sinking into the snow at Sazquiel's feet in a flattened, perfectly circular disk.

Even as Sazquiel puzzled over the silver bird's strange behavior, a second shell hurtled toward the two angels, blasting from the Scorpinaut's turret appendage.

Damiel stepped ahead to greet this one, but Sazquiel warned him back. Together, they sidestepped, allowing the heavy shell to zip past them and smash against the metal wall of the mobile base with resounding violence.

In response, a cataclysmic explosion rocked the wall.

RUNNING WITH Brigid in his arms, Kane watched the first shell's progress as it slammed into the angel with a burst of explosive. The angel had staggered, but when the smoke cleared Kane saw that the shell had dropped uselessly to the snowy blanket of ground and the angel seemed remarkably unfazed.

Kane turned away as the second shell was launched, engaging his Commtact as he hurried along the metal wall of the temporary base. "Grant, we need to get out of here right now," he instructed. "Pull back. These things are impervious to gunfire."

Grant's voice came back to Kane over the medium of the Commtact, and Kane noted that the large man sounded out of breath, his voice shaking as he continued to pepper the area with bullets. "I hear you, pal, but what do we do?"

"Keep running," Kane concluded. "Right now that's the only option we have."

WITH RELUCTANCE, Grant agreed. He wasn't a man who liked to back away from any situation, especially one where combat was concerned. Holstering his Sin Eater, he ducked as another 40 mm shell whizzed by overhead and slammed into the glowing body of one of the willowy angels. Carver was pulling the Scorpinaut around now, clear of the sheltered garage so that he could unleash the fearsome vehicle's full barrage of armament on the angelic figures. The twin .50-caliber machine guns blazed from the foreclaw-style arrangement at the front of the boxy vehicle, and missiles and bullet strings blasted from various ports all over the surface of the remarkable wag.

Grant ran, head down, keeping well clear of the Scorpinaut's vicious onslaught as he raced back to the sheltered area by the side of the domed base. "What happened to Brigid?" he asked over the Commtact. "She okay?"

"Woozy and unsteady on her feet," Kane responded via the Commtact relay. "I'm bringing her back to the gara— Oh, shit!"

Grant turned as he ran, trying to locate Kane through the cascading snowfall. "What's happened, Kane?" he snapped. "What is it?"

For a long, anxious moment there was no response from his partner, and Grant felt the fear rising in his belly. Ahead of him, he saw the second Scorpinaut pulling out of the garage shelter, its gears grinding as its driver urged it across the snow.

Then Kane's voice finally came to Grant's ear over the Commtact link. "Look sharp, we have more company."

KANE HAD STOPPED in his tracks at the side of the circular base, the lolling form of Brigid Baptiste balanced in his arms. Ahead of him, another door had been pulled apart, its hinges twisted beyond recognition, and yet it still clung to the metal wall at an absurd angle. An angel was floating there, just above the ground, its frosty gaze playing over Kane and Brigid as a smile tugged at its perfect bow lips. Behind it, Kane saw, three more angels were swooping closer, moving effortlessly through the air like papers drifting on the breeze, inquisitive looks etched across their fiercely glowing features.

Grant's voice came from the Commtact, close to Kane's ear. "How many?" Grant asked.

"I have four angels—" Kane began and then he corrected himself as he saw another glide through the open doorway closest to his position, moving with all the urgency of a cloud on the wind. "Make that five."

"Can you hold them until I get there?" Grant asked doubtfully.

"Just get here," Kane snapped, raising his arm as he called the Sin Eater back to his palm, struggling to balance Brigid's slumped form.

Brigid had slipped into unconsciousness now, but Kane didn't have time to concern himself with that. He didn't even think about it. He just snapped off shot after shot at the angels, knowing it was a futile exercise but consoling himself that the bullets at least seemed to slow the graceful creatures while they considered the nature of the attack.

The angels seemed to be mostly inquisitive in their actions, Kane realized as the Sin Eater spit bullets at the lead figure. They didn't really battle with their foes in the sense of normal combat. Instead, they were intrigued by their surroundings, almost as though every experience was a new one.

Perhaps it was, he realized. Perhaps these angels, or what-ever they really were, had never seen the Earth before. That was a credible theory in that they certainly didn't seem concerned with normal requirements, including many of the basic principles of physics. They floated above the ground without any visible means of support, moved swiftly and yet never seemed hurried, displayed no urgency to their progress. Even as he watched, the lead angel—a female, Kane decided—reached for the bullets he was firing at her and just brushed them aside, knocking them from the air with no noticeable sign of exertion or distress. And throughout it all, each angel smiled, as though a parent indulging a child in some silly game.

The smiles were dangerous, Kane concluded, swinging Brigid's limp body around as he turned away from the quintet of glowing figures. The angels' smiles possessed some kind of hypnotic quality, burning into an observer's thoughts, locking them in place like the mesmeric effect of a cobra. This was new territory, Kane knew, a battleground that existed both in the physical and the psychological realms, that played one off the other with such cohesion, such perfect synergy, that an unwary foe might be tricked into welcoming his or her own demise. That very thing had happened to Simona Jurist back in the control room.

Kane understood the physical; that was a realm he could cope with with absolute mastery. But the mental plane, an enemy who could turn your thoughts against you merely with a smile—that was something outside Kane's realm of expertise. He glanced down at Brigid as he rushed across the snow. "Come on, Baptiste," he muttered, "we're going to need your smarts if we're to survive this one."

As he ran across the snow away from the angels, the light around Kane grew brighter, his shadow before him lengthening and then shortening as though the sun was just overhead. He peered behind him and saw the lead angel following, just three feet away from him, that terrifying, benevolent smile playing across her perfect lips. Snow fell in thick swirls around her, and above that the sky continued its beautiful display of colors as the aurora australis flared across the darkening heavens.

Just ahead of Kane's racing form, another 40 mm shell rocketed through the air, missing the angels who had touched Baptiste, slamming into the metal structure of the base and rocking the wall in a ferocious explosion. Kane turned his back on the fiery wall as he ran past it. Shielding Brigid with his own body, Kane felt the heat even through his shadow suit.

GRANT SPRINTED across the snow, watching the dark, lumpy figure of Kane run along the outer perimeter of the spherical consortium base as a shell exploded in his path. Behind Kane, almost lost in the swirling whiteness of the falling snow, the glowing chalk form of an angel closed in on Kane and his red-headed burden.

"Hang in there," Grant muttered into the Commtact. "I'm almost there."

"Do you have a plan?" Kane's breathless response came back over the Commtact receiver.

"Sure is a fine time to ask that," Grant snarled as he leaped high in the air, swinging his fist at the floating angel at Kane's back.

At the last second, the angel turned, suddenly aware of another player in the battle, just as Grant's pile-driver blow slammed into her chin. Remarkably, the angel reeled from the force of Grant's blow, overbalanced and crashed into the side of the temporary base where flames were still licking up its metal sides.

Grant stepped back, adopting a fighting stance as the angel's eyes assessed him with utter tenderness. "There's still one Scorpinaut in the garage area," Grant shouted as Kane halted in his tracks. "If we get to that we can get outta here. Back to the Mantas, maybe."

Kane looked all around him, getting his bearings once more. In the haze of the falling snow it was becoming increasingly easy to get lost, especially while the deadly pursuit continued. The garage area was just a little way to his right, and Kane reckoned he could be at the Scorpinaut's door in twenty seconds.

"Seems like a decent enough plan," Kane said, turning his attention back to Grant. What he saw there took his breath away.

Grant's powerful form had locked the angel in a powerful hold, shoving with all his might, his feet digging deep tracks in the soft snow as he forced the glowing figure back toward the wall.

"Keep the hell away from my friends, glow star," Grant shouted as he shunted the angel against the wall.

The angel's back slammed into the wall and, just for a moment, her smile slipped. "You are rambunctious, child," the angel Abariel said, her voice like raindrops splashing against the churning sea. "It is an admirable quality."

Grant's booted feet pushed harder against the ground, struggling to find traction as he shoved the angel backward against the wall.

Abariel loomed like a glowing fish in the depths of the sea, and her expression seemed to be one of sadness now. Her right hand reached out, palm extended, to touch at Grant's forehead and begin the judgment.

Grant leaped back, spinning as he ducked beneath that glowing palm, and his leg swept out as he did so. Grant's thick leg smashed against the angel's calf muscles, a little way below her knees, and she seemed to totter like a skittle, unsure of whether to fall.

Abariel put out her arms, regaining her balance as Grant's

blow knocked her. She swayed a moment, and in that instant, Grant was moving once again, driving his fist upward as his whole body sprang from the ground, propelled by his powerful leg muscles. His clenched fist cleaved a path through the falling snowflakes.

Wham! Grant's fist smashed into the angel's jaw with a bone-jarring crunch.

Before Abariel could react, Grant was readying a second blow, driving his knee into the glowing form's belly, swinging a roundhouse punch at her face.

As Grant struggled with the angel, another shell from one of the Scorpinauts cut through the air with a whistling howl, crashing against the wall beside Abariel with a clobbering crash. Grant fell back as the explosion billowed from where the 40 mm shell had hit, while Abariel dropped backward through the ruined section of wall.

Seizing the opportunity, Kane urged Grant to follow him to the roofed garage area where he was swinging the drooping body of Brigid Baptiste into the remaining Scorpinaut. As Grant reached the sheltered area, Kane glanced at him, a look of incredulity on his face. "Did you just bitch-slap an angel?" he asked.

Grant laughed, a wide smile appearing beneath his gunslinger's mustache. "Bullets didn't seem to be doing squat, so I figured what the hell," he said.

"Full marks for taking the direct approach," Kane told him as the big man reached the garage area.

"Wouldn't want to do it again, though," Grant admitted. Then he looked at his hands before he pulled open the passenger door to the remaining Scorpinaut. "No burns," he muttered.

"What's that?" Kane asked as he ducked out from the Scorpinaut where he had just placed the unconscious form of Brigid on one of the rear seats.

"I half expected glow star there to burn me," Grant explained as he joined Kane inside the vehicle. He shook his head, dismissing the idea.

The Scorpinaut's engine roared to life and Kane pumped the accelerator, swinging the vicious-looking vehicle out from under the open-sided shelter.

Beside Kane, Grant flipped open a panel on the dashboard and brought up the fire control board. He armed the Scorpinaut's main cannon and brought the other weapons to life. "All systems are go," Grant told Kane as they bumped over the snow.

Grant reached for the telemetry helmet as Kane pulled the Scorpinaut around to face their attackers.

THE OTHER TWO Scorpinauts were bumping across the snow, their formidable array of weapons targeted on the glowing figures of the seven angels who had emerged from the infinity breach and now mingled around the snow-locked base.

Everyone in the base was dead now. The angels had judged some, while others they had simply swept aside like a furious tide raging against the shore. They were coming to a consensus now, reaching an agreement on what had to be done. As bullets and shells blasted all around them, the angels ignored them and discussed their next step.

"The children have been corrupted," Vadriel stated, his voice as bright as petroleum separating on water. "All of them exhibit the same strand of impurity, as though they have been infected."

Bateliel pulled away from the spot on the snow where he and Damiel had judged Brigid as another volley of gunfire blasted past and through him. "Something invaded the garden," he stated in a voice of sifting sand. "It has spoiled the children."

Beside him young, inquisitive Damiel looked fearful. "What if this impurity has affected everything?" he asked as a stream of bullets blasted unnoticed through his head of light. "What shall we do then?"

"We would feel it," Sazquiel, Damiel's master, assured him.

"But you have always told me that all of the things in the garden are interlinked," Damiel complained, "which is why we must protect it from the externalities. If one strand of the web is damaged, the whole web will surely fall."

Sazquiel nodded as another huge shell hurtled toward him from the left-hand Scorpinaut's taillike cannon. He held up his hand and the shell slapped against it, shunting him three feet backward. He didn't care, simply watching impassively as the shell crumbled in on itself, a flattened metal disk. "We shall excise the cancer and save the garden," Sazquiel stated, his voice like sparks on flint.

"How?" Adriel asked, her voice the purest note of a bird's song as the machine guns of the Scorpinauts blasted .50-caliber slugs through her ethereal form.

"Seek out and purge the garden of the impure children," Sazquiel explained.

"But perhaps they are all impure," Domos cried, "and we would have to lose all of them."

"They shall be replaced, reborn, pure once more," Sazquiel assured the others. "It is His will."

Another 40 mm shell exploded against Sazquiel's hardlight body, shaking him to the core. He stood there, feeling the sensation, the new thing, and he smiled. "They play anger games," Sazquiel said then, his tone taking on the darkness of shadow. "That will make it easier."

"Yet each of the children is unique," Damiel's other master, Vadriel, said. "Shouldn't we judge them all individually?"

"We must act with alacrity," Sazquiel stated as he brushed at the broken parts of the shell, swiping them from his luminescent robes. "The decision is made."

A cluster of rockets zipped toward the angels, their dark exhaust trails marring the whiteness of the snow-filled air. Bateliel tracked them with patient eyes, watching their curving arcs as they swam through the air toward their prey. As they neared, Bateliel swept his hand through the air before his face, as though batting aside an annoying insect. The pointed nose cones of the rockets snapped at his touch, sparking into explosions of brilliance, of noise and light, as they broke apart.

The metal detritus of the rockets slumped to the ground by Bateliel's feet, smoldering with fire, dark smoke churning into the air. Bateliel looked down at the pieces and smiled, dismissing them from his mind.

Abariel floated closer as the bullets continued to sing all around, ignoring their little bites at her divine body. "There are many children in the garden now," she said, her voice like the whisper of satin on flesh. "Many more than when the Garden was planted. They live in pockets all over the garden, pollinating and procreating to swell their numbers."

"The task will be harder, then," Sazquiel said, "but not impossible. We simply find them and excise them."

As one, the seven angels turned and flew toward the nearest Scorpinaut.

"It seems sinful," Damiel said as they flew, "to extinguish sparks without first judging the children."

"Sin begets sin," Vadriel reminded his pupil.

The seven figures swarmed toward the first Scorpinaut, like sharks scenting blood.

INSIDE THE VEHICLE, the millennialist foot soldier called Scriver was working the weapons rig on his own, leaving the engine idling. He was alone in the Scorpinaut and had been unable to work the fire controls and drive at the same time. Scriver flipped switches, launching rockets from their pods at the indicated targets, setting them to automatically reload. He glanced up as something bright caught his eye from the reinforced glass of the windshield. Ahead, he saw seven glowing figures hurtling toward him through the falling snow, lighting their surroundings with their luminescent forms.

Scriver smashed his fist against the launch control of the tail gun, blasting another of those punishing 40 mm shells at the angels as they rushed at him. The Scorpinaut rocked, and, through the glass screen, Scriver saw the shell fire ahead with a tail of dust, cleaving a path through the air as the snow swirled all about it. The shot was going to the left, and one of the angels plucked it from the air and pulled it to her breast, as if holding a baby. It seemed to do her no damage and, after a moment, she tossed aside the useless shell, letting it spin through the air before it fell to the ground twenty feet away in a puff of dislodged snow.

Ahead of Scriver, the machine guns were spewing fire, the weapons ports blasting bullets and rockets, shaking the body of the vehicle and lighting up the air all around it with fiery explosions. Suddenly, something drummed against the side plating of the Scorpinaut and Scriver realized that he was under fire from another Scorpinaut, the one commanded by Carver.

The radio squawked to life and communications officer Lacea's perky voice came over it in an urgent shout. "Get out of there, Scriver! Get out now!"

Carver's voice piped up from the communications rig a moment later, shouting to be heard by the microphone of his own Scorpinaut's radio pickup above the sound of the rockets launching. "You're in the line of fire, son. Move your shit! Now! Now!"

Scriver glanced through the windshield again, seeing the angels closing in, feeling the Scorpinaut rock as projectiles smashed against its armored shell. There was no time left. His finger jabbed at the buttons on the fire control board, launching whatever artillery he had loaded as he scooted across to the driver's seat and pumped his foot down on the accelerator. Then the windshield shattered, thick chips of safety glass spraying across the interior cockpit of the Scorpinaut as Sazquiel powered two pointed fingers through the fragile barrier.

Scriver looked up just in time to see the angel's hand of purest light rushing toward him, fingers outstretched as they drove through the sockets of his eyes, pushing his eyeballs back into his brain.

As he powered his hand through the child, Sazquiel said just one word in his most haunting voice: "Infection." It was the same voice that had been known to bring his peers to tears, such was the beauty of his divine singing.

Scriver screamed as those ghostly fingers drilled into his face, his vision disintegrating into an awful checkerboard of red and black. Something inside him hurt, and he felt the warm blood pouring from his ears, drizzling down his face like human rain. And then nothing.

HUNCHED OVER the steering column inside the third Scorpinaut, Kane was grinding gears to swing the vehicle around when the communications array burst to life.

"Grant? That you in there?" It was Carver's voice, bellowing to be heard over the complaining growl of his own vehicle's engine.

Kane's eyes roved across the dashboard until he spotted the mike pickup overhead. He toggled it and began speaking, trusting the hidden mikes to pick up his voice. "This is Kane," he said. "I'm here with Grant and Baptiste. Grant's just bringing the weapons systems online."

"Forget it," Carver said. "You can see as well as we can that none of our weapons are doing anything. We need a better plan."

"We already have one," Kane answered. "We're going to lay down cover fire and get the hell out of here. You with us?"

Lacea's voice came over the speaker, its trembling tone betraying her genuine fear. "Where are you going to run to, Kane? These things move like lightning."

"We have a couple of birds parked out in the snow," Kane explained. "You guys have something similar?"

"No," Carver said. "We were dropped here with our equipment and the facilities to build the temporary base. We were to radio in when we were ready for evac."

"So radio," Kane growled as Grant fired up the main cannon and blasted off a shot at the swarming angels as their glowing forms played across the hull of the distant Scorpinaut.

"That's a negative, Kane," Lacea stated. "We need the booster aerial to get that kind of signal out there, and even then this blizzard would play havoc with any broadcast beam right now."

"How about giving us a lift?" Carver asked. "For the old fraternity—a favor from one old ex-Mag to another."

Though he knew that the Millennial Consortium would likely steal and strip down the Mantas given half a chance, Kane wasn't about to leave two people stranded here in the path of the murderous otherworldly creatures. "It'll be a tight squeeze," he grumbled in a low voice.

"Say again, Kane," Lacea stated. "Did not copy."

Kane was about to respond when he heard Brigid's voice coming weakly from over his shoulder.

"It won't work," Brigid said in a breathy voice close to Kane's ear.

When he glanced over his shoulder, Kane saw Brigid was kneeling in the space just behind the front seats, looking a little exhausted but otherwise herself once more.

"What won't?" Kane asked, realizing that there was no time to check on his partner's well-being.

"We can't outrun them in the Mantas," Brigid explained. "Angels can fly."

"We're out of options, Baptiste," Kane spit. "I'm willing to give this a try."

"No," Brigid shouted, wincing as she shook her head. "Ow."

"You okay?" Kane asked. "What is it?"

"Head rush," Brigid admitted. "Got up too soon."

"Then lie down and we'll take care of this," Kane assured her, turning his attention back to the escalating situation outside the windshield. Beside him, Grant was using a VR control helmet to assign targets and drill the angels with a relentless stream of bullets and rockets from the various ports on the surface of the Scorpinaut.

"No," Brigid announced. "We need a better plan. Something to stop the angels following us."

Carver's voice piped up from the internal speaker once more. "Kane, do you have a plan or not?"

"Give me a minute," Kane replied.

"They've just killed Scriver," Carver explained. "Your minute's already up."

"Crap," Kane snarled, shifting the gears of the heavy wag. "Come on, Baptiste, time to blind us with science."

"I'm thinking," Brigid screamed back at Kane, "just let me—"

Kane pumped his foot on the accelerator and spun the steering wheel in a sharp turn, pulling the Scorpinaut away from the devastated Millennium Consortium mobile base. "Carver, you're bringing up the rear," Kane shouted.

"Acknowledged," Carver responded. "You know where we're going?"

Kane glanced at Brigid, his look full of meaning. "Well," he asked as the snowstorm almost obliterated the view through the windshield, "do I?"

"Dammit," Brigid cursed. "I can't think of anything. We need…"

"Need what?" Kane snapped, flipping on the rearview monitor and watching as Carver's Scorpinaut bounced over the snowy terrain behind him, the glowing forms of the angels following, barely visible through the thick curtain of falling snow.

Beside Kane, Grant's fingers played across the fire control board, unleashing and reloading a barrage of shots at the distant angelic forms.

"Think, Baptiste," Kane urged. "This is either your show or we're taking our chances in the Mantas."

"We need help," Brigid stated, somehow calmer than she

had been just moments before, the realization settling into place in her mind.

"Yeah, I hear that," Kane shouted. "Any ideas?"

"Just one," Brigid told him. "Professor Abraham Flag."

Kane and Grant both turned to Brigid, stunned expressions straining their faces, even where Grant's was partly masked by the VR helmet. "What?" they asked in unison.

"Take me to Abraham Flag's laboratory," Brigid said, a determined smile crossing her lips.

# Chapter 19

"You get that, Carver?" Kane asked over the radio as he pulled at the wheel and angled the Scorpinaut toward the hidden entrance tunnel to Flag's Laboratory of the Incredible.

"You lead and I'll follow," Carver replied over the comm. "Where are we heading?"

"Back where we started," Kane said. "Baptiste has some kind of plan."

"'Some kind'?" Carver repeated, clearly concerned.

"My reaction exactly," Kane said, "but I trust her."

Crouched at Kane's side, Brigid caught his eye and mouthed the words "Thank you."

Grant continued to work the fire control board as they raced across the frozen wastes as the snow billowed all about them. "So, what is this plan?" he asked.

"Professor Flag was a revolutionary inventor," Brigid began. "Although he preferred not to advertise it, many of his inventions had military applications. In fact, the very reason that the U.S. government kept files on him—the ones we used to locate his secret laboratory—is because they wanted access to those inventions."

"And you reckon that there will be something in his lab that we can use," Kane concluded. "An 'angel gun' or something?"

"The man made copious notes for everything he did,"

Brigid said. "If he has something we can use, it shouldn't be too hard to locate it."

"If it's still there," Kane somberly reminded Brigid.

"If it ever even existed," Grant added.

THE TWO SCORPINAUTS sped across the snow, turning in the direction of the tunnel entrance as seven angels floated over the ground in pursuit.

"Why do they run from us?" Domos asked, perplexed. A rocket raced past him, missing his head by inches, and yet he didn't even flinch. "Are the children scared of us now?"

Leading the pack, her beautiful form cutting a path through the falling curtain of snow, Abariel turned back to Domos and smiled. "The children could never be scared of us," she assured him. "It defies belief."

"But without belief…" the apprentice Damiel began, horrified at the notion, his toes brushing at the twinkling snow covering the ground.

"Purity of thought, Damiel," Vadriel reminded him as a 40 mm shell cut through his body, passing harmlessly through it as though he were made of nothing more than intangible thought.

Damiel focused his thoughts as instructed, feeling his buoyancy return, lifting a little higher off the ground.

All around, explosions and gunshots wailed as the Scorpinauts continued their relentless assault on their luminescent pursuers.

IN THE DRIVING SEAT of the lead Scorpinaut, Kane was wrestling with the steering wheel as the boxy vehicle bounced and jostled its way over the snowy ridges, struggling to maintain traction while traveling at such high speed.

"Anyone remember where this tunnel entrance was?" Kane asked, peering hopefully through the windshield as he tried to locate it, the curtain of falling snow almost entirely obscuring his vision.

"It's marked on my heads-up display," Grant replied from beneath the VR helmet. "Hang right and you'll see it."

Kane did as instructed, the suspension of the Scorpinaut groaning as they raced over the shifting surface of the frozen snow.

"Fifty feet," Grant told Kane as they plowed onward. "Forty. Thirty."

Kane's teeth were clenched as he tried to spot the entrance amid the falling sheet of snow. "I don't see—"

From over Kane's shoulder, Brigid leaned forward and pointed toward the right. "There," she said. "You see it?"

Kane looked, locating the little patch of shadow amid the almost total whiteness of the scene before him beneath the multicolored sky. Nodding, he adjusted the Scorpinaut's direction and the vehicle hurtled into the tunnel entrance, barely missing the right-hand wall.

A moment later, the Scorpinaut was speeding toward the hidden Laboratory of the Incredible inside that secret tunnel. The tunnel itself was dark now, the overhead light strips providing just a little illumination as they reflected the greens and reds of the aurora australis into the tunnel's depths.

"Hang on, people," Kane muttered. "We'll be there in no time." His foot jammed the accelerator to the floor, urging the heavy, tanklike vehicle onward.

INSIDE THE SECOND Scorpinaut, Carver worked the controls and battled with the steering as the vehicle churned up snow in its wake. He could hardly see anything through the windshield, just the dark blob of Kane's vehicle amid the shifting whiteness of the snowstorm.

Lacea was using a VR feed to track the path of the angels behind them, watching their tagged forms on a three-dimensional telemetry display. They were running short of ammunition now, and she was staggering her bursts of fire accordingly, as she had been advised by Carver.

"Do you think Kane's plan will work?" Lacea asked as the Scorpinaut jounced into the darkened tunnel after the first.

"I can't rightly say I know what it is," Carver admitted as the falling blanket of snow disappeared, replaced by the strange cascade of reds and greens playing off the tunnel walls, "but we are running damn short of options."

"I've tried raising the base on the radio, but no one's answering," Lacea said.

Carver ignored her, working the controls silently, concentrating hard as he negotiated the low-ceilinged tunnel at a much faster speed than the Scorpinauts were comfortably controllable.

"Everyone else is dead," Lacea said, her voice hollow. It was as though the realization had only now hit her.

"That seems about the sum of it," Carver growled, stomping his foot on the accelerator in a desperate bid for more speed that the Scorpinaut simply could not give. "How close are the hostiles?" he asked, glancing briefly at the rearview monitor.

Lacea watched the tagged forms fluttering behind them through the medium of the VR telemetry display. Despite following the Scorpinauts, the angels' movements were like spindrift, eerily directionless in their meandering paths. "Thirty feet," she stated. "Their ETA to tunnel entrance is five seconds…four…three…two…one…in."

"Kane," Carver shouted into the radio pickup he now wore clipped over his ear. "They've followed us into the tunnel. You have any ideas yet?"

"Just one," Kane's voice came back over the radio speaker. "Blast the roof, see if you can block their way."

"You're crazy," Carver spit. "These things can burn through fucking doors, man."

"All we can hope to do right now is slow them," Kane responded. "Blast the roof, Carver."

"And how do we get out of here with the tunnel scragged?" Carver shouted into his radio mike, panic coloring his tone.

"We have that covered," Kane assured him, his voice level. "Now blow the roof or we'll do it for you."

Carver glanced across to where Lacea sat at the fire controls. "You heard him," he said. "Bring down the roof."

"Targeting," Lacea responded, her voice trembling.

With the angels rushing through the tunnel just a few wag lengths behind the Scorpinauts, Lacea rotated the tail gun around so that it pointed a little way behind their vehicle. She altered the angle on the tail cannon, pointing it in an almost upright position. The cannon was so long that it very nearly scraped against the ceiling. Suddenly, that great gun boomed as Lacea blasted five shells in quick succession from its nose. Each 40 mm shell powered from the cannon in a flash of explosive, slamming almost immediately into the tunnel ceiling. The roof quivered at the impacts, a powdery dusting falling through, closely followed by great chunks of white tumbling to the ground, painted in multicolor by the curious lighting of the tunnel itself.

Aboard the Scorpinaut, Lacea automatically turned her head in flinch reaction as she watched the tumbling roof crash to the ground on her heads-up display. "Shells launched," she announced, flipping switches to launch a further volley of fire from the rocket pods that littered the surface of the vehicle.

His eyes on the tunnel road, Carver saw a swell of powdery snow race past them as the debris continued to crash to the ground from behind. "Was it a success?" he snapped. "Lacea? Report."

Lacea, who was primarily a comm officer and had had little genuine combat experience, looked at the VR display for a few seconds, trying to make out the picture that was being piped there. "I think so…" she began, her voice tentative.

"I need a solid report, Lacea," Carver snapped. "Is the roof down? Have we lost our pursuers?"

"Roof is down, sir," Lacea announced. "No sign of tagged pursuit at present, but I couldn't tell you how long that will hold them."

"Stow the speculation," Carver instructed.

THE ANGELS PULLED to a halt as the explosions began and they saw the roof above them tumble down to the ground. To their eyes it was a strange thing, seeing the snow fall like this, in huge, solid chunks where all the fallen snowflakes had melded together, as though holding on to one another for comfort. It reminded Sazquiel of an avalanche, only it didn't really build; it just fell and then it stopped, over before it had really begun.

The explosions had been bright, abrupt things that also seemed far too sudden. But they had done something to the packed snow outside the roof, dislodging it and making it drop.

"The children did this," Bateliel observed, his glowing body hovering in place before the heaped snow as it continued to pile up in the tunnel, blocking the way.

"But why would the children do this?" Damiel asked, confused.

Abariel stepped forward, placing a hand on the snow to make sure that it was what it appeared. In less than a second, she split the heaped snow in her mind into all of its component dendrites, re-creating their unique shapes as they had originally drifted down from the sky, freeing them from the mass that they had elected to form. A beautiful smile crossed her full lips. "The children are playing," Abariel said, her voice like the sloughing of a snake's skin. "They like to toy with the things they find in the garden."

"I think not, Abariel," Vadriel corrected, his voice like sunrise in the fall. "I think they are scared and now they are trying to hide from us."

"The children could never be scared of us," Abariel stated firmly, reiterating the point she had made a few minutes before.

Kneeling by the newly formed wall of snow, examining the patterns it shaped within the focus of his magnificent angel's eyes, Sazquiel spoke softly. "They are corruptions. Impurities course within their systems." He turned to the others, looking up at them sadly with his pale blue-on-white eyes. "That is why they are scared."

"We must judge them quickly then," Bateliel decided. "They must not run loose in the garden any longer than is absolutely necessary."

"This barrier is firm," Sazquiel announced. "It will not part as easily as the things the children make with their hands."

"They use the rules of the garden against us," Adriel whispered, her voice as brittle as a crone's bones. "The impure children have run amok in the garden for too long. They have learned how to use its rules of up and down against us, employing them to their advantage."

"But they do not manipulate the rules as we do," Sazquiel stated, reaching his hand into the tightly packed snow barricade. Where his hand touched it, dark streaks began to appear, cutting across the white surface of the snow.

"KANE? YOU GET THAT?" Carver asked over the radio.

In the lead Scorpinaut, Kane was studying the footage from the rearview monitor as Grant talked him through the heads-up display report.

"Looks good," Kane said into the radio pickup, "but it's just the start. You're not going to much like what we're going to do next, Carver."

"What's that?" Carver asked over the comm.

"As you say, the collapsed roof won't hold them for long," Kane began.

Beside him, Grant read out a figure from the tactical display: "One mile."

"We're one-third into the tunnel," Kane explained to Carver. "I want to set up a blockade at the midpoint. Old crowd-control technique back in the Tartarus Pits."

"I remember," Carver replied. "Sounds good, but what do we use?"

Kane grimaced, letting the tension wash over him, clarifying his thoughts. "I need you to park at the midway point and bail out," he explained. "We'll blast your wag and blow up the roof there to create a bottleneck."

Carver took a few moments before he responded. "Acknowledged," he said in a resigned manner. "You guys going to stop long enough to give us a ride?"

"Well," Kane drawled, "I was going to leave you for the crazy aces out there, but since you asked so nicely…"

"Much obliged, Kane," Carver acknowledged. "Tell me when we reach the blockade point and I'll pull her to a halt."

"Copy," Kane replied, his eyes focused on the darkness of the tunnel as it stretched on ahead.

THE ANGEL Sazquiel pushed his hand into the snow barricade, feeling the intricacies of the patterns therein, hearing the song of the snowflakes. With a twist of his hand, Sazquiel located the flaws within the barrier, mapping its fault lines in his mind.

Sazquiel pulled, turning his hand as it came loose from the snow wall. He stepped back, rejoining his six companions as they waited behind him in the oddly lit tunnel, their glowing forms burning whitely amid the eerie colors on the walls. There was a small hole in the barricade now, where Sazquiel's arm had reached into it. The angels watched impassively as the snow wall began to split around the hole, cracks appearing like veins across its surface. The cracks spread across the whiteness, coiling like snakes as they located more and more faults in the compacted snow barrier.

A few seconds after the cracks had begun to appear, the first chunk of snow fell from the great barricade, flaking from the wall like sun-scored paint.

The angels watched as the snow dropped to the floor of the tunnel, disintegrating to nothingness as it fell away.

KANE WATCHED the shifting colors of red and green as they played across the tunnel walls before him through the Scorpinaut's windshield. The inside of the vehicle shook and rattled as Kane pushed it to its limit, urging more power from the complaining engine.

"Hit the brakes," Grant stated as he watched their progress on the three-dimensional tactical display of the VR helmet. "We're at the midpoint."

Kane's booted foot pumped the brake pedal and he sent a quick command to Carver over the rig's radio. "We're here," he said.

Behind Kane's Scorpinaut, Carver pulled his own vehicle into a sharp turn as he locked the brakes, forcing the vehicle to fishtail on the slick surface of the tunnel floor before sliding to a halt across the tunnel itself. As Kane brought his own vehicle to a stop, he watched Carver's maneuver in the rearview display, admiring the man's control. Carver had placed his Scorpinaut in such a way that it almost entirely blocked the width of the tunnel, leaving just a little space to front and rear.

Kane revved the engine, pumping power through his Scorpinaut, making it strain against the emergency brake like an angry dog held on a leash. As Kane continued to watch on the monitor screen, his foot pumping at the accelerator, the side door of the other Scorpinaut opened and Carver and Lacea stepped out. The girl looked a little shaky on her feet, but otherwise they appeared to be fine. Together, they ran across the slippery surface of the tunnel, making their way swiftly to where Kane's Scorpinaut waited, its engine snarling.

Watching in the monitor, Brigid reached across for the door release, and the side door opened to grant their two passengers entry.

"Good control," Kane said to Carver as the ex-Mag climbed through the doorway. "Excellent placement—we couldn't have asked for more."

"I've had a little experience with these wags," Carver replied modestly as he took a seat in back beside Lacea and Brigid. "We all set?"

In response, Kane disengaged the emergency brake and gunned the engine, and the Scorpinaut arrowed forward once more, its mighty engine growling like a jungle cat.

Beside Kane, head immersed in the VR hood, Grant targeted the stalled Scorpinaut that Carver had left blocking the tunnel behind them, watching the distance between them increase. With the target lock in place, Grant unleashed the full fury of the Scorpinaut's impressive arsenal at its twin, firing the tail gun, rockets and rear-facing machine-gun placements at the parked vehicle as they surged away from it down the strangely lit tunnel.

The barrage smashed against the side panels of the Scorpinaut, rocking it on its wheels. A moment later, the stalled vehicle caught fire as rockets impacted all across its surface. In another two seconds, the parked Scorpinaut blew, chunks of metal plating blasting everywhere as fire ravaged across its surface. Grant ignored it, his attention already on the roof above where he targeted the remainder of his arsenal, reloading the tail gun with another of those devastating 40 mm shells. The Scorpinaut shuddered as Grant let loose the second salvo, drilling the ceiling with projectiles just a little way beyond the burning barricade of the Scorpinaut.

The ceiling tumbled under the assault, and huge chunks of snow and ice crashed to the floor of the tunnel as Kane and his crew sped away, blocking off the tunnel just past the burning shell of the other Scorpinaut.

"Second blockade's in place," Grant stated, pushing back the VR helmet and rapidly blinking his eyes as he peered around the Scorpinaut's cabin.

"Think it will hold them, Grant?" Carver asked, leaning forward from his position in the rear of the Scorpinaut.

Grant shook his head. "Not for long," he rumbled.

EVEN AS GRANT said it, the seven angels were making their way past the first snow barricade. The whole structure had lost integrity with the effect of Sazquiel's touch, and now it tumbled all around them, disintegrating and evaporating as the angels strode through its remains.

They were barely a mile away from Kane's fleeing Scorpinaut.

# Chapter 20

Inside the remaining Scorpinaut, Lacea was looking pale and decidedly shell-shocked. She hadn't seen much in the way of combat in her short career with the Millennial Consortium, and this had been nothing less than a rude awakening.

"What the hell did we unleash here?" she asked, her voice trembling. "Angels? I mean…what the hell?"

Sitting facing her in the back of the vehicle, Brigid fixed the younger woman with her emerald eyes, willing her to calm down. "Yes, they're angels," she stated, "or, at least, whatever angels really are. I think Carver here hit the nail on the head when he described them as antibodies. We perceive them as angels, see them in human form, but if we suppose the universe is an organ that, in some religions, we might call God, then the angels are there to fight infections and repair damage. When the multidimensional knife was used, it some-how cut an impossible hole—a breach in infinity—that crossed through multiple fractals."

"Are we talking about casements here?" Kane asked, re-ferring to the Cerberus team's experiences involving parallel time lines.

Brigid shook her head. "No, this is something far more fundamental than that," she stated solemnly. "This is the kind of stuff that reality itself is constructed from. The Annunaki blade opened a multidimensional hole that needed the universe's antibodies—the angels—to heal. They didn't come out of the hole—they came because of it."

"So," Carver asked as the Scorpinaut rumbled beneath them, "are they protecting the body from the inside or from without?"

Brigid bit her lip in thought. "It's a good point," she reasoned. "The breach seemed to open *into* something—flowing blood that the lights, the angels, emerged from. By that logic, we're on the surface—the skin—of whatever it is we construe to be the body."

"God's body," Carver whispered in awe.

Lacea looked distressed, trying to follow the philosophical conversation over the roar of the Scorpinaut's straining engine. "But I thought angels were meant to be the good guys," she said. "Why would they come to hurt us? They killed Simona and probably all the others."

"We're impure," Brigid told her unhappily, and then she addressed the point to everyone. "I saw it when they touched me, when they *judged* me. The whole thing flashed through my mind and I realized what it was they were seeing."

"Which is?" Grant asked, peering up as he checked the tactical display for signs of pursuit.

"What I saw was something that we've heard about before now," Brigid explained. "When the Annunaki first came to Earth…"

Carver stopped Brigid with a gesture. "Think you can explain it for all of us," he requested, "from the beginning?"

Kane ground the gears as the Scorpinaut slipped on the icy surface of the tunnel, racing beneath the changing colors of the lights. "The Annunaki are a lizardlike alien race who came to Earth out of boredom. Once here, they were so far advanced that they became revered as gods by the primitive peoples they interacted with," he growled. "We've met a few of them over the years—one mean son of a bitch called Enlil has been a thorn in our side for far too long. These lizards just love to meddle in human affairs, and—what's more—they always have."

"And by always, we really do mean *always*," Brigid explained.

"It's like a game to them," Grant added unhappily from the passenger seat.

Brigid took up the story once more. "The Annunaki are incredibly advanced," she explained. "They have technology that we can only dream of, they literally re-create their bodies through a memory download."

"Ouch," Carver spit.

"There were stories," Brigid continued, "that the Annunaki have engaged in genetic manipulation and intervened in human affairs for centuries."

Lacea gulped. "They must have a reason," she insisted, pushing her blond bangs out of her eyes.

"To them, it's like a disruptive child pulling the wings off flies," Brigid said. "They wouldn't even give it a second thought. It's something to do."

"That's horrible," Lacea stated, her nose wrinkling in disgust.

"Whatever it was that the Annunaki did," Brigid explained, "is what the angels are picking up on now. They think that we've been corrupted by some kind of infection. Not just the people here—we're talking the whole human race."

"So, you're saying," Carver summarized, "that once they've finished with us, they're going to keep seeking more and more people and then—what?—burn them to oblivion. Until there's no one left."

"As far as the angels are concerned, we're cancerous cells in the body now," Brigid said. "And you're right. It's fair to assume that they'll keep going until there isn't a single human being left alive."

SIDE BY SIDE, the angels passed through the spray of falling snow that had barred their way. The hard-packed snow had been changed, shifted, returned to its old form as the single snowflakes that had fallen from the skies hundreds of years before. The dendrites drifted upward this time, for the angels cared little for the wants and the needs of gravity in the garden.

With their bare feet never quite touching the ground, the glowing angel forms moved on through the strangely lit tunnel as the whirring patterns of red and green played across its walls. Ahead of them, they now saw the second barricade that their quarry had left. This one was made of metal, and it burned brightly with fire.

To Domos, the whole thing looked like an upturned insect, magnified a thousandfold, left to struggle on its back as though unable to right itself. The flames licked at its sides, a pretty pattern of yellows and reds with other colors, subtler colors, hidden within those dancing streaks.

And behind that, Domos saw, the white snow roof was falling down, caving in like the one that Sazquiel had been forced to shift aside before they could pass.

Such games the children played.

Beautiful Adriel was the first to approach the burning shell of the Scorpinaut, and she watched the flames reaching up with crimson-and-gold fingers, sharp nails of fire clawing at the fractured ceiling. Fascinated, Adriel placed her hand into the flames and watched as their red-yellow tongues lapped at her fingers, then ran up her arm, playing along its pale length.

"It's so pretty," Adriel said, the flames reflecting in her delighted eyes.

Damiel frowned. "What does it feel like, Adriel?"

Adriel was thoughtful for a moment before she spoke. "Like the sun," she said. "It feels like the sun."

The flames continued to play along the length of her porcelain-white arm, and Adriel slowed her vision, watching the bright little things running back and forth as though creatures seeking somewhere to hide. Fire was a strange thing to the angel's eyes, a great mass of little things that held together in one big thing, but was ever breaking apart again, little sections forming new shapes, rushing toward the heavens, only to lose themselves and dissipate, shattering like dreams. Adriel wasn't sure, but she thought she could grow to like fire.

Adriel stepped closer then, letting the flames run across her body, feeling them at play on her skin. They felt warm, of course, but it was a friendly feeling, the warmth of laughter, of company. Dipping her head, Adriel let the fire touch her cascading white locks. The flames reached for her hair for a moment, then settled there, rushing across her scalp and the whole of her perfect face, playing in the crevices and cavities that formed her breathtaking, perfect features.

Adriel looked back at the others, who were now watching her with great interest. She could see them still, but now there were flames running before her eyes, shining across her vision the way the falling snowflakes had played there before, when they had all been outside. She slowed time's input and peered past the flames, reminding herself how her companions looked without the heat haze, before switching back to peer through it once again. It had a curious effect, like a reflection in flowing water. Which was strange, Adriel realized, for she knew that fire and water were opposites. But, like all the opposites in the garden, fire and water were really the same thing.

"We must remove the barrier," Bateliel reminded the others as they watched Adriel turn before them, now just a pillar of flame.

As one, the angels approached the flames.

As THE LAST remaining Scorpinaut sped along the tunnel, the rear tail gun began booming for one final salvo. Grant was working the main controls, with Carver at the secondary fire control board backing him up. Together they blasted a continuous stream of shells and rockets at the tunnel's ceiling, disgorging the remainder of the vehicle's formidable arsenal, knocking the densely packed snow ceiling and walls loose so that they tumbled free and crashed down to the floor, blocking the tunnel.

The Scorpinaut rocked under the stress of multiple launches, and Kane fought with the steering wheel as the falling ceiling exploded all around them. Up ahead, he could see the large hangar doors of the hidden laboratory now, just a hundred yards away.

"Show's over," Kane instructed, and Grant and Carver ceased fire; none of them wanted to damage the integrity of the ceiling too close to the secret base itself.

With Kane's foot jammed on the accelerator, the boxy, tanklike vehicle hurtled onward along the tunnel, its wheels sliding along icy patches as Kane powered it through the open hangar bay doors.

At the driver's controls, Kane wrestled with the wheel,

pulling the Scorpinaut into a sharp turn as he slammed on the brakes. The armored vehicle raced through the hangar, speeding toward the far wall as Kane pumped at the brakes. Suddenly, a dark shape appeared in the windshield as something heavy slammed into them, bumping over the tilted windshield and crashing against the roof of the Scorpinaut as the two impacted again and again. Kane recognized the skeletal metal construction as it sped out of his field of vision; it was the one-man gyrocopter.

With a whine of straining gears, the Scorpinaut shuddered to a halt, its twin foreclaw-style machine-gun armatures just two feet away from the rearmost wall.

"Cutting it a bit close, weren't you?" Brigid said, cocking an eyebrow as she peered through the windshield.

In response, Kane shrugged. "Tough to find a space," he suggested.

Discarding the VR telemetry helmet, Grant reached for the door release and leaped from the vehicle.

As Carver followed, he turned back to Kane. "You're sure you have another way out?" he inquired, concerned that they had now blocked the main tunnel and hence the only exit.

"Hey," Kane told him, pointing a finger at his own chest, "I got in, didn't I?"

"We spent a long time working to get those main doors open," Carver explained. "Just how did you guys get in here?"

Kane grinned. "Made our own entrance," he explained. When Carver offered a querulous look, Kane elaborated. "Used my charm. My friendly nature. My acetylene torch."

Carver nodded. "Ah, now I get the picture."

Lacea was just making her way from the Scorpinaut, and she addressed Carver and Kane as they hurried away from the vehicle through the main doors into the lab. "That snow outside is pretty thick," she said. "Are you sure your homemade entrance will still be there?"

"We can always make another," Kane assured her.

"Kane's good at that," Grant added when the blond comm officer looked worried. "He won't leave anyone behind, don't you fret."

The five of them rushed through the hangar door and into the vast Laboratory of the Incredible. Everything was just as they had left it a few hours before. The icy roof twinkled overhead, somehow lit via that secret power source. The workbenches waited, filled with 250-year-old experiments that would never be completed, notebook compendiums filled with observations and analyses written in Abraham Flag's elaborate hand. Shattered vials and beakers indicated where the Cerberus field team had been challenged by the Millennial Consortium prior to their uneasy alliance.

Having never been in the lab before, Lacea drew a sharp breath when she saw the interior. "It's amazing," she said, her voice a hushed whisper.

Behind her, Grant was working the controls to seal the hangar door, shutting it off from the main lab. As he secured the lock, he glanced across at the nearest workbench. "Might be an idea to put a table or two here," he suggested, "to bolster up the door a little."

Carver nodded in agreement. "I'll help you, Grant," he said, and the two of them stepped over to the nearest heavy workbench and grabbed either end.

While Grant and Carver shored up the doorway, Kane and Brigid rushed through the vast laboratory room with Lacea hurrying to keep up.

"Where are we heading?" Lacea asked, her blond bangs bouncing over her face as she ran.

"Weapons," Brigid explained. "We need to find weapons."

"Anything particular?" Lacea asked as she rushed to keep pace with the two Cerberus warriors.

"Something that has enough kick to knock down an angel," Kane growled.

# Chapter 21

Kane and Brigid rushed through the vast laboratory, their eyes roving over the mismatched items that littered the many worktables, and Lacea hurried to keep up with them.

Kane picked up a small hidebound notebook and flicked rapidly through its pages as Brigid rushed ahead to the next desk.

"So what exactly would this zap gun look like?" Lacea asked Brigid, already sounding out of breath with the exertion.

Brigid turned, offering the younger woman a bright, reassuring smile. "It's not the weapon we need to find," she explained, "not yet, anyhow. Check through the journals and notebooks and see if you can find an inventory of some sort. Once we find that, we can use it to locate items of interest."

Lacea's eyes widened, but she moved on to the next table and began to rummage around the notebooks there, reading their covers and checking their contents. "Do we really have time for this?" she asked.

Kane patted Lacea on the shoulder reassuringly as he passed her. "Looking for a way to stay alive is never time wasted," he assured her as he made his way to a stack of notebooks that rested on a shelf beside some glass tubing.

Despite his words of reassurance, Kane felt his heart sink as he pawed through his fourth notebook of Boolean algebraic equations.

OVER AT THE hangar entrance, Grant and Carver shunted a second worktable in front of the doors and began stacking more heavy equipment atop it, piling it high to completely block the entryway.

"This isn't going to hold them for long, you realize," Carver grumbled as he maneuvered another desk into place in the center of the barricade.

"Right now I think every second might just make the difference," Grant told him, muscles tensing as he hefted a desk across the room to add to the barricade.

Carver stopped, looking at the barrier for a moment. "We can add some of the heavier desks," he suggested, "maybe wedge them tight so that they reinforce each other."

"Yeah," Grant agreed, reaching into his jacket. "I've got a better idea." When his hand reappeared it was holding what appeared to be two thumbnail-sized ball bearings.

Carver looked at the round items resting on Grant's palm. "Should I ask?"

"Miniexplosives," Grant told him. "They'll make a lot of noise and release a little gunpowder once they're tripped." He leaned down, priming one of the little explosive charges before placing it at the foot of the door.

"How many do you have?" Carver asked, full of admiration.

"Half a dozen," Grant told him. "Kane and Brigid should have some, too."

Carver looked around, seeing that the other two Cerberus warriors were already halfway along the vast length of the laboratory area, rapidly checking through cabinets and desks in their search for details on a weapon. "They're kind of busy with their own thing," he pointed out. "You have anything stronger?"

Placing the second charge, Grant shook his head. "Not with me," he lamented.

"Then let's keep working on blocking the door," Carver said, "and we'll place the remaining charges as strategically as we can."

Grant nodded, stepping out from the huddled desks to help Carver shift another piece of furniture. "Maybe Kane will find us something a bit more powerful we can use," he growled.

BRIGID, KANE AND Lacea had covered three-fourths of the laboratory area and found nothing other than lists of experiments into various energy sources, studies of aerodynamics and airflow and a theoretical periodic table showing an additional fourteen elements that Brigid had never heard of.

As the frantic search lengthened, Kane's good humor began to fade. "It's a dead end, Baptiste. There's nothing here."

Brigid looked over to him from where she was flicking through the pages of another notepad at a desk with a built-in sink. "There has to be something," she said. "Flag was a genius, not a pacifist."

"What about the junk room upstairs?" Kane suggested, reminding Brigid of the trophy area through which they had initially entered the laboratory.

Brigid held up her index finger, calling on Kane to be silent. "Wait," she breathed, her emerald eyes working over the open page of the book in her hand. "Here—sonics."

Brigid tossed the book across to Kane, who grabbed it from the air and studied the open page. It showed a diagram of what appeared to be a cannon, with a wide aperture at the front from which a waveform was being emitted.

"Sonics?" Kane repeated dubiously.

"Just find the cannon," Brigid told him. "I've had another idea."

"Okay," Kane said, turning to where the blond comm woman was still searching. "Lacea, you're with me. We need to find *this*—" he held up the diagram for her to see "—as soon as possible."

"ASAP," Lacea said, offering Kane a brisk salute.

Kane was pleased to see that the young communications officer was keeping her spirits up. For a while, he had wondered from their radio communications if she might be about to lose it, but it seemed that getting her out of the Scorpinauts had calmed her sufficiently that she could be of assistance. Probably her first time in a tank during combat, Kane realized as he walked with the blond-haired woman across the laboratory.

"It says here," Kane explained, "that this sonic cannon was used to excavate this place."

"Creepers, that's one tough sonic beam," Lacea said, astounded.

"Well, that's the kind of power we need right now," Kane reminded her. "Says here that Flag stored it in a locker coded like this." Kane showed her the reference that Flag had written in his careful, elaborate penmanship.

"So, we need to find the equipment lockers," Lacea realized, "then we'll find this sonic zap gun."

"And who knows what else," Kane said, suddenly feeling a little more optimistic. He glanced back to the far end of the lab, where Grant and Carver continued to work at their makeshift barricade. In relative terms, things were going well.

As Kane and Lacea rushed off examining Flag's notes, Brigid stood in place, feeling the vastness of the high-ceilinged laboratory area all around her. There was a far more obvious solution to their problem, she had concluded, albeit with a little touch of madness to it. With a determined stride, Brigid made her way toward the double helix staircase, her eyes on the prize that waited in the shadows beneath the stairs.

AT THE OTHER END of the lab, Carver stood admiring the barricade that he and Grant had constructed before the locked doors. It stood over ten feet high and now looked like a solid, immovable knot of furniture. Grant had added several more tiny explosive globes from his miniarmory, and they had placed these at strategic points. They were positioned to blow outward into the hangar and away from the laboratory area if they were triggered by the angels.

"It's good working with someone who can keep a calm head under pressure," Carver said with admiration.

"Thanks," Grant replied. "Right back at ya."

Carver turned to the dark-skinned man then, his brow furrowed. "Do you ever miss it, Grant? The life of a Magistrate?"

Grant shook his head. "I never regretted leaving," he said. "Cobaltville was a lie. That whole world of barons and subjugation—it was all built on a lie. And as Mags, we were a part of that lie—you, me and Kane."

Carver nodded. "Still, it was a cozy life for a while, huh? You knew where your next meal was coming from."

The two of them turned from the barricade and, side by side, trudged through the huge laboratory area beneath the icy ground.

"Why did you leave?" Grant asked. "I mean, really why? You had a pretty good career ahead with your skills. Could have gone into administration, got yourself off the beat if you wanted to."

Carver was quiet for almost a half minute as he contemplated Grant's question. "I met a girl," he finally said, "if you really want to know. I was young and impressionable, just graduated from the Hall of Justice. I guess she just…well, women. You're with them and you think you can take on anything, you know?"

Grant nodded silently, thinking of his girlfriend, Shizuka.

"I guess we just thought, 'To hell with the world,'" Carver explained. "Took off one day, left everything I had behind. Went out into the hills, hooked up with a group of outlanders, roamed for a while."

"You make it sound easy," Grant said.

Carver snickered. "There were a few complications at first. Baron Cobalt doesn't take too kindly to Mags resigning, I guess. But the heat died down, and it's not like we stuck around much to face it, anyway."

"And what happened to her?" Grant asked.

"The girl?" Carver smiled. "Oh, she's long gone. Went off with one of the roamers, had to be a free spirit. I dunno, it was a long time ago."

Grant peered back over his shoulder, checking the barricade as he thought over other things. "Do you regret it, Carver?" he asked after a moment. "Leaving?"

"I regret *her*," Carver said, "but leaving? No, I don't regret that. I've traveled all over, and I've seen such things that you wouldn't believe."

"Sometime when we're not running for our lives, we'll have to swap stories," Grant told his fellow ex-Mag.

They were past the midpoint of the laboratory when they heard a rumbling coming from off to the left. The two ex-Mags turned, their combat senses alert, ready for whatever was making the racket. A moment later, a curious-looking one-man wag appeared from an alcove, its engine chugging with the loud rumble they had heard. The wag appeared to be in two sections. The bottom half was five feet long, with caterpillar tracks running on a three-wheel system at the front and a large ball-like wheel to the rear beneath where the driver was located in a standing position. The top half appeared to be a separate section, a long, conical barrel carved into a series of bubblelike shapes that stuck out three feet beyond the length of the vehicle's base.

Kane worked at twin levers on the dashboard, navigating the walkway between the scientific worktables as he pulled the vehicle around. Lacea followed, taking brisk strides to keep pace with the slow-moving vehicle.

"Look what we found," Lacea hollered over the beastly rumbling of the wag's engine.

"What is it?" Carver asked as Kane pulled the vehicle around toward them.

"Sonic boom box," Kane shouted, a broad grin etched across his face. He pulled at the twin levers once more, adjusting the weird vehicle's path and aiming for the far end of the laboratory that led to the hangar bay.

Grant took two quick steps and jumped up beside Kane at the driving area of the rig, hanging on to its frame. "So, what does it do and how do we work it?" he bellowed over the noise of the rumbling engine.

Kane passed Grant the notebook that detailed the weapon's design. "It's a sound gun," he summarized as Grant began scanning the page. "Emits a very low frequency beam that can be used as a drill. It's how Professor Flag opened up this whole underground base in the first place."

"A sonic drill," Grant said as realization dawned.

"Right." Kane nodded. "And if it had the oomph to carve out this place, then it might just have the power to keep our glowing friends at bay."

Grant nodded slowly, a smile forming beneath the dark lines of his gunslinger's mustache. "Worth a try," he agreed.

Kane pulled the bulky vehicle to a stop within sight of the door to the hangar. "I'm not sure what kind of range this thing has," he explained, "and we don't really have much opportunity to test it."

"Just show me how to fire it," Grant rumbled. "I'll figure out the rest."

As Grant and Kane fiddled with the control panel on the sonic cannon, Carver and Lacea came to meet them.

"We can use this to hold them back once they bust through the barricade," Kane reasoned. "I've got no idea what hard sound does to an angel, but it can drill through well-packed snow so I'm guessing being caught in its beam won't do anything much good. Even angels."

"You think it might discorporate them?" Carver projected.

Kane offered the shaved-headed ex-Mag a sly grin. "That's the dream."

"Do you think we'll find anything else here that we can use?" Lacea asked.

Kane gestured to Carver. "Ask your boss—he's spent more time here than any of us."

Carver shook his head. "Other than the stone knife, Flag seemed pretty antiweapons," he said. "Even this thing—" he slapped a hand firmly against the side of the sonic blaster "—is essentially a drill that we can adapt for use as a weapon, am I right?"

"You called it," Kane agreed. Just then, his Commtact

came to life; Brigid was paging him from the far end of the laboratory.

"Kane, Grant," she began, "forget the drill—I've had a better idea."

Kane held his hand up to show Grant that he would respond. "Need help?" he asked.

"Come here and I'll show you," Brigid said, "and bring an extra pair of hands."

Hearing the whole exchange over his own subdermal Commtact, Grant ushered Kane away. "You go," he said. "Me and Carver will cover things here. If this sonic blaster works, then we need to get it in place."

Kane leaped down from the sonic drill's rig and left Grant to maneuver it to just where he wanted it.

As he began striding back across the laboratory toward Brigid's position by the far staircase, Kane turned back and addressed Lacea. "Fancy being an extra pair of hands, Officer?"

Lacea smiled. "What else was I going to do with the rest of today?" she said as she fell into step beside him. She seemed much more buoyant the more time they spent away from the avenging angels.

THE FLAMING Scorpinaut lit the tunnel in red-and-gold hues, long, shimmering shadows running up and down the curved walls. Beautiful Adriel still burned, for she had welcomed the fire's play upon her perfect body, encouraged it to nest there where it would be safe. She walked alongside her companions, a few inches above the floor, as they passed the ruined shell of the vehicle and continued onward down the tunnel.

Bateliel glanced at Adriel for a moment, a look of disdain

creasing his flawless white features. "Must you burn so?" he asked. "It is a distraction."

Adriel smiled. "I like it," she said, her arms outstretched, the fire playing along their lengths. "It feels like—" She stopped.

"Like what?" Bateliel encouraged after a few moments, while the other angels bent to the task of shifting the fallen roof that stood between them and their quarry.

"Like the issue of my procreation," Adriel said. "I have offered the flames security and now they look to me to keep them safe, to provide for them. This must be what it is like to have children of one's own."

Bateliel shook his head sadly. "We shall never know, Adriel," he said, his voice sounding like cracking ice. "Put the thought from your mind and extinguish your new friends."

"No," Adriel said, her own voice as bright as paint. "They do me no harm. I shall travel with them for a while, see how they like the sights we see."

"As you will," Bateliel said, dismissing Adriel's whims for foolery.

Ahead, Sazquiel and Vadriel stood to either side of Damiel as all three communed with the snow, finding its fault lines and teasing them apart. With an eerie shushing sound, the snow began to break apart at the angels' touch.

BRIGID BAPTISTE came to meet with Kane and Lacea about twenty feet from where she had been standing beneath the curving stairwell. She held an ancient notebook in her hands.

"So, Baptiste," Kane began, "what's the big plan?"

Brigid held up the notebook, waving it in her hands. "We're going to get us a little extra help," she said, "from Abraham Flag."

"From his secret books or something?" Kane asked.

Brigid shook her head. "Why, when we can ask him to help us himself, Kane?"

"Flag's the guy who owned this place, right?" Lacea recalled. When Brigid nodded, she looked perplexed. "He's dead, right?"

"Only temporarily," Brigid said with an enigmatic smile.

Kane raised his eyebrows. "If you're planning what I think you're planning, it doesn't sound very smart."

Brigid turned and strode toward the cryogenic cylinder that waited beneath the staircase. "Come on," she shot back. "It'll be fun waking the dead."

"Yeah," Kane muttered as he followed his Titian-haired companion. "That kinda fun I don't need."

# Chapter 22

Abraham Flag stood before them, six foot six, his head resting atop wide, muscular shoulders as the bluish gas of the cylinder wafted about his naked body. His eyes were closed, but the jut of his square jaw still seemed to hold a certain pride—even arrogance—as Brigid, Kane and Lacea studied his striking form through the glass.

"Is he asleep?" Lacea asked, her voice timid, as though she was afraid of waking the man who stood naked before her.

"He's a freezie," Kane explained, his eyes on the figure in the glass tube. "Put himself under over two centuries ago."

"Could they do that then?" Lacea questioned with genuine surprise.

Brigid turned to the blond comm officer. "Flag could," she told her. "The man was a genius of the highest echelon."

Lacea looked over the powerfully built figure in the glass tank with approval. "He's…very impressive," she said, and a blush rose to her cheeks.

Brigid glanced back at Lacea as she strode over to the control podium that was connected to the cryogenic hardware. "Professor Flag may be our only hope of getting out of this alive."

Chastised, Lacea nodded and averted her eyes from the statuesque naked form within the glass cylinder. "Sorry," she said. "What do you need me to do?"

Kane followed Brigid, making his way across the room to join her at the podium. "This is Baptiste's show now," he told Lacea. "From here on in, we just run the errands she gives us."

Brigid winked when she caught Kane's eye. "I love when you talk dirty," she told him playfully. "Now, I'm going to need to hook up the power here, so we'll need cables—make sure they haven't rotted—with attachments to fit here and here," she said, pointing. "The man's going to wake up feeling really cold, so let's see if we can find some blankets, maybe a portable heater, something like that. And clothes, he's going to need clothes."

"There was a room upstairs," Kane recalled, "just off from the trophy room. My guess is it's the living quarters in this crazy place."

Lacea pointed to the double helix staircase and took a single step toward it. "I'll go," she told them.

"Keep your eyes open for anything useful up there, too," Kane called after her.

"Such as?"

"Weaponry, anything we might use at a barricade." Kane shrugged. "Whatever you think. It's mostly junk up there, but I can give you a hand with the big stuff if you locate something worth shifting."

Lacea's fingers brushed against her brow in casual salute. "Will do, sir," she assured Kane as she trotted up the stairs.

Kane couldn't help but chuckle when he saw Brigid's look.

"'Sir'?" Brigid asked. "That's what she's calling you now?"

Kane shrugged. "It's a Magistrate thing, Baptiste. The old authority never leaves you. You wouldn't understand."

Brigid nodded slowly. "Sure, not just because she's young and impressionable."

"Maybe there's a bit of that," Kane admitted.

"And you're an old man in her eyes," Brigid told Kane, and she chuckled as she turned back to the control panel.

Kane looked at the powerfully built man waiting silently in the glass cylinder. "Not as old as he is," he muttered as he walked across to where Brigid was working.

"Do you know what you're doing?" Kane asked.

Brigid ran her finger across the open page of Flag's journal, slowing momentarily as she found a section that seemed pertinent to her intentions. "Flag wrote that he was unable to finalize the wake-up protocols. But he says here that freezing himself was necessary in the circumstances he faced. 'My body must be frozen, a timeless thing, that the monster lurking in my blood not be set free to enact its apocalyptic rampage.'"

Kane shook his head with annoyance. "Was this guy a poet, as well? I mean, what the hell does that mean? If you wake him up, are we unleashing something even more troublesome than our angel pals?"

Brigid looked up at Kane for a moment. "Find me a generator and some jump leads," she said. "We can worry about everything else when it happens."

"Yeah, that's the ass-backward way we usually do stuff," Kane grumbled as he rushed off to a dark corner of the vast laboratory where he could see numerous odd items stashed in a series of cagelike mesh shelves.

He found a small generator there, along with some ancient storage batteries that were as big as a person's head. When Kane played the beam of his pocket flashlight over the storage batteries, he saw that they were corroded, with ugly streaks of greenish-brown liquid staining their surfaces. The generator, however, looked unmolested, and Kane brushed the dust off of a notice that had been pasted to its side. The notice gave clear instructions in its usage, and Kane searched until he found several canisters of fuel over in another of the cratelike shelves. The fuel was liquid based and smelled like paraffin, and it had stored well in the freezing temperatures of the hidden laboratory. Other than a little natural evaporation, the tanks seemed to be pretty much as they had been left centuries earlier.

ALMOST DIRECTLY above Kane's position, Lacea crossed from the staircase, past the radio apparatus and on into the vast trophy room. She walked among the weird collection of treasures there, admiring them for the first time. Several of the tall glass cabinets had been shattered during the earlier gun battle, and the blond-haired comm expert tiptoed around the broken glass strewed across the floor, peering at the bullet holes that now decorated the icelike walls.

At the far end of the room, off to the right, was the little recessed area that Kane had told Lacea about. She walked past six cabinets containing such exotic treasures as a sculpted hand, a brightly colored metallic feather and a ring with a scarlet gemstone that twinkled in the diffuse lighting of the odd room. When she reached the recessed room, Lacea saw that its door had been forced from its hinges, and there were scuff marks around the lock where someone had tried to jimmy it open.

Inside, Lacea saw a neatly made double bed, upon which several cabinet drawers had been overturned, their contents scattered all about. There were some odd things here, flashlights and acoustic devices that Lacea only half recognized, such was their antiquated nature. She picked up a large silver coin from the bed, glancing at the eagle design across its surface before tossing it back where she had found it.

A small basin stood in the corner of the room, really just a bowl on a podium, and when Lacea looked inside she saw that there was a powdery coating across its concave bottom. Beside the basin was a bowl with a wide opening that Lacea presumed had been used as a toilet centuries before when the Laboratory of the Incredible was in use by Flag.

There was a low cabinet beside the basin, and a half-dozen copies of *Scientific American* rested atop it. Peering at the top copy, Lacea saw that it was dated February 1930. When she went to touch it, its cover began to flake apart. She pulled at one of the drawers of the cabinet and found it contained under-wear, socks and several white undershirts. Lacea ran her hand along the edges of the drawer, feeling for any hidden objects or perhaps a hidden catch, but her hand came back with noth-ing other than a little covering of sawdust on her fingertips.

Closing the top drawer, Lacea wiped her hand and checked through the other drawers to find that they contained nothing of particular significance: a few more copies of *Scientific American* and similar journals, some newspaper clippings, several dealing with military operations and archaeological discoveries and one that outlined an exploit in which Abraham Flag himself had been engaged.

Lacea skimmed over the final newspaper clipping, which came from *The New York Times,* dated 18 January, 1924, and told of an assassination attempt on a policeman called Allen. Flag was quoted several times in the piece, downplaying his involvement in apprehending Commissioner Allen's would-be killer. To Lacea's mind, Flag sounded staid and withdrawn, a man with little time for the journalist's line of questioning.

Lacea replaced the newspaper article and turned to the other side of the room.

Three doors stood side by side, making up the farther wall, and Lacea strode over to these. The doors were on sliders and one of them was halfway open. The youthful comm officer pushed it back and peered within.

Lacea found that the doors formed the front of a walk-in wardrobe. Despite its size, the wardrobe was almost empty, with just a half-dozen shirts, two jackets and a few pairs of pants hanging on the rail that stretched along its whole length. At the far end of the rail, several bulky weatherproof coats hung, doubtless for use in the snowy conditions outside. Other than that, there were three pairs of boots at the bottom of the wardrobe along with a pair of what she took to be dress shoes. A raincoat lay on the floor beside the shoes, where it had fallen from its hanger.

Reaching inside the wardrobe, Lacea took a shirt and a pair of pants, along with one of the pairs of boots that rested on the floor in the shadows. Then, folding the clothes over her arm, the blond woman went back to the top drawer of the cabinet and took out a set of underwear and a pair of socks. Then she took the two topmost blankets from the bed before she exited the living quarters and made her way back through the trophy room. As she passed the weird items in the remaining glass cabinets, she wondered at their purpose.

CLOSE TO THE HANGAR doors, Grant was running through a prep sequence on the sonic drill unit. He had directed it toward a solid wall just a little way along from the hangar doors, a wall that he was sure was backed by solid snow.

"It's a one-man job," he told Carver from atop the wheeled rig, "but I'm going to need all the cover fire you can give me."

Carver nodded somberly. "Can't see how that's going to

do much, Grant," he said. "You've seen what these angels do to bullet attacks. They either cast them aside or they walk right through them. It's pointless."

"No, it's not," Grant said. "Though they're impervious to gunfire, the angels—for whatever reason—are slowed by it. They don't seem to quite know how to deal with it, and that distracts them."

"But is a distraction going to be enough?" Carver wondered.

Grant patted a hand against the surface of the sonic drill. "If the angels come through that door, I'm going to use this thing on its maximum setting," he explained. "Looks like it packs quite a punch, but I'll need time to recharge for the settings I'm using."

"How long?"

"About eight seconds between blasts," Grant estimated. "The coils take that long to reach full capacity. Shall we test it to make sure?"

Carver looked up at him and nodded.

Grant set the coils to charge and counted down as the twin display needles shuddered toward full capacity. "Now," he stated as he pushed at the button marked Drill Engage.

The sonic cannon shuddered beneath Grant, feeling like an earthquake as a blast of white noise was unleashed. The blast was invisible to human eyes and unheard by human ears, and yet its effects were immediately obvious: the wall of ice that stood eight feet from the nose of the drill bit began to cave inward and a rapidly deepening tunnel appeared in its glasslike surface.

Carver was laughing as Grant shut off the beam and set the drill to recharge.

"One…two…three," Grant counted aloud until he reached eight. Then the cannon had charged and he worked the drill engage button once again, blasting a second burst of white noise at the rapidly diminishing wall.

After several seconds he shut it off.

"I think we have ourselves a sonic cannon," Grant said happily.

"I think so, too," Carver agreed. "But how on earth did this Flag guy use this thing to carve the whole base out of the ice?"

Grant worked at the steering levers, pulling the drill around to face the barricade before the sealed doors to the hangar. "I'd guess he used a lower setting, so it didn't need to keep recharging," he explained. "But we don't really have a lot of time for low settings, wouldn't you say?"

Carver nodded. Sin Eater in hand, he made his way to a workbench a little way off from the doors, so as to provide cover while Grant was charging the cannon. "We're going to need a whole lot of luck for this, you realize?"

Grant nodded. In his experience, luck was one commodity that was always in short supply.

KANE HAD HAULED the generator and fuel tanks back to where Brigid worked at the cryogenic cylinder beneath the stairs. As he set them up, his eyes were drawn to a cupboard in the far corner of the lab. The cupboard had a lightning-bolt symbol on its double door.

"You have any idea what's in there?" Kane asked, pointing out the cupboard to Brigid.

The red-haired archivist looked up from her work at the cryogenic cylinder, where she was busy disengaging the main feeder tube that slowly pumped gas around the glass container from a large cube with dented metal sides. "Not sure, but the lightning bolt says 'power' to me."

"Me, too," Kane agreed, placing the heavy fuel canisters on the floor and marching swiftly to the closed doors.

The lightning-bolt doors were quite low, and when he reached them, Kane found that they barely came up to his chest. Warily, he undid the catch and pulled the doors open, peering inside. The first thing that struck him was the abominable stench that came forth from the darkness, so strong that it felt like a physical blow. Kane turned his head, covering his mouth and nose even as his eyes began to water.

Cursing, Kane peered inside.

The room itself was dark, though it appeared quite large, going well back into the wall of the Laboratory of the Incredible. The whole structure had been carved from the ice, Kane reminded himself, and as such was not designed like a normal building; new rooms could have been added at any time simply by burrowing farther into the surrounding ice.

Ducking, Kane took a step into the stinking room, reaching for his penlight once more and flicking it on. Despite the low doors, the room itself had a ceiling of normal height or perhaps a little higher, stretching about two feet above Kane's head. Inside were buckets of various sizes that were brimming with mushrooms growing in what appeared to be fecal matter.

"Shit," Kane muttered, running his flashlight beam across the contents of the nearest bucket.

The mushrooms were huge, some bigger than Kane's chest, and they had swamped the room, overwhelming it and growing over one another in their quest for survival in the utter darkness.

Kane stepped out of the room, slamming the doors behind him before he strode back to where Brigid adjusted the hoses connecting the cryogenic cylinder to the control desk.

"What did you find?" Brigid asked, not bothering to look up.

"Mushrooms," Kane stated blankly. "A whole room full of them."

"Really?" Brigid asked, intrigued.

"I think they're taking over," Kane said with a shrug. "Reeks like you wouldn't believe."

Brigid leaned closer to Kane and sniffed at his jacket for a moment. "Fermentation," Brigid suggested. "They're still growing."

"How's that?" Kane asked.

"Some mushrooms grow very, very slowly," Brigid explained, calling the information from her eidetic memory. "They prefer darkness where they form colonies and keep expanding and expanding. The fermentation is what you smelled, and it's a chemical reaction that produces an incredible amount of energy."

"Energy that we can use…?" Kane suggested hopefully.

Brigid looked up at him for a moment, a bright smile on her face. "We can try."

THE SEVEN GLOWING angels continued to make their way through the blocked tunnel that led to the underground Laboratory of the Incredible. The fallen ceiling was proving to be a greater obstacle than anything that they had hitherto come across, because of both its size and the density of the compacted matter.

Sazquiel, Vadriel and Damiel worked at the fallen snow, convincing the dendrites to break away, to assume their original forms so that they might be parted from the fallen roof. Although this approach was successful, it remained time-consuming.

"This must be what it feels like to be trapped," Damiel said, his voice sounding like the wind in the trees.

"We still have an exit," Vadriel pointed out, impatient with his pupil's musings.

"Yet we feel caged," Damiel continued.

Domos snatched one of the falling snowflakes from the air as it reverted to its original appearance and danced on the breeze. The six-pointed star twinkled beneath the eerie red-green lighting of the tunnel as Domos laid it carefully on the palm of his hand for closer inspection. The snowflake did not melt, for Domos's temperature remained constant. An angel may feel warm or cold, but this was merely a fallacy, a creation that it projected for others; an angel itself never changed.

Close to Domos, flaming Adriel peered over to see what it was that her companion studied, examining it with her own wonderful angel's eyes. "It's very pretty," she said through the fire that burned all over her white body, and her voice resounded like the dawn chorus. "May I hold it?"

Domos nodded, holding his hand out to her, palm flat that she might take the white dendrite. As she reached for it with the flames that were dancing across her hands, the snowflake melted, turning into water.

"What happened?" Adriel asked, perplexed at this turn of events.

"I don't know," Domos admitted, and they both turned to wise Bateliel for an explanation.

"The fire's heat," Bateliel explained. "It burns and melts things."

Adriel rolled her fingers, turning them this way and that before her incomparable eyes, watching as the bright flames continued to play there like little children in the sun. "There are so many rules in the garden," she whispered, "that it is hard to keep track of them all."

"Perhaps," Domos began, "this is why the children have

become ill. Perhaps it was all the rules that made them commune with the lizard things."

Bateliel glared at Domos and Adriel. "It matters little," he said, his voice like boot heels on gravel. "Soon they shall be gone."

Domos looked saddened at that, as did Adriel.

"The garden is paramount," Bateliel reminded them. "The garden must survive the infection."

The other angels agreed with Bateliel's statement. The garden had to always be protected.

Along the tunnel, Abariel had joined the other three in their work at the collapsed ceiling. "The children are not far away," she said. "They would never run far from us."

LACEA HAD RETURNED from her jaunt upstairs, carrying a bundle of clothes and blankets. She found Kane and Brigid working at the final connections for three generators, one of which stank of what she assumed was fertilizer. Though young, Lacea had been on enough field missions with the Millennial Consortium to recognize the way in which the two Cerberus teammates had set things up. The generators had been hooked in parallel to the control console and the cryogenic cylinder, almost like a triple buffer between the two. Effectively, this would create a single surge of power rather than an increasing current had they been connected in series.

"You've been busy," Lacea observed as she placed the clothes in a pile on a nearby chair.

Kane glanced up at her. "Brigid's idea. You find everything we need?"

"Got some clothes for Mr. Flag here," Lacea said, "but there wasn't anything I could see worth using as a weapon."

"Nothing you fancied stealing anyway?" Kane goaded, his dislike of the Millennial Consortium coming through.

Lacea was oblivious to Kane's allusion. She responded in the negative as she looked at the generator hookup with wide eyes. "How will this work?" she asked.

Brigid glanced up for just a second as she used a wrench to tighten a connector tube with a steel clamp fastening. "Flag had noted some investigations into the principle of waking up a freezie," she said. "Working off those, I've jury-rigged this to pump a sudden shock through his system. If my calculations are correct, it will work a bit like a defibrillator, shocking Flag's heart back to life."

Lacea's hand went over her head in a swift stroke. "You've totally lost me," she admitted.

"Frankenstein science," Brigid said. "One single big burst of energy and we wake the subject."

"Okay," Lacea said tentatively. "Is it going to hurt?"

A wry smile crossed Kane's lips as he answered the young comm officer's question. "He's about to get hit by quite a few volts of energy after being asleep for almost three hundred years," he said. "Probably going to be a bit of a shock to the guy."

Brigid sighed at Kane's statement, consoling herself that his terrible pun wasn't intentional. "Let's just do this, shall we?" she stated as she locked the final connector in place.

A moment later, Brigid was standing back at the control board, a pair of little square-framed spectacles now perched on her nose, while Kane and Lacea waited before the glass cylinder containing the motionless form of Abraham Flag.

"Well," Kane muttered as Brigid started the power-up sequence on the generators, "here goes nothing."

Within seconds, the generators whirred to life, chugging

in place as their power slowly started to build. Two generators sounded fine, but the third rumbled twice and then shuddered to a halt, visibly rocking in place. Brigid peered up, looking over the frames of her glasses, annoyance creasing her brow.

"I've got it," Kane called as he saw Brigid take an irritated step away from the control board to look at the malfunctioning generator. Kane walked briskly to the jenny, kneeled and checked the connections, tightening them with strong hands. "Any better?" he asked as the generator chugged back to life.

Brigid examined the readouts on the control board that was inset beneath the main glass plate of the podium-style desk. There were five semicircular needle displays that were gradually ticking in unison toward the one-third point. Next to the dials, an analog counter showing white numbers on black wheels was moving at a gradual speed, fast enough to be perceptible but far from racing. As long as it kept steady, Brigid knew she shouldn't have anything to worry about. Beside that, another analog register showed a counter running down toward zero, and the display beside it looked like a clock face, circular with a thin needlelike hand that flitted this way and that, like a confused compass searching for magnetic north.

Brigid checked the comprehensive notes that Professor Flag had left before she leaned forward, flipping two switches and tapping at the circular dial until the needle settled at a point that was roughly at the ten-o'clock position. Now and then, the needle would spin around 360 degrees, but it seemed more settled now than it had before.

"Baptiste?" Kane asked again, still kneeling beside the erratic generator that was chugging angrily to itself.

"Better," she assured him without looking up from the display board.

Kane rose and made his way back to where he had been standing with Lacea at the front of Flag's cryogenic cylinder. The generators continued to groan, but they seemed to be firing regularly now, their charges building in parallel.

Brigid quickly flicked back a few pages of the notebook, checking for something she had only skimmed before. The procedure was simple enough. She was to extract the cryogenic mist first, and then fire the shock through the cylinder where it would be automatically channeled through Flag's resting body. Hit with the charge, Flag should be woken from his dreamless sleep. At least, that was the theory. But there was a big risk attached. For one thing, Brigid estimated that they would only have time for one jolt; if it didn't work they simply could not waste any more time dealing with the old freezie while the angels stalked just outside the secret base. Furthermore, once the cryogenic mist was extracted, the man in the tube either had to be revived or he would die. Given more time and better equipment, Brigid was certain she could bring Flag back to consciousness, but that was a luxury she simply did not have.

Brigid's pale hand reached forward, and she twisted a black knob counterclockwise. Inside the glass tube, pumps started to thrum and the bluish cryogenic mist began to be extracted through the vents.

Brigid peered at the control board, watching as the quintet of needles wavered on their pivots before finally passing the halfway point. Beside the cryogenic cylinder, the generators banged out their angry symphony as the power of the charge continued to build.

APPROXIMATELY one mile away, in the tunnel leading to the hangar entrance, the seven angels were moving ahead once more. They walked through the wall of snow that had been dislodged from the ceiling, burning a perfectly circular tunnel through it as they paced ahead, having communed with the snow stuff and made a convincing argument for its discorporation. The snow barrier parted now, fluttering away as the angels neared, pretty six-pointed dendrites whirring all about their beautiful glowing forms.

Through the gap in the snow wall, the angels moved onward, part flying, part walking as they continued through the eerily lit tunnel. Beyond the fallen ceiling, the tunnel was empty once more, just an icy road leading forward, lit by those peculiar bars that lined its ceiling. Six of the angels simply glowed, while the seventh—Adriel—also burned with fire.

The garden had to be purged.

# Chapter 23

Back in the lab, Brigid watched as the display needles flickered past the three-fourths mark and made their shuddering way toward maximum. She was holding her breath now, albeit unconsciously, as the charge built further and further.

Kane stood before the cryogenic cylinder, waiting for some sign of the man inside returning to life. Lacea watched from behind Kane, feeling trepidation at the mad science that was being performed before her.

Brigid spoke softly then, her voice carrying even over the thudding sounds of the generators. "Shocking in five seconds," she said. "In four. In three…"

AT REST IN THE cryogenic mist, Abraham Flag had thought of nothing in over 250 years. Utter blankness had consumed his mind, a tragedy when one considered that it was arguably the most accomplished mind of his day. Now it contained only nothingness, swirling and turning, waiting patiently for thought to someday return.

Once Brigid engaged the wake-up sequence, the generators chirruping to themselves as they rumbled beside the glass tube, Abraham Flag's mind had begun to awaken. A jolt had blasted through his body, but he had not felt that, as it had come while he was still asleep in the embrace of nothingness.

But after the jolt to his body, his awakening was like a rebirth. His synapses fired, the tiny electrical currents leaping across the centers of his brain, running in their natural playground once again, like frogs leaping from lily pad to lily pad.

The mind of a human being worked in pictures. Visual references, the use of color to represent emotion and mood—that was how the human brain was hardwired. When people slept, they dreamed, and when they awakened they could see thoughts as clearly as they saw the world. People were creatures of pictures, and Flag understood in that instant how all the words were just thought-forms, ways to make the pictures appear.

Stuck between slumber and awakening, Abraham Flag saw the white sheet he had seen one time before, back when he had peered into the impossible hole in the air above Isle Terandoa. The sheet was a beautiful, crisp white, the pure virgin whiteness of fallen snow. But it was marred already, the black splotches splattering across it in their disturbing patterns, clumping into little blocks. And now, as Flag watched the strange shadow play in his head, he saw something he had not perceived before. That virgin white plain was changing, losing its luster, turning from its brilliant whiteness to the off-white color of milk.

The edges of the yellowing expanse wizened, curling inward in the same way that fingernails will begin to curl if they grow too long. As the edges pulled away, Flag saw the dark color of the bleed that the whiteness had rested upon, that the white sheet had covered. Then the bleed was revealed once more in all its hideous scarlet substance, pulsing with demented life.

Was the sheet there simply to hide the bleed, or did the bleed feed the sheet until it bloated, curled and was destroyed?

Disturbed, Flag pondered that question, his synapses firing faster, bringing him back to life.

And suddenly his eyes snapped open, twin amethysts in his hard-planed face, and he saw a mishmash of bright colors where the Laboratory of the Incredible stretched out before him, its icy ceiling high over his head.

"HE'S COMING OUT of it," Kane said, peering at the waking figure in the glass cylinder. Instinctively the ex-Mag pushed Lacea back as he himself approached the cylinder.

Brigid looked up from where she worked at the control board of the cryogenic sequencer. "How does he seem?"

"I can't tell," Kane replied. "I don't think his eyes are focusing yet."

Beside the cryonics cylinder, the generators were powering down, their shock pulse spent. One of them shook for a moment, and then it sparked as something blew inside it. A moment later, a small electrical fire burst to life on its metallic surface, spitting sparks in a little explosion.

"Lacea, can you—?" Kane began.

"On it," Lacea assured him, running across to the fire and smothering the flames with one of the blankets that she had brought for Flag. Grayish-white smoke plumed from the blanket for a moment, and Lacea stamped at it until it stopped sparking.

"I'm going to open the cylinder," Brigid called across to Kane. "You may want to stand by to catch him if he falls."

Kane nodded, watching as the last of the blue gas was vented from the cylinder. "Just count me in," he said, stepping closer to the transparent pod.

"In three," Brigid said, turning a dial on the inlaid desk, watching as the quintet of needles slowly reverted to zero with the loss of power from the generators.

Kane spread his arms wide as Brigid counted down to

zero, and they both watched as the glass front of the cylinder pulled away on hidden motors, sinking down into the base of the unit.

Naked, almost godlike, the statuesque form of Abraham Flag stood fully revealed, icy wisps trailing from his artificially cooled skin.

Very slowly, Flag's eyes drifted downward until they lit on Kane where the ex-Mag was standing before him, ready to catch him should he fall.

THERE WAS SOMETHING in the bleed, Flag realized, as the redness that swirled before his eyes began to take shape. His skin felt strange now; it tingled and yet it was such a distant sensation, so much so that it might, he thought, have been the skin of someone else that was merely being described to him. The red swirl of the bleed was before him, all around him, and he saw the bland colors beyond it, the whiteness of the weird plain. Was it truly there, or was it simply something he saw, a fault in his vision, a scratch on the lens of his eye?

He peered down, conscious that the something that was in the bleed was standing before him, a human figure painted in vilest red, its features a frightening blur.

*The devil.*

KANE WAS READY for the semiconscious form of Abraham Flag to fall toward him, but he wasn't prepared for the freezie to snap awake and take a pop at him. Flag's right fist powered forward and down, connecting with the left side of Kane's face with sledgehammer force, knocking the ex-Mag off his feet.

Kane was disoriented for a moment, but his body went into an automatic routine, rolling to avoid Flag's follow-up.

With cool wisps of cryogenic gas trailing in his wake, Flag leaped from the open cylinder and lunged for his fallen foe, the man he believed to be the devil. He crouched, swinging his shoulders as he drove another sledgehammer punch at Kane's rapidly retreating form.

Kane rolled swiftly to one side, and Flag's forceful blow cut the air beside him, missing his head by no more than an inch. Kane's senses were still reeling from that first punch, but already he was trying to piece together what had just happened, to make sense of the chaos. Abraham Flag had been violently awakened from a near three-century slumber, and he was either expecting trouble or had convinced himself he had already found it.

Rolling to the side, Kane reached for a workbench and pulled himself back up to his feet, spreading his legs as he assumed a wrestler's stance. Across from him, standing close to the open casket of the cryogenic cylinder, the powerfully muscled form of Abraham Flag raised himself from the floor and glared at Kane, his amethyst eyes burning with hatred.

"We don't mean to harm you," Kane called, raising his empty hands in a gesture of peace.

Flag either didn't hear or he didn't care. Instead, like a charging bull, he ran at Kane, head down, back bowed, driving his right shoulder into Kane's gut as the Cerberus warrior tried desperately to get out of the man's whirlwind path. Ancient freezie or not, Flag moved incredibly fast, Kane realized as his boots scuffed against the tiled floor and he was driven backward into a desk full of glassware. The glass was thrown everywhere as Kane toppled over it.

From her place at the control desk, Brigid Baptiste watched, wondering at the speed of the sudden battle that had erupted mere feet away from her.

"What's happening?" Lacea asked, looking up from where she was stamping out the final evidence of the burning generator.

"I don't know," Brigid admitted as the two powerful figures crashed past her.

Kane stopped abruptly as his back was slammed into a workbench, and he toppled backward over it, the pain of the blow screaming through his kidneys.

Flag's body held enormous power, and Kane recognized the fighting techniques that the man was employing—he was using weight and momentum to ensure every one of his attacks caused the maximum amount of damage.

Kane pulled himself off the floor as Flag's bare foot whipped toward his face, clipping him across the chin in a glancing blow. Even that glancing blow had incredible impact, Kane noted as lights flashed before his vision.

Kane stumbled backward as this juggernaut of a man took another swing at him, left fist rushing toward Kane's face. Even as Kane sidestepped the blow, Flag drove a low punch into his gut, connecting with such force that Kane was lifted off the floor, his breath blurting out of his mouth in a sudden, strained gasp.

Kane fell back, knocking over a holder full of test tubes, their cylindrical glass shapes spinning free and shattering on the floor beside him where he landed.

"Please, Professor Flag," Kane said, the words coming through loud, gasping breaths. "We mean you no harm."

Flag ignored Kane's pleas, lunging at the floor and reaching his hands around Kane's neck.

That's it, Kane decided as Flag's hands closed around his throat. *You want a fight, you'll get one.*

Kane's arms whipped up, and his hands clapped hard against Flag's ears, the sound echoing through the ice-walled room. Flag grunted, and his grip on Kane's neck loosened fractionally as he pulled himself away. Kane didn't hesitate. His hands were already down at the man's belly, jabbing him in the sides with twin flat-palm blows. The man's skin felt awesomely cold, as if he were something carved from marble.

Flag growled as Kane's blows connected, and he spit his breath out of his open mouth. Kane gripped at Flag's wrists, pulling the man's grasping hands away from his throat, feeling the soreness there where his windpipe had been scratched in the tussle.

Flag struggled out of Kane's grip, swinging another almighty punch at the ex-Mag's head. Kane turned his head away, and the potent blow struck him in the left shoulder instead, immediately making the whole of his arm go numb.

Swiftly Kane drew his legs in, wrenching them under Flag's body and then kicking them out in a rapid snap that dislodged the man from atop him.

Flag fell backward, bare feet sliding on the icy floor as they sought purchase, wisps of cryogenic mists floating up all around him. And then he was back on his feet, his head whipping around to pierce Kane with his purple stare as he raised his hands in those brutal, bone-shaking fists.

In a heartbeat, Flag's powerful figure leaped from the floor, his left leg snapping out to deliver a savage kick to Kane's chest. Again Kane was knocked backward, struggling to keep his balance at the continued onslaught of the raging figure before him.

Flag swung another blow at Kane's head, his left fist rocketing through the air in a formidable cross. With his own left arm still numb, Kane blocked the blow with his right, absorbing its force and letting himself drop just a little with the impact. As he dropped, Kane's leg swept out and hooked behind Flag's knees, whipping the man from his feet.

As Abraham Flag slumped to the ground, Kane danced backward on light feet, keeping a low center of gravity as he watched his exceptional opponent warily.

Slowly, with no sign of irritation on his chiseled features, Abraham Flag stood up once more, his eyes locking with Kane's.

"There's been a heck of a mistake here, Professor," Kane said as he readied himself for another attack. "I'm not your enemy."

FLAG LOOKED at the figure before him, seeing the swirling red of the bleed playing across the man's skin. It was something in his eyes, he realized now, like a trick of the light. The man was saying words, distant, like echoes from within a cave. He was saying that he wanted to help.

Tentatively Flag unbunched his fists, and saw for the first time the streak there, on the surface of his right hand. That tiny wound, like a paper cut, where his index finger met with his palm. The cut shifted as he watched it, pulsating in place on the surface of his flesh.

"Professor?" the devil asked, his voice coming to Flag's ears as though from a long way off.

Flag looked up once more, seeing the man standing amid the roiling sea of the bleed. "I'm infected," he said simply, holding out his hand for the other to see.

KANE STEPPED closer, watching Flag intently as the man held out his hand. The fight seemed to have left him as suddenly as it had appeared, Kane realized, and instinctively he felt he was in no more danger.

Still keeping a wary distance, Kane peered at the tiny wound on Abraham Flag's hand and wondered at its relevance. It was a red streak and it seemed a tiny, inconsequential thing, but that didn't mean it was unimportant. As he looked at it, Kane saw the streak move, shifting in place like a leaf caught in a draft. It pulsed, as red as blood.

"Baptiste," Kane called. "You need to look at this."

Brigid was already running over to them, her eyes on Kane where the man's face was bruised and bloodied. "Are you okay?" she asked.

"Forget me," Kane snapped, shaking his head. "Look at the professor's hand."

Brigid peered at Abraham Flag's outstretched palm and saw the tiny sliver that marred the skin beside the joint of the index finger. As she watched, the wound pulsed, redness visible through the space as its sides parted like lips, tiny white lights dancing within.

"Oh, shit," Brigid said.

Flag's mysterious eyes widened at Brigid's response. "With all due respect, I hardly think there's need for that kind of language, ma'am," he told her.

A self-conscious smile crossed Brigid's face as she responded. "My name is Brigid Baptiste and I'm—*we're*—here for your help, Professor."

"Mrs. Baptiste," Flag said politely, "I'd offer my hand but under the circumstances, as you can see, that may not be prudent."

Brigid gestured toward Kane, who was rubbing at his left arm to bring the sensation back. "This is Kane, my partner."

Flag nodded. "I think that perhaps I owe you an apology, sir," he said. "I'm not entirely sure what I saw when I awoke, but it wasn't you."

Kane shrugged, and then winced at the aching pain it caused in his shoulder. "Think nothing of it. We all wake up grumpy sometimes."

Brigid introduced Lacea, who came over with a second blanket, which she placed over Flag's wide shoulders.

"I must apologize for my appearance," Flag said to her, seeming to only now realize that he had been fighting naked.

"Quite all right," Lacea assured him, her eyes on the man's well-defined pectorals.

Pulling the blanket over his shoulders, Flag turned back to address Kane. "You all seem to know who I am," he observed. "Perhaps you would be so kind as to explain who you are and what you're doing in my laboratory."

Kane winced as he felt the feeling beginning to return to his arm in a sensation of pins and needles. "We're adventurers and explorers, I guess you'd say, much like you," he said. "We came here looking for help with an urgent problem, and what we found was…well, you, frozen in stasis."

"Can I presume that you are the leader of this team, Mr. Kane?" Flag asked.

Kane ran a hand through his hair. "Well, kind of," he said, "although Baptiste calls the plays more often than I do. And Lacea here's just along for the ride.

"Baptiste's the one who revived you," Kane added, "not me."

Brigid removed her spectacles and returned them to her inside pocket. "I bypassed the wake-up protocols to rush through the failsafe mechanism you'd installed," she said, "which allowed me to jolt you to life in the manner of a defibrillator."

Flag pulled at the blanket he had wrapped over his shoulders, briefly exposing and examining his own chest. "The application of electrodes to the heart," he muttered. "But there's no surgical wound with which one might—"

"I employed the conductivity of the cryogenic tank itself," Brigid explained.

"Remarkable," Flag said. "You seem to be a very capable woman."

"Thank you," Brigid said as a blush rose to her cheeks.

Abraham Flag looked from Brigid to Kane, and he was clearly deep in thought. "The only capable woman I ever met in my line of work turned out to be a fascist temptress," he said wistfully.

Kane nodded. "Oh, they're still around," he said. "Always the pretty ones."

A broad smile tugged at Flag's lips. "I suspect that you and I have a lot in common, Mr. Kane," he said.

Brigid had made her way back to the control panel and was checking that the jury-rigged system was powering down correctly. "Why don't you get dressed, Professor," she suggested, "and I'll take a look at that wound while we explain our current situation to you."

"I have a medical kit in my quarters," Flag said as he reached for the pile of clothes that Lacea had neatly stacked on the chair. "Of course, I have a few questions of my own, yet. To begin with, what year is this?"

Kane took a deep breath as he phrased his response.

THE ANGELS WERE now just a few hundred yards from the doors to the Laboratory of the Incredible when they encountered the final obstacle. This was where Grant had unleashed the last salvo from the Scorpinaut, destroying yet another section of the roof, creating an artificial cave-in.

This barrier would be easy to pass now that the angels understood snow so much more fully than they had when they had first entered the garden. They could simply speak to it in its cold tongue, requesting that it part for them.

Sazquiel stepped forward and began to speak in the language of the ice.

# Chapter 24

"This is the part I hate," Carver said, and though he spoke quietly, his voice carried across the now silent room. He was standing across from the sonic drill, a desk before him for cover, and his eyes were fixed on the barricade that hid the hangar door.

"What's that, Carver?" Grant asked from his position at the driver's post atop the drill.

"Waiting for something to happen," Carver said. "That's the part I never liked about being a Magistrate. Investigating crimes, busting perpetrators—all that 'doing stuff' was great. If the job had just been that, I think I probably wouldn't have walked away from it."

"Kane doesn't like waiting for stuff, either," Grant replied after a moment's consideration. "He gets antsy. I don't mind it so much. That's why we make a good team, I guess. It's all a balancing act."

From beyond the doors, Carver and Grant heard just the faintest echoes of movement as the angels drew ever closer, destroying the final snow barricade.

DESPITE THE MANNER in which they had first met, it struck Kane that Professor Abraham Flag was among the very calmest individuals that he had ever met. Flag had taken in stride the news that he had been woken in the twenty-third century. Now fully dressed, the man sat on his bed in the Spartan adjunct room that served as his living quarters next to the trophy room, wrapping a bandage around his right hand.

Brigid had examined the wound and silently recognized what it was—a scar to another world. The cryogenic process had held it at bay, and for the moment it remained in stasis as Flag's body warmed up, neither growing nor shrinking. But that was a situation that could not conceivably last long.

Kane stood near to the door, his body adopting a naturally upright position, a habit from his years of service as a Magistrate. Brigid crouched beside the bed, offering Flag her assistance with the bandage, which he politely declined.

Lacea was just outside the room, examining the trophies in their cabinets while things were quiet.

"It's not a normal cut, is it?" Brigid finally said, her eyes meeting Flag's as he snipped at the bandage with a small pair of scissors, trimming it to size.

"No," he said. "I received this cut from a supernatural knife."

"Godkiller," Brigid said, nodding. "That's why we're here, Professor."

"I saw that stone blade cut a nonsensical hole in time and space," Flag said pensively. "It was a terrible thing, a wash of sensory input exuding from that rent in the air. The blade took control of my—" he stopped, sadly recalling Demy Octavo once more "—an acquaintance of mine. It began to eat at her, blotting her mind, writing over her thoughts. I saw it and I wondered at what I could do. And then the hole in space appeared and I saw something."

"Saw what?" Kane asked from where he stood beside the doorway.

"Something red," Flag said. "It's difficult to describe."

"We saw it, too, Professor," Kane told him. "Felt it in our heads."

"It's called the bleed," Flag said. "Don't ask how I know that, because I could not provide a logical explanation. I simply know."

"We think," Brigid proposed, "that this bleed is in actuality a part of the inner workings of the universe, the building blocks of reality."

Flag nodded, placing the scissors back in the first-aid kit that sat beside his bed. "I think there's another level," he said in his smooth voice, "something we're not meant to see."

"What kind of something?" Brigid asked.

"The bleed exists for a reason," Flag told them. "I feel as if I know what it is, as though the reason is there, in front of my eyes, and yet I can't quite make it out."

"What about the cut on your hand?" Brigid asked softly.

"That's a part of it," Flag told her. "When that knife touched me, the bleed infected my body. It's small now, but it will grow unless something can be done about it. Another hole will open up, and then it will all start over. That's why I froze myself. I could think of no other way to stop the bleed spreading. I'm afraid that I still can't."

"And now we've released you," Kane groaned. "Sorry, man, we should have realized when we read over your notes."

Flag considered the new dressing on his hand. "No matter," he decided. "You woke me for a reason, and my wound is a difficulty that we shall address in its own time. Why did you wake me, Mr. Kane?"

Kane drew a deep breath before he spoke. "Things came

out of the hole that Godkiller created," he began. "Things we don't know how to stop."

"And if we don't stop them," Brigid added, "they're going to kill everyone on the planet."

Flag nodded, considering the problem. "What is the precise nature of the things that we are talking about?"

"We think they're angels," Kane said.

OUTSIDE THE LITTLE room that formed Flag's meager living quarters, Lacea was examining the remaining cabinets that held the odd treasures Flag had saved over the years. One cabinet contained the hand of a statue, and as Lacea peered at it, the hand appeared to move, to shift inside the glass box.

Lacea's heart pounded in her chest, and she scooted away from the eerie marble hand, her heels clacking against the broken glass that covered the floor. She watched for a moment, wondering if the hand would move again, but nothing happened.

As she stepped closer, the carved hand seemed to flinch just momentarily, and Lacea realized what it was. The hand was like one of those paintings, the ones where the eyes seem to follow you around the room. Somehow the marble hand had a similar property. It seemed to move, but it never did; it just remained, guiding the viewer with its pointing finger.

Bolder now, Lacea placed her palm against the transparent front of the locked cabinet, closely watching the frozen hand until her breath misted the glass. "I wonder where you came from," she whispered.

Unmoving, the hand did not reply.

*April 11, 1929*
*Sendai City, Japan*

IT WAS LIKE one of those nightmares where you're running as fast as you can but getting nowhere, like wading through quicksand and slowly sinking. Flag's amethyst eyes darted around, searching for anything that would help him find his way to the center of the maze while listening for the heavy clunk of metal that told him his pursuers were catching up.

Everything was crumbling and rusting and overgrown. The maze was almost impassable in places, where the hedges had reached toward one another and begun to entwine. But Flag determinedly fought his way through, ignoring the cuts that now covered much of his face and arms.

Waking whatever was inside those suits of samurai armor had been a mistake, and he was now paying for it. At least the rust that dulled their once-shiny surfaces was slowing them and giving him a slight advantage. Not much of one, though, because their swords made easy work of the burgeoning undergrowth. Looking over his shoulder without slowing his pace, Professor Flag could see the flash of metal slicing up the greenery that he had just scrambled and struggled through.

As he turned back, Flag ran past an ivy-covered statue standing where there used to be an archway in the hedge. Was it his imagination or did it really stick a hand out from the greenery and point one of its long marble fingers? He didn't have time to check.

Flag instantly ran in the direction that the statue dictated, following its silent instruction without question. He had to trust that the statue was putting him on the right track and not leading him into the path of a living suit of armor.

Finally, with the statue's help, Flag reached the center of the maze and for the moment even his keen ears could not hear the suits of armor behind him. But there was nothing in the center bar four more statues surrounding a mossy, circular slab of stone. Flag took a second to catch his breath and think.

As he frantically gulped in the warm air, all four statues slowly moved and pointed straight down, toward the slab on the ground between them. Quickly following their direction, Flag scraped some of the chartreuse moss off the slab and saw that the stone there was heavily cracked. He took a little run-up and jumped onto the stone slab, praying that the momentum and his weight would be enough. It was. The slab crumbled beneath him and Flag fell into the darkness, surrounded by fragments of shattered stone. The last thing he saw before the daylight disappeared was the glint of metal as the suits of armor finally reached the center of the maze above him....

"ANGELS," FLAG repeated quietly, showing no emotion.

"They're beautiful beings of light," Brigid told him, "and they fly. We see them as angels, but we think they're probably some kind of antibody that was attracted here when the knife Godkiller cut a breach in reality."

"They came and sealed the hole," Kane explained.

"But once the hole was sealed," Brigid continued, "they began 'judging' and then killing everyone in sight. *Everyone.*"

"Angels," Flag said again, still shocked by the term. "Angels that kill."

"They sense something in us," Brigid told him. "An impurity that shouldn't be there, something that's been wired into our genetic structure for millennia."

"This impurity is in everyone?" Flag queried.

Brigid nodded somberly. "Everyone."

"If mankind is broken, is flawed," Flag lamented, "then that would explain many things. About the human race. Why man has a propensity to turn to evil."

"That's not true," Kane told him, an edge to his voice.

Abraham Flag looked up at Kane with sorrowful eyes. "I have seen many sights in this world, Mr. Kane," he said, "and the vast majority of them can be explained through man's inhumanity to his fellow man. A few of us, myself and I would hope you and Mrs. Baptiste here included, may try to stem that tide of inhumanity, may try to hold back the evil, but there are truly very few of us indeed. Evil isn't cold and calculating, it isn't the sinister machinations of a man who hides in the shadows and asks that he be addressed only as 'Master.' It is in the tiniest acts, the petty selfishness, the quick temper that people display every day.

"When I locked myself in my cryogenic apparatus," Flag continued, "I had a greater reason than simply preventing the release of the infection I had inside my body. I had begun to wonder if the world was broken, and what I saw there, in the bleed, made me suspect that, fundamentally, I was right."

Kane's blue-gray eyes locked with those of the three-hundred-year-old adventurer. "You're wrong," he said. "The bleed was messing with your head. The very fact that people like you exist is proof that the system is not flawed."

"Like me?" Flag asked.

Kane stepped forward, reaching his hand out to firmly grasp Flag's. "Like *us*," he said.

Flag shook Kane's hand. "Are there others? Like you and Mrs. Baptiste?"

Kane nodded. "There are a few. We work together, kicking

down the old statues, exposing the lies that placed them on their pedestals to begin with."

Abraham Flag sat there in silence, considering everything that Kane and Brigid had told him. Finally he nodded, as though having made a difficult decision. "Beings of light, you said," he mused, rising from the bed and pacing through the doorway.

Brigid and Kane followed as the man stalked through his obscure trophy room, searching for something he clearly knew to be there. Lacea stepped aside as the mightily proportioned man brushed past her.

"So what do you propose, Professor Flag?" Brigid asked, walking fast to keep up with him.

When he turned to her, there was a grim smile on Flag's face. "We'd need to consider basic optical theory—how is it that we see these creatures, do they exist as anything more than light waves?"

"They have substance," Kane told the professor. "They can grab things, and my partner Grant slugged one in the chin."

For the first time in over 250 years, Abraham Flag laughed, a pleasing, genuine sound in the chaotic surroundings of the debris-strewed trophy room. "It's refreshing to hear that some things never go out of fashion," he said.

"Grant can be kind of direct," Kane told him. "You'd probably get along."

"It sounds as if we might, at that," Flag agreed before turning his attention back to the problem. "So, hard light principles come into play in our equation."

"The angels are mutable," Brigid said. "We've seen them catch bullets, and we've seen bullets pass straight through them."

"Catching bullets," Flag muttered, chuckling a little to himself once again. "Now, that really does take me back."

Once Flag had finished chuckling, he addressed Brigid and Kane once more. "Have you considered employing the principles of refraction?" he asked. "Have you studied those with respect to these angels of yours?"

"I'm afraid we haven't had a whole lot of time for study, Professor," Brigid lamented.

"No matter," Flag said, standing before a glass-fronted display case. Within the cabinet there stood a plinth atop which was a blue velvet cushion on which rested a single item of jewelry—a gentleman's signet ring with a large sunset-red gemstone in its center.

"We don't have a lot of time now, either," Kane reminded the man as he peered at the ring through the glass panes. "You need that, Professor?"

"I remember the day I was given that ring," Flag said, ignoring Kane's question.

"What is that, a ruby?" Brigid asked.

"A very rare type of ruby, yes," Flag breathed. "Look at the way that it captures the light, bending it around its many facets."

"That's great," Kane said, unimpressed. "Real pretty." Kane found himself beginning to question the freezie's sanity.

"What you're looking at there is refraction, Mr. Kane," Flag stated, turning to look the ex-Mag in the eye. "The way that the light bends is a result of its changing speed as it enters another medium."

Kane nodded impatiently, listening to the ancient adventurer.

"This is how we shall trap your angels," Flag explained. "By refraction."

"We're going to need a pretty big ring there, ice pop," Kane told the older man.

Professor Flag smiled, turning from the cabinet and exiting

the room. "I believe that we have one," he said, looking to Brigid, "don't we, Mrs. Baptiste?"

For a moment, Brigid was mystified. Then, realization dawned and a broad smile appeared on her face. "As big as the whole of your laboratory," she said, marveling at the way that the light was held by the scarlet ring.

*January 10, 1927*
*Brooklyn, New York*

WITH THE MENACE of the winged stalker and his Olympian strongman ally finally ended, Abraham Flag looked around the darkened streets of Gotham, his keen eyes seeking his own ally in the shadows.

All he found was a glimmering bit of jewelry atop a heavy manila envelope.

Flag picked up the ring, and even his keen knowledge of precious gemstones was stymied by the unusual nature of the crimson jewel set within its plain golden band. His finely attuned sense of touch told him that this trinket was truly gold, and the cost of the setting would be prohibitive in terms of leaving such an item lying around where it might be lost. His ally's wealth had to have been far greater than Flag initially surmised.

He read the note within.

I am glad my misgivings about working with you were proved wrong. Make no mistake, your presence is not wanted in my circles, but should the need arise, wear this ring in public. It will be the signal that we must unite again.

The note was unsigned, and Flag knew that his mysterious counterpart would be impossible to trace through handwriting.

Flag pocketed the ring, then threw the note and its envelope into a trash can that had been lit to allow the hobos some warmth. It would be good to return to the environs he was more familiar with.

OUTSIDE THE Laboratory of the Incredible, in the tunnel leading to the hangar, the seven angels willed the last of the snow aside and pushed through the hangar bay doors. Beautiful Adriel continued to sparkle and fizz with the flames playing across her perfect body, while the others stalked ahead, reaching out with their minds in their search for the children.

The hangar was a strange place to the angels, one full of new things. As one, they marveled at what they saw there, the funny mechanisms that the children had created with their clever hands.

"Despite the infection," Domos observed as he peered at the dartlike airplane that Abraham Flag had used hundreds of years before, "they still make beautiful artworks."

Adriel peered at the fixed-wing aircraft, too, watching as her flames were reflected in its glossy surface. "What does this one do?" she asked.

Bateliel glanced at the aircraft for just a moment. "It is shaped like a fish. Perhaps it swims."

"But there is no water here, except for the frozen water," Domos complained. "How would a fish swim without water?"

"Perhaps it flies, then, swimming in the air," Bateliel said, his voice like drifting dust motes caught in the sunlight. "It matters not."

Abariel was close to the main entry doors, hovering past the Scorpinaut that Kane had parked at the back wall. "The children are through there," she said in her voice of song. "I can sense them, waiting for us. Waiting for judgment."

With a serene smile, Abariel reached forward and placed her left hand against the doors, pushing harder and harder, watching as its fragile structure began to bow.

GRANT TURNED the dial on the control board and felt the sonic cannon vibrate as it warmed up.

Ducked behind a desk close by, his retrofitted Sin Eater in hand, Carver gestured to the barricade and shouted, "They're coming through!" as if Grant hadn't already realized.

The artificial barricade shook one final time as the doors finally gave, and the first of the glowing angelic forms peered through. Even as the topmost desk tumbled to the floor, the miniexplosives triggered and the first four explosions went off, one after the other in rapid succession. The doors blew outward, crashing into the hangar bay as the pile of furniture shuddered and caught light. Then the stack crumpled just a little but held where it stood, smoke pouring from it toward the high, icy ceiling of the lab.

From outside, Grant and Carver could hear another blast as something in the hangar exploded. Most likely it was the gas tank of one of the vehicles, Grant guessed—the roadster, maybe.

As Grant turned the sonics dial to its maximum setting, watching the twin flickering needles whir as the charge built, his Commtact burst to life with Kane's voice.

"We heard an explosion. What's happening down there?" Kane asked urgently.

"Company," Grant explained as he engaged his Commtact's pickup, "of the angel variety."

"Are they in?" Kane demanded over the Commtact.

"Not yet," Grant told his partner. "I'm going to try the sonic blaster on them if they ever get past the door."

Kane gave a swift acknowledgment before breaking the communication link and getting back to whatever it was that was concerning him and Brigid.

Grant glanced up from the rising needles displayed on the dashboard as the sonic charge increased, and he saw the first of the angels stepping through the broken doors, shoving a heavy workbench aside, flames licking at her flesh.

"This had better work," Grant muttered as he eyed his target and depressed the button marked Drill.

The sonic cannon shook as Grant stood behind it, waiting to see what would happen next. There was a tickling within Grant's eardrums, a little like the way static was occasionally transmitted over the Commtact, and a wide beam of white noise blasted out of the drill bit, blaring toward the hangar door.

UPSTAIRS, ABRAHAM Flag was sketching a triangular design on a sheet of notepaper, working out dimensions in his head.

Kane cut into Flag's thoughts as he disengaged the Commtact communication with Grant. "They're here," he explained. "Downstairs. Coming through the hangar doors."

Flag showed the sketch he had created to Brigid. "Is this possible?" he asked her.

Brigid's green eyes roved over the design for a moment, considering the massive dimensions that Flag had proposed, and she nodded. "How will you cut it?" she asked.

"We'll use the drill," Flag replied.

BESIDE GRANT, Carver was firing short bursts from his Sin Eater, knowing that they were nothing more than irritants to the angels but still hopeful that they would keep the otherworldly beings in place long enough for Grant to use the drill. He turned to Grant, his teeth gritted. "I can't hear it," he shouted, "but I sure as hell can feel it."

Grant toggled a switch, adding power to the drill beam, feeling the change like a low bass note thumping through his body from another room.

The remaining desks were blasted aside under the power of that sonic blast, and then Grant saw something he had imagined was impossible. The angel—a willowy female figure floating just above the ground as she passed through the doorway—suddenly became larger as she took the full brunt of that furious beam of noise.

# Chapter 25

Pushing through the doors, Abariel stepped over the threshold and made her way past the explosive furniture to enter the vast, hidden room under the snow. Fires played across the stack of furniture as she pushed it aside, and another explosive charge went off, blasting over her left shoulder like an erupting volcano. As she shoved the furniture away, ignoring the explosion, a brutal blow slammed into her like a construction ball crashing against her rib cage, and she felt her breath—and more than that, her very substance—lurch out of her unbidden.

She could hear it, too, that strange frequency, powerful and all-commanding, so much like the word. As the sonic beam blasted into her, Abariel felt her body expand, doubling, then tripling in size in the space of a second. It was hard to keep hold of her shape now. Her fingertips seemed so far removed from her fingers, and they in turn seemed incredibly distant from their joints at her hands, hands that had left her wrists.

Abariel's luminescent form blasted in all directions, glowing particles firing off from her body like fireworks.

And her mind cried out, "The body must prevail."

GRANT WATCHED, amazed, as the angel expanded beyond the edges of her body, a star going supernova. He turned away, clenching his eyes closed as the angel disintegrated, a millions tiny flecks blasting in all directions, floating away like clouds dissipating on the wind.

Grant felt no satisfaction at the destruction of such a thing of beauty, but he assured himself it was the only way for him and his teammates to survive. Engaging the Commtact, Grant announced, "We got one."

Kane and Brigid's delighted response came through a moment later, and Kane demanded a full report.

"Not right now," Grant said, turning back to the doorway. A second angel, this time a male, peered warily through the gap there. Grant's hands played rapidly across the control board of the sonic drill, watching the needles flicker as it went through its recharge sequence. "Come on, you son of a bitch," he muttered, "let's see you judge your way out of this."

The needles reached optimum level and Grant's finger stabbed out, unleashing a second boom of white noise from the nose of the drill, blasting through the revealed doorway to the hangar.

The angel Damiel caught the full brunt of the blast of white noise, feeling its all-powerful blow clobber against his body.

"GRANT'S GOT THEM on the run," Kane explained to Flag as they hurried toward the exit of the trophy room. "Maybe we won't need you after all, Professor."

Flag's amethyst eyes burned with intensity as he worked the problem over in his mind. "The sonic beam won't work," he realized.

"It just has," Kane assured him. "Angel down. We're home free."

"The principles of sound say different," Flag corrected in a solemn tone. "A sound wave can influence a beam of light, but the influence in this instance will only be temporary. Once the audio waveform abates, the effects of its interference will cease."

Brigid peered back at all the weird mementos that stood silent vigil in Flag's trophy room. "You mean, the cannon— the drill—will run out of charge?" she clarified.

"More than that," Flag explained. "The intensity required to disrupt light can only be held for a brief period of time. The drill itself will burn out long before its effectiveness could make any true difference to your situation."

"*Our* situation," Kane corrected, locking eyes with the older man. "We woke you up for a reason, Professor."

Flag nodded. "Are you suggesting that that reason was to lie to make you feel safer, Mr. Kane?"

Kane spit a curse as he turned away from the unruffled three-hundred-year-old man.

A moment later, Flag led the way from the trophy room, his long-legged strides eating up the distance. Kane trotted at his side, while Brigid noticed that Lacea, the young communications officer, was holding back. She looked terrified. Seeing Lacea's reaction, Brigid stopped before her, taking the young woman's hands in her own and meeting her eyes with her own sympathetic gaze.

"Are you joining us, Lacea?" Brigid asked.

Lacea shook her head. "I thought… I hoped that they'd gone. That they'd leave us alone," she admitted. "I don't think I can help anymore, Brigid. I don't want to die."

Brigid nodded. "There's an old communications set on the main balcony," she said. "Wait there and see if you can use it to radio your friends in the consortium. Perhaps they can provide backup or organize an evac for everyone."

Sniffling, Lacea struggled to meet Brigid's gaze, and Brigid saw now that there were tears glistening on the young woman's cheeks. "You don't mind?" she asked. "If I don't fight, I mean."

Still holding one of Lacea's hands, Brigid turned and began to lead the way past the trophy cabinets after Kane and Flag. "In my experience, Lacea, heroes aren't always the people who fight the monsters," Brigid said. "Sometimes they're just the people who do what they can and don't run away."

Lacea wiped the tears from her face as she trotted through the trophy area with Brigid, running after the two men who hurried across the balcony.

"We'll have to create a distraction so that I can get to the drill," Flag was telling Kane as they ran toward the spiral staircase.

"These angels can be pretty mean bastards," Kane explained as he summoned the Sin Eater into his palm from its hidden holster. "You'll need to go get your gun."

"I've never needed one, Mr. Kane," Abraham Flag assured him, a twinkle in his eye.

Kane was muttering something as Brigid appeared behind him. "This guy's either cocksure or foolhardy," Kane growled as he hurried down the stairs.

Brigid smiled. "Remind you of anyone?" she asked suggestively.

Kane glanced at her, seeing the coquettish grin that was playing at her features. "Ah, stow it," he chastised, but there was humor in his friendly tone.

Behind them, Lacea had found the radio unit that Brigid had mentioned, tucked away in the far corner of the balcony, past the door to the trophy room, and she began working at the dials, trying to equate the antiquated system to her modern knowledge of radio transmission.

GRANT SET the sonic drill to recharge as the third angel stepped through the open doorway. This one was aflame, fire racking over her perfect body, and yet she seemed to be in no evident pain. The doorway with its furniture barricade had worked well as a bottleneck, trapping the angels and forcing them to enter one at a time. But they had become wary now, having seen two of their number—beautiful Abariel and the youthful Damiel—rent apart by the sheer force of the white noise beam.

Flaming Adriel stepped through into the main lab, and Grant spit a curse as the sonic cannon continued its recharge; he had never known eight seconds to last so long. Then suddenly the needles clicked to maximum. Grant peered up as he directed another brutal blast of hard sound at the doorway, but the flaming angel had already stepped out of its path, her feet whipping across the floor as she sped toward him.

The sonic drill shook as it unleashed another three-second burst of white noise, slamming into the remaining furniture that stood burning around the doorway to the hangar before blasting through, driving some hunk of whining machinery back in its wake.

The beam missed the lead angel, and her burning form leaped atop the vehicle that contained the drill. The whole of her glowing body was covered in flames like some awful human torch. With Carver busy continuing to rake the doorway with bullets from his blaster, Grant did the only thing he could: he punched the flaming angel in the face as she closed in upon him. It was like hitting a brick wall. Grant's knuckles struck the angel's burning flesh and they seemed to simply stop, his whole body lurching as he tottered in place atop the drill with the force of his own blow. Instantly, his hand began to throb with the pain of his punch. Before Grant, the angel's palm reached forward for his forehead, flames licking at her fingers.

As the angel made to touch him, Grant fell back, dropping from the edge of the cannon. Adriel snatched at him, but all she got was a handful of air—Grant was gone.

Over at the doorway, Bateliel, Domos, Sazquiel and Vadriel stepped one by one across the threshold, their perfect glowing forms lighting the whole of the laboratory. Carver held the trigger down on his Sin Eater, blasting a steady stream of bullets at their approaching figures.

Bateliel dismissed the bullets without even thinking, bored now with the silver-shelled insects since he'd seen too many of them in his brief time in the garden. He shifted his form, working through the spectrum in a picosecond, allowing the hard bodies of the bullets to pass through his own with no effect.

Behind him, the ever-inquisitive Domos reached for one of the bullets and plucked it from the air, feeling the kinetic energy of its momentum shuddering through it as he halted its progress, bringing it to a dead stop. The other bullets he ignored, and they drilled against his pure white body, their pointed noses flattening as they met his ideal form.

Carver watched with dread as the four angels neared, their glowing forms like sunlight reflected on water, their feet never quite reaching to the floor of the hidden laboratory. With a dull clack, Carver's Sin Eater ran out of ammunition and clicked on empty. The angels were six feet away, stalking toward him with no rush to their movements, simply determination. There was no time to reload, to try drilling another wave of bullets pointlessly at the impervious, incredible beings of light. With a frustrated holler, Carver drew back his hand like a baseball pitcher and threw the reconditioned Sin Eater at the lead angel.

Bateliel watched as the gun flew through the air, slowing time through his angel's eyes to better observe its movement. To Bateliel it was another nest where silver-shelled insects lurked, ready to unleash their tiny specks of irritation on the garden. His hand snapped out, moving with breathtaking speed, the fingers held flat and straight. The thrown Sin Eater pistol was cut in two as it met with Bateliel's hand, and the split halves flew off in different directions, one slapping into a twinkling wall of ice while the other flew across the room, shattering a glass beaker on a desk before it finally landed in a basin with an echoing clatter.

AS HE HURRIED down the stairs, Flag gave instructions in a raised voice. "Kane and I will distract the angels," he said, "while Mrs. Baptiste will find a space to create our special trap."

"How does this triangle thing work anyway?" Kane asked, raising his voice to be heard.

Flag sprinted ahead, taking the steps three at a time. "First we need to construct it," he said, "and I'll require the drill for that."

Kane glared at Brigid, irritation marring his features. "If we're not careful, this old guy's going to be the death of us," he muttered.

"The dividing line between genius and madness is very thin, Kane," Brigid reminded him.

Flag led the way down the stairs, huge strides powering down the stairwell at a frenetic pace. Kane and Brigid hurried after the large man, their eyes flicking across to the action on the far side of the laboratory. They could see the distant figure of Grant as he fell from the sonic cannon at the same time that the glowing form of an angel swooped up and reached for him. The glowing angel appeared to be on fire, dark smoke billowing from her skin.

Over by the doorway, more of the glowing figures had emerged, clumped together and so bright that it was hard to tell just how many there were.

Flag leaped the last few steps of the staircase and sprinted along the walkway between worktables. He glanced back at Brigid, issuing his instructions. "Find a weak spot on the wall," he called, "and mark it up as rapidly as you can. There won't be much margin for error."

Kane looked annoyed as he chased after the retreating figure of Abraham Flag.

"He has a plan, Kane," Brigid assured him as she sprinted toward one of the sheer ice walls that surrounded the underground base.

"I just wish somebody would clue me in," Kane muttered as he hurdled over a workbench in pursuit of the revived adventurer.

Abraham Flag glanced back over his shoulder and shouted a command to Kane. "Cover me while I get the sonic drill," he called.

Sprinting after Flag, Kane engaged his Commtact. "Grant, we need the drill," he explained.

Flag looked at Kane, confusion marring his chiseled features. "What are you talking about?"

"Radio communication," Kane explained, indicating his ear. "My partner will help us if he can."

"Remarkable," Flag said, clearly impressed at the concept of Kane's hidden radio receiver.

As Kane explained, Grant's voice came back to him over

the Commtact receiver. "Kane, I am in a whole load of trouble here," Grant said. "Whoa!"

"What is it?" Kane asked.

AS THE ANGEL Adriel reached for him, Grant leaped away from the sonic cannon, moving in a snap-roll across the floor to evade his blazing pursuer.

"Got me an angel who just won't quit," Grant snarled over the Commtact. "Could do with a rescue if you have anything in mind."

Kane's voice came back over the Commtact a moment later. "I'll think of something," he assured his partner.

A little way from where he had landed, Grant saw Carver being mobbed by four of the glowing angel forms, their right hands stretching out to touch the man. Even as Grant struggled back to his feet, the angel quartet opened their mouths in that eerie way they had and spoke two words in unison, like a beautifully harmonized choir. "Impurity discovered."

Then Carver began to shriek as the angels cast judgment, turning around and around him. Carver's body began to disintegrate from the feet up as had Simona Jurist's back in the mobile base. Grant called the wrist-sheathed Sin Eater to his hand and began blasting bullets at the four glowing figures even before his brain had consciously made the decision. At the same time, Grant was running, head down, focused on the closest figure—the wise angel called Sazquiel.

Head down, Grant barged into the luminescent form of the angel, impacting against the dancing form of Sazquiel with all the force he could muster.

Sazquiel moved just three inches with the impact of Grant's attack, but it still shocked him more than anything had in millennia. He turned on Grant, studying this bull-like child of the garden, wondering at his incredible strength. His hand had disengaged from the screaming form of Carver, the child he was judging, and the dance of judgment had been broken. Such a thing had never happened, not in the *Book of the All*, which was the history of the garden.

"Child," Sazquiel spoke, his voice like rumbling thunder in the distance, "what have you done?"

Grant shoved the nose of the Sin Eater in Sazquiel's face, blasting a stream of bullets into the angel's blue-white eyes, the muzzle-flashes bright even against the angel's skin. Incredibly, Sazquiel felt annoyance then, a tiny, inconsequential thing that rankled at him. It was a new feeling, a new thing, and yet he did not treasure it as the angels had with the other new things that they had experienced. No, Sazquiel simply lashed out, anger overwhelming him at the thought of the broken dance of judgment. His pure white hand snapped out and batted Grant across the top of his chest.

Grant yelled in pain as he was shoved backward by the angel, tumbling over and over as he lost his footing. The world spun for a second through Grant's eyes, and then suddenly his head met with something solid and the world stopped in place once more. He peered up, pain hurtling through his skull, and saw Carver still standing ahead of him, standing and screaming. But there was something wrong— very, very wrong. Carver stood amid the icy walls of the Laboratory of the Incredible, his jaw open, a penetrating scream generating from his throat, and yet he had no feet. He just hovered there, completely static, his legs ending abruptly above the ankles where the judgment had disengaged.

Grant watched, horrified, as the five remaining angels

stepped across his vision, poised to judge him now, too. Behind them, two more glowing forms took shape, like people appearing in a mat-trans—it was the two angels that Grant had blasted apart with the sonic drill; somehow, they had pulled themselves back into solidity.

Together, seven angels—Heaven's number—approached Grant's fallen form, preparing to do the dance of judgment and forever excise him from the garden.

AS THEY CLOSED IN on the angels, Kane began firing triple bursts from his Sin Eater. The bullets raced ahead, but their effects were negligible.

Seeing that, Abraham Flag reached out and grabbed two ancient fire extinguishers from their resting place beside one of his worktables. Still running, he turned to Kane and thrust one of the red-painted extinguishers at him. "Do you know how to use this?" Flag asked.

"Sure," Kane said, sending his Sin Eater back to its hiding place in his sleeve, "but how old is it? Won't it have dried out by now?"

"Powder based," Flag explained as he twisted the nozzle open and leaped over a fallen stool. "It will be like throwing sand in their faces."

With that, Flag was on the angels as they loomed over Grant, spraying them with a blast of white powder from the fire extinguisher.

Kane followed, pulling at the chain that held his own fire extinguisher closed. An instant later, the fire extinguisher in Kane's hands started to blast a spray of cream-colored powder ahead of him.

Distracted, the angels swept at the cascade of powder,

hands in front of their faces. To the angels, the white powder was a thousand individual spots, all of them rushing through the air at them. It was fascinating and baffling all at once, like a cloud of gnats.

At the forefront of the angels, Vadriel reached for the powder, trying to bring it into one mass as it blasted toward his eyes. A second source added to the spray as Kane let loose with his own fire extinguisher.

"This is going to work for about three damn seconds," Kane growled as he sprayed the angels with more of the dampening powder.

"That's all I need," Flag assured him, leaping past the group of glowing figures in the direction of the sonic drill.

AT THE OTHER END of the laboratory, Brigid Baptiste was eyeing one of the glasslike, icy walls, appraising it as quickly as she could. It looked clean, and the light played off it in bright patterns with even the distant glow of the angels reflected there like a mirror.

"This is it," Brigid decided as she reached for a glass beaker that rested on a nearby work surface. Flipping the beaker in her hand, she smashed it against the edge of the desk, watching it shatter. Then she reached down and took one of the large shards, examining its sharp edge. It wasn't perfect, but it would do the job she had in mind.

A moment later, she was using the sharp shard of glass to mark out an isosceles triangle on the wall, rapidly comparing its dimensions to those in Flag's sketch as she clambered onto a chair to score the triangle's apex. The shard cut into the ice, leaving a tiny mark of about half an inch in depth, but Brigid felt certain that that would be sufficient. The triangle just needed to be used as a guide for Flag's endeavor, and the way that the glass cuts dulled the ice made their lines clear even from a distance.

Brigid stepped back and examined her handiwork approvingly. It looked as if a ten-foot-high triangular door had been cut there in the ice.

Glancing back to the scene of the battle, Brigid pulled her TP-9 pistol from its holster at her hip and prepared to lend her own covering fire for the final showdown.

# Chapter 26

Casting aside the powder-based fire extinguisher, Abraham Flag climbed atop the sonic drill unit and began working at the levers, turning the vehicle on its rear steering ball. He acknowledged Brigid with a curt nod, and his strong fingers played across the controls of the drill. It was fully charged, he realized, since Kane's partner had left it running when he had become enmeshed in the fracas with the glowing interlopers.

As the sonic blaster turned, Flag lined up the angels before him, estimating the range of the makeshift weapon in his mind. Kane was there, battling with the willowy, glowing angels, using up the last of his own extinguisher's contents in the face of the one nearest to him. Beside Kane, lying on the ground, a dark-skinned man was reloading the pistol in his hand, shouting instructions to Kane. A little way over, and strangest of all, another man was screaming as he stood rooted to the spot. As more of the attacking angels came into view of the drill bit, Flag's finger jabbed at the Drill button and he unleashed a shocking beam of white noise from the sonic blaster.

There was perhaps just the faintest of hums, felt deep inside the inner ear of Abraham Flag as the drill went off at its maximum setting once more. Then he watched stoically as four of the glowing creatures expanded like white paint dropped in water and seemed to disappear under the force of the incredible sonic beam. Kane and the other man seemed to reel from the blast of white noise, too, though its only effect was to thud against them like a strong wind. Purely physical creatures, neither of them could be affected by such a blast of sound in the way the ethereal beings of light were.

As Flag spun the drill in its tight turning circle, Kane's fire extinguisher ran dry. Kane glared at the three remaining angels, then flipped the metallic cylinder of the fire extinguisher into the gut of the nearest. It was like taking a hammer to a wall—it hit and knocked the angel slightly back, but the damage was minimal. The angel just hovered there, a curious smile tugging at his thin lips.

Kane growled as he swung the fire extinguisher in a looping arc, bringing it all the way around his body, building the momentum before he smashed it into the angel's smiling face. In return, the angel simply accepted the attack, peering at Kane with those pale, sympathetic eyes.

"Child," the struck angel—Sazquiel—said, "why must you harbor such anger for your games?"

"It's not anger," Kane spit. "It's survival."

Sazquiel seemed oblivious to the statement. His only response was to reach forward, palm flat, preparing to judge the errant child who had attacked his heavenly presence.

From behind Kane, Grant began blasting rounds from his Sin Eater, 9 mm slugs whizzing through the air just over Kane's shoulder, rocketing onward in the direction of Sazquiel as he reached forward.

Kane leaped aside as the stream of bullets continued to cut the air, and watched as they passed through the angel's glowing form.

On the balcony overlooking the vast laboratory area, Lacea had got the radio unit working and had sent out a distress signal on all frequencies. Whether anyone would hear, let alone respond, she couldn't guess. All she knew was that she didn't want to die this day.

Now she stood at the head of the staircase, staring down at the vigorous battle that continued at the far end of the vast, ice-walled room. The glowing beings she knew to be angels were fighting with her new friends. In the distance, Lacea could hear a terrible screaming coming from a man's throat, cracking in absolute pain as he held that awful, impossible note.

Suddenly four of the angels blew up like fireworks, their virginal white forms expanding with breathtaking speed before disappearing in a burst of incredible brightness. Lacea felt optimism at that, but it lasted less than a half minute. Even as she watched, the first of the blown-up angels re-formed from nowhere, his pure white form amassing as though from the very air itself, a cloud of fireflies that assumed glowing, humanoid form.

"They're indestructible," she breathed. "We don't stand a chance."

At the same moment, Abraham Flag was directing the cutting beam of the sonic drill, now set to a much lower frequency, on the ice wall of the laboratory, where Brigid had marked out the points of the isosceles triangle with the shard of glass. Flag channeled the cutting beam of hard sound inward so that each side of that triangular shape went in on itself, carving a three-sided pyramid the way one might cut a slice of apple. Ice chunks flew all about as the unseen beam of white noise ripped into the wall.

Beside the forming shape in the wall, Brigid watched the continuing battle at the far end of the lab. "They need help, Professor," she stated, and she began to run toward where Kane wrestled with the ghostly form of Sazquiel.

Flag leaped from the sonic drill and held his hand up to halt Brigid in her tracks. "No place for a woman," he said. "You finish things here."

Damping down her irritation at the man's comment, Brigid climbed atop the sonic cannon to take Flag's place as the time-lost adventurer began sprinting back to the glowing forms at the end of the laboratory.

He turned back just for a second, calling a further piece of advice to her. "Remember, it doesn't need to be perfect. It just needs to work. Have faith in science."

Brigid grimaced as she worked at the controls of the sonic cannon. "Just needs to work," she muttered, blasting the invisible sonic beam at the wall. "Right."

CLOSE TO THE hangar doors, Carver was still screaming, as though he had been locked in a fragment of time.

Grant was standing once more, looking a little woozy as he fired his Sin Eater at the glowing angel looming before Kane. Six other angels hovered close by, approaching where Kane battled with Sazquiel.

"We're running out of options," Kane barked as the angel ignored the bullets that passed through his heavenly form.

"There are always more options, Mr. Kane," Flag assured him as he leaped over the nearest desk and plowed into the angel Sazquiel. The glowing form just rocked in place, spinning as Flag rolled from him.

Grant watched in amazement as Flag ducked the angel's

lightning-fast grasping hands, moving just quickly enough to avoid the angel's attack. "Is that who I think it is?" he asked.

Kane nodded. "Abraham Flag, no longer on ice. Professor Flag, this is my partner, Grant."

Flag leaped out of the path of the attacking angel as Kane and Grant drilled it with bullets.

"Your friend here speaks highly of you, Mr. Grant," Flag acknowledged as he assessed the ex-Mag. "Although you're not quite what I pictured."

"Well, I hope I don't disappoint too much," Grant said as he scampered back from the looming forms of the luminescent angels.

"I have traveled the globe," Flag told him, grasping Grant's shoulder, "and I have learned that the color of a man's skin does not determine his ability."

Grant frowned. "Good to hear it," he said, though he wasn't entirely sure of the point that this olden-day adventurer was making.

ON THE LEVEL ABOVE, Lacea rushed back to the radio unit, stabbing at the resend button and willing for someone to hear the distress beacon she was broadcasting. She reached for the microphone attachment, a surprisingly heavy piece of equipment made of dull metal, and spoke into it.

"We need help," she said. "We need help."

It seemed to be all she could think to say.

At that instant, Lacea's attention was drawn by a cracking noise coming from below her, and she panicked for a moment that the balcony was going to give way. Running back to the stairwell, Lacea peered over its side and saw the tiny figure of Brigid, clearly identifiable because of her fierce red hair, using the sonic drill on one of the ice walls. Uneven fragments of discarded ice littered the floor where Brigid had sliced them from the wall.

As Lacea watched, the drill carved a large section from the wall with near surgical precision, causing a large triangle of ice to fall forward and rock in place gently, in the same careful way that a lumberjack might fell a redwood. The triangle— an elongated pyramid, Lacea saw now—was one-third of the height of the towering wall, approximately ten feet in all.

Lacea watched in curious amazement, wondering if Brigid planned to use the sharp tip of the ice pyramid to impale the angels.

STANDING ASTRIDE the sonic drill, Brigid shifted the controls and watched as the section of wall that she had carved broke loose, rocking forward in a beautiful demonstration of the application of the cantilever principle. Finally, the raised-back "hinge" of the ice triangle snapped away and it slid two feet across the floor, just a little way away from the wall.

Brigid looked at the glistening shape with openmouthed approval. "I can't believe this idea actually worked," she said to herself, before glancing back at the continuing battle at the far end of the lab.

Engaging her Commtact, Brigid called to Kane. "Tell Professor Flag that it's ready," she said. "For what it's worth," she added to herself grimly.

"GOOD WORK," Kane acknowledged Brigid as he unleashed another volley of shots from his Sin Eater at the luminescent forms.

Beside Kane, Grant was adding his own gunfire to the assault while Abraham Flag was rubbing at the bruised knuckles of his left hand where he had punched Sazquiel in his rockhard jaw. Furthermore, the bandage around Flag's right hand was turning red now from all the movement, where the awful wound had begun to break through.

"Baptiste says she's ready," Kane told Flag and Grant.

"We need to lead the angels to the far end of the laboratory," Flag explained. "Any ideas?"

Kane reloaded his blaster, never taking his eyes off the beautiful, glowing forms. "Oh, if we run they'll follow," he assured Flag. "They're like bloodhounds."

"Then let's start running," Flag said, ushering Kane and Grant ahead toward the ice pyramid.

Back amid the wreckage around the hangar bay doors, ex-Mag Carver continued to stand in place, his mouth locked open, emitting an awful, strained scream. Seven glowing angels hovered between the three men and the screaming figure.

"Someone has to do something for Carver," Grant decided, and he turned back. "You go on."

Kane looked at his partner for a moment. "It has to be all of us, Grant," he said. "Right now."

"Fine," Grant barked, "but I'm going back for him when we're all done."

Together, the three men began to run the football-stadium length of the vast laboratory, fists pumping, legs striding ahead as they sprinted through the room.

The angels sang as they pursued the scuttling forms of Flag, Kane and Grant through the main area of the laboratory, rushing toward where Brigid had carved the strange pyramid of glistening ice.

Grant glanced over his shoulder, seeing the beautiful, glowing forms as they hurtled ever closer.

"Keep going," Flag instructed, steely determination on his face.

Head down, Grant sprinted ahead, hurdling a fallen cabinet as he hurried toward the spiral staircase.

Brigid Baptiste waited by the ice pyramid, watching with frantic eyes from atop the sonic drill. Then she blasted a burst of white noise at the angels, keeping the settings below maximum now, just enough to slow them without temporarily discorporating them. As Brigid worked the drill controls, smoke began to pour from the back motor where it had overheated. She jabbed at the controls once more, trying to send another blast of white noise at the onrushing forms, but the display needles remained static; the sonic cannon was dead.

Brigid leaped from the smoking vehicle, her TP-9 in hand, and sent a stream of bullets over the heads of her companions.

As Kane and Grant ran past her, Brigid fired shots from the pistol, lashing the angels with 9 mm bullets. The angels ignored Brigid's attack, bored now with the silver-shelled insects that seemed to accompany the children wherever they went.

As they caught up with Brigid, Kane and Grant slowed, releasing their Sin Eaters from their hidden holsters once more and joining their teammate in her assault on the angels. Abraham Flag was fifteen paces away, still weaving through the walkways between the worktables. Kane couldn't quite comprehend how that had happened. The older man appeared to be incredibly fit, and he had been just paces behind them when he and Grant had set off. Had he deliberately slowed to allow the angels to catch him? Was he offering himself as bait for the trap that he and Baptiste had concocted?

"What the hell is he doing?" Kane growled, his pistol recoiling as he blasted another burst of fire over Flag's head, targeting one of the luminescent beings. Before Brigid could respond, Kane took a pace forward. "I'm going to help him."

"No, Kane," Brigid shouted, grabbing Kane's wrist. "Wait."

"He's just going to get himself killed," Kane spit. "That isn't a plan—it's suicide."

"Have faith, Kane," Brigid said, repeating the words that Flag had said to her just shortly before. "Faith in science."

As the three Cerberus warriors watched, Flag reached the ten-foot-high ice pyramid and stopped there, letting the angels swarm toward him. Their beautiful luminescence sparkled off the ice walls like stars in the night sky, and the pyramid seemed to glow all the more as it caught the light.

Flag waited, holding his arms out to his sides, looking up at the glowing angels hovering toward him. The bandage on his right hand was bloody now where the multidimensional gash was seeping out into the world, breaking free of its unsteady moorings. "Judge me," Flag ordered. "I'm ready."

The seven angels swooped down, arms outstretched, and placed their palms on Flag's flesh, communing with his inner being.

"He is going to get himself killed," Kane realized, wondering what he could do now to stop this. They had stopped the judgment of Brigid, but that had been with just two angels. There had to be a way.

As urgent thoughts rushed through Kane's brain, each one vying for attention, two words came to his ears, spoken in a chorus so tranquil it made him feel sad: "Impurity discovered."

The shining forms of the angels began to turn then, twirling around Flag as they performed their dance of final judgment, the dance that could disintegrate a human being.

Standing beside Brigid and Grant, Kane ejected the empty clip from his Sin Eater and slammed another into the breech. "What? Did he think he was too fucking good to be judged?" he growled, looking at Brigid with angry eyes.

"Wait, Kane," Brigid said again, and there was something in her face that made Kane trust her, made him realize that the final hand had yet to be played.

The angels swirled around Flag, eerie and beautiful. Flag's mouth opened as he prepared to let loose that horrifying scream that every one of the judged shrieked during the final procedure. But remarkably the scream never came. Instead, Abraham Flag, adventurer of another era, closed his mouth and a grim expression set on his handsome features.

As Kane, Brigid and Grant watched, the angels' spinning dance took them past the ice pyramid, forcing them to brush against it with their glowing forms. As each of the seven beings of light touched the triangular structure, their light was caught up in it and they seemed to be sucked into the pyramid, pulled inside.

And then a spectrum of color burst forth from the pyramid, painting the icy walls of the laboratory with harmless rainbow streaks.

It wasn't a pyramid, Kane realized now. It was a prism. Abraham Flag, that exceptional champion of science, had employed the most basic principle of light against the angels, dividing it into component colors through the process of refraction.

The Cerberus warriors watched in amazement as each of

the angels' bodies was ripped apart as they neared the prism, dissipated into harmless colors that lit the room.

Vadriel and Sazquiel watched as their twirling companions were sucked into the prism and broken down like so much fog, splattered across the walls of the room in streaks of red and gold and green. Vadriel stopped his uncanny, beautiful movement as Sazquiel was yanked into the prism, his song bursting out for a sliver of a second.

Abraham Flag looked at the angel who remained, and then he grabbed his glowing wrist where his palm was brushing against his forehead. A wry grin tugged at Flag's lip then. "See you in Heaven," he said as he called on all of the power in his mighty muscles to flip the angel toward the ice prism.

Vadriel's bare feet touched the edge of the ice structure, and he felt them split as his pure light became a bloody red, a fiery orange, a sickly yellow. As he fell into the prism, Vadriel's arm reached back and he snatched for this impure child, pulling Flag with him even as his spectral form was split apart.

Flag felt that angelic hand grab him, and he resigned himself to its grasp, letting it pull him into the prism. Perhaps he could have struggled, perhaps he could have shrugged away from the weakening pull of this heavenly being, but he knew that this was his time. The infection in his hand, the bleed that waited there like a tiny land mine, hidden just beneath the surface of the skin, was plucking at reality, striving to break free.

Effortlessly, Flag passed through the smooth surface of the prism, turned into light as he was pulled by the supernatural touch of the angel Vadriel. Within the prism, the beautiful colors of Heaven flowed all around, and Flag realized that the angels were not really being pulled apart at all. As they became finer creatures, their substance shredding as the prism slowed the movement of their forms of light, they were being called back, returning from whence they had come.

Flag let the colors wash over him like the waves of the sea, no longer enduring—just enjoying—as he journeyed with them through infinity.

KANE, GRANT AND Brigid stood before the ice prism, watching the last of the bright colors seep from its far edge. As they watched the pretty patterns play across the walls and finally fade entirely, Grant looked across to the others. His face was cut, and his body sagged with exhaustion. "What just happened?" he asked.

"An old soldier died," Kane said, his eyes on the surface of the prism where it was once more a blank plane of ice.

"And the angels?" Grant queried.

Kane shook his head, a grin forming on his lips. "He's probably still fighting them."

"Even now," Brigid proposed, "Abraham Flag is doubtless bringing justice to the hereafter."

"Amen to that," Grant said quietly, and the others echoed his sentiment.

Together the three Cerberus warriors saluted the memory of Abraham Flag, a man whose exploits seemed to be so much an ancestor of their own.

# Chapter 27

Lacea had joined the others on the lower floor of the Laboratory of the Incredible. Her radio pleas had finally elicited a response from her Millennial Consortium employers, and they had promised to send a pickup craft sometime in the next twelve hours.

"Did you tell them what happened here?" Brigid asked as they strode side by side toward the hangar bay doors.

Lacea shrugged. "Some of it," she said, "but I didn't really know what to say. I figure they might be interested in the stuff upstairs, and maybe they'll be able to salvage some of the equipment from the base."

At the far end of the laboratory, Carver's static form continued to scream in that bloodcurdling, never-ending cry. Grant and Kane were discussing what to do with the man, when Brigid and Lacea joined them.

"We're going to have to put a bullet in his head," Grant determined. "He's clearly suffering."

"I don't think he's even conscious," Kane said, peering in fascination at the empty space between the floor and the start of the man's calves.

"We can't just leave him like this," Grant insisted. "He was a good guy, one of us despite his allegiance with the millennialists."

He glanced across at Lacea with a hangdog expression. "Sorry."

"It's okay, Grant," Lacea said, sweeping her blond bangs out of her face. "I realize that the date's over."

Brigid stepped closer to Carver's impossible figure. His mouth was locked in that hideous scream. Like the others, she had come to block out the awful sound of that shriek; it had gone on for too long to do otherwise. After walking around Carver's static form, peering at it from all sides, Brigid looked at the others. "That was almost me, you realize?" she reminded them.

"Then what would you have wanted us to do?" Kane asked. "If it had been."

Brigid waved her hand before Carver's face, but his eyes were nonresponsive and they merely continued to stare off into the distance. "I don't know," she admitted. "It doesn't seem right to just kill him."

Angrily, Grant began to say something but he checked himself and took a deep breath. Then he turned to Lacea. "Do you have a opinion?" he asked. "He's your partner."

"I hardly knew him," Lacea admitted. "He was just my boss."

"As your boss," Brigid said gently, "what do you think Carver would have wanted?"

Lacea looked at the hanging figure that bellowed that endless scream. "He'd want this to be studied," she decided, "to see if anything could be learned from it."

Kane nodded. "Sounds reasonable. Grant? Brigid?"

Brigid nodded and, after a moment, Grant did, too.

With everyone in agreement, Kane turned back to Lacea and offered her his hand. "We're going to have to get out of here before your crew arrives," he said. "Different viewpoints, you understand?"

Lacea took Kane's hand and smiled coyly. "Yeah," she said. "Oil and water."

"You'll be okay here on your own, right?" Kane queried.

"Sure," Lacea told him. "And thanks."

"Don't thank us," Grant rumbled, still staring at the floating figure of Carver. "You're the only survivor of this clusterfuck."

"No, I'm not," Lacea told him. "If you guys hadn't done what you did today, it would have been—well—everyone on the planet."

"Take care of yourself," Kane said, "and if you ever find you're looking for a new outfit to work with, put the word out, okay? I'm sure we can find something at Cerberus that'd suit you."

"I'll do that," Lacea assured him.

With that, the Cerberus warriors made their way to the staircase in the shape of a double helix, leaving Lacea alone with her screaming boss. The screams carried through the underground structure as the trio walked up the stairs and onto the balcony. By the time they reached the trophy room with its carpet of shattered glass and bullet casings, the screaming could still be heard, but just barely.

Grant peered about the room for one final time before joining the others at the shelves that doubled for steps up to the surface. "Do you think we'll ever have something like this, full of all the crap we found?"

"Us?" Kane said. "No. Baptiste maybe, but not us."

"Me? Why me?" Brigid asked with irritation.

"Because you'll get old and you'll file it all in alphabetical order and write up little notes about everything," Kane said as he pushed at the covering that led to the snowy ground above. "You can't help yourself."

Grant sniggered and Brigid shot him a fierce look.

"Is that what you both think?" she demanded.

Climbing from a gap in the snow-covered ground, Kane reached back and offered Brigid his steadying arm so that she could follow. The sun was just rising over the horizon, painting the slopes of snow in reds and golds.

"Don't bother denying it, librarian. We know you too well," Kane told her as he began to chuckle. "I mean, come on! Have faith in science?"

Brigid jabbed a finger in Kane's face. "If you're not careful, I really will set up a trophy room when we get back to Cerberus," she threatened. "And the first thing I'm going to put in there are your surgically removed—"

"Whoa," Kane cried, stepping back. "Let's just find where we parked and get out of here."

A FEW MINUTES LATER, the graceful bronze shapes of twin Manta craft swooped up from the frozen plain of the Antarctic as the rays of the modern sun played off their wings. The storm had finally abated and, below, the snow had settled as a crisp white blanket. The whiteness of that blanket spread from horizon to horizon as, piloting the Mantas, Kane and Grant employed the air pulse engines to power away to the north, heading for their distant home in the Montana hills.

Sitting behind Kane in the cockpit of one of the banking Mantas, Brigid Baptiste looked out of the window at the ground below.

The white sheet stretched onward beneath them, and the twin shadows of the Mantas raced across it, forming their own inky patterns there as the rays of the sun lit the edges of the scene with a swirl of red. And just for a moment, Brigid thought she saw the thing that Abraham Flag had spoken of, back when they had revived him.

"I think there's another level," Flag had said in his smooth voice, "something we're not meant to see."

Brigid watched the ink-spot shadows of the Mantas playing across the snow and reluctantly she dismissed the thought from her mind.

# JAMES AXLER

# DEATH LANDS®

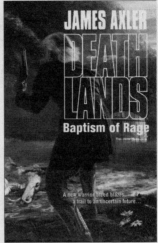

## Baptism of Rage

In the Deathlands, the future looks like hell—and delivers far worse...

Of all the resources Ryan Cawdor and his group struggle to recoup, hope for escaping the grim daily life-and-death struggle has suffered most. But reports of a fountain of youth appear to be true, luring Doc and the others on a promising journey. But the quest proves to be tainted and the survivors soon discover the deadly price of immortality....

*Available July 2010 wherever books are sold.*

---